Albert Wendt

Albert Wendt is one of our foremost writers and has been an influential figure in the development of New Zealand and Pacific literature since the 1970s. He has published numerous novels, collections of poetry and short stories and edited several notable anthologies of Pacific writing. His work has been translated into various languages and taught around the world.

He has been awarded many literary prizes and honours. Most recently he won the 2010 Commonwealth Writers' Prize for the South East Asia and Pacific Region with his novel *The Adventures of Vela* (Huia Publishers).

The unpublished manuscript of *Ancestry* was overall winner of the 2011 University of the South Pacific Press Literature Prize.

He is a member of the 'Āiga Sa-Maualaivao of Malie, the 'Āiga Sa-Su'a of Lefaga, the 'Āiga Sa-Patu and 'Āiga Sa-Asi of Vaiala and Moata'a, of Samoa and Aotearoa.

He is Emeritus Professor of English at the University of Auckland and lives with his partner Reina Whaitiri in Ponsonby, Auckland. He continues to write and paint full-time.

ANCESTRY

ANCESTRY

Albert Wendt

First published in 2012 by Huia Publishers
39 Pipitea Street, PO Box 17–335
Wellington, Aotearoa New Zealand
www.huia.co.nz

ISBN 978-1-77550-037-7

Copyright © Albert Wendt 2012

This book is copyright. Apart from fair dealing for the purpose of private study, research, criticism or review, as permitted under the Copyright Act, no part may be reproduced by any process without the prior permission of the publisher.

National Library of New Zealand Cataloguing-in-Publication Data

Wendt, Albert, 1939-
Ancestry / Albert Wendt.
ISBN 978-1-77550-037-7
I. Title.
NZ823.2—dc 23

Published with the assistance of

For Tuaopepe Felix and Marita,
Kube and Michael,
Jeannette and Vilsoni,
and Anne and Robert.
Thank you for your alofa and agalelei.

CONTENTS

Robocop in Long Bay	1
Interrogation	23
Friendship	45
Absences	65
Hour of the Wolf	91
First Visit	111
Neighbours	127
Ancestry	147
First Class	167
Hawai'i	193
Fast	221
Rantor	253
One Rule	269
Family	289

ROBOCOP IN LONG BAY

Who cares about picnics and picnics at Long Beach? Yeah, our parents and their generation, who never had picnics in Samoa and who do everything our boring Faife'au, Rev. Loa, and his humongous wife, Faga, want. The Reverend and our deacons (one of them being my obedient dad) have again decided to have our church annual New Year's picnic at Long Bay: Long Boring. Fourth tedious year in a row! Apart from being boring, picnics are uncool and a lot of work for us, the 'Au Talavou, serving our elders hand and foot and looking after the horde of little kids. No matter how old you are – and I'm twenty and at varsity – you're at your demanding elders' beck and call. I and most of our 'Au Talavou just want to do our own thing at New Year's, like going to see Arnold with-the-unpronounceable-but-cool name in his latest movie *End of Days*, or being with my girlfriend Caroline.

But it's to be Long Boring again, playing boring kilikiti and volleyball and doing all the barbecuing. Even the mea'ai's going to be the usual: sapasui, pisupo, barbecued steak and chops and sausages – rich with fat that'll kill ya. Our FOB elders *will* insist on feasting on their favourite FOB meaʻai.

Last week I tried to get out of the picnic: I asked my mother to tell Dad I had to work at my holiday job at the Warehouse and continue earning money for my varsity fees and to help support our large hungry ʻāiga. Mum tried. I heard her in their bedroom. But Dad, in his *quiet* way, was bloody adamant that, being the leader of our ʻAu Talavou, I *had* to be there. What would the church and everyone think of our ʻāiga if his son, the Taʻitaʻi o le ʻAu Talavou, didn't turn up? I then tried my Aunt Umi, the only person in our family Dad tolerates in an argument. But he turned her down with a flat voiceless shake of his small head. While she was fuming about his dismissal, he said, matter of factly in Samoan, 'That's right, keep spoiling him and he'll end up being a bus driver.' Poor Aunt Umi – she's a bus driver. He left before she could get at him.

With Dad and his FOB generation, it's always appearances and doing the right and proper thing. The public face is the most important face! I learned that early and have lived my life accordingly.

I've been bloody unlucky all my short life because I'm the only son – I have four older sisters – and the only heir in our ʻāiga to be going to university, where I'm expected, by Dad and Rev. Loa and our church and my ʻāiga, to qualify as a lawyer. I was born into my parents' undeniable expectations of my being the brightest, cleverest kid at school, Sunday school, high school and varsity. I wasn't even allowed to do any sports at school so I could concentrate solely on my schoolwork. My poor unfortunate sisters had to work during the school holidays to help support our family. My parents refused to let me do that: I had to stay home and devote my time to my studies! When my sisters finished the fifth form – they all passed five subjects in School C, two with exceptional grades – Dad got them to go to work. Varsity wasn't for girls, he insisted. My mother and Aunt Umi were silently bitter about that – they'd wanted my sisters to go to university and were willing to keep slaving, my mother at the hospital laundry and Aunt Umi in her bus, to pay their varsity fees.

In most Hamo 'āiga, the children work, give their full pay packets to their parents and get some spending money back. My smart sisters resented having to do that, and got their own back on Dad when, within three years of leaving school, they were all married and living away from home, with their money. When the grandchildren came swiftly, my sisters dumped them on Mum and Dad whenever possible, and on Dad sometimes for the whole school holidays – after all Dad doesn't have a job! Whenever Dad tries to foist them on me, I insist politely and respectfully that I have a lot of study to do.

When my Dad first came to Niu Sila, he worked in a tyre factory and hated it because, in his estimation, it was 'low uneducated work for low uneducated people,' but he worked hard because he didn't want 'any ignorant Pālagi to think I was a lazy ignorant Samoan.' Then he was a cleaner at Farmers and hated that too because of the shame – every work day was full of his trying not to be seen by the numerous Samoan shoppers. When his cousin Lopaki got him a job at Ford's Car Plant, he was a happy man because he could now boast he was a highly skilled motor mechanic. But shock of shockers, after ten years of Dad's unquestioning loyalty and dedicated service, the Ford Plant closed down. He's spent since then working for our church and our local rugby league club for free. Briefly he tried to get another job, but, in his own unique words, 'I'm not going to continue exposing my aristocratic Christian tolerance and spirit to those uncivilised Pālagi racists!' And he didn't.

However, our 'āiga's been all right financially, with Dad's redundancy money and the dole, and my Aunt Umi's and Mum's and our three cousins' wages. We own our own house (most of our church members live in rented accommodation); have a fairly new Mazda van; always have enough food to feed ourselves and the schools of relatives and friends who swim by; pay all our bills on time; and contribute, at the aristocratic level of our Dad's matai and deacon status, to church, 'āiga and community fa'alavelave here and in Samoa. 'No one can accuse us of not contributing at the generous appropriate level expected of us,' Dad keeps telling our relatives. It's a philosophy that keeps us, if not poor and poverty-stricken, at a fairly modest level of existence. It is certainly not the Warehouse Way, which I believe in fervently.

It's a fine Sunday morning. 'And it's going to get hot, very hot,' Dad predicts. We've been up since 6 a.m. packing the things for the picnic. I put on my Ray-Bans – Caroline's Christmas present – and throw my sports bag into the back of the van. 'Let's go!' Dad orders. I get into the driver's seat, beside Dad. On our family outings Dad trusts only me to drive. That's because he suspects Aunt Umi, the long-time experienced bus driver, of drinking secretly. (Everyone in the family, apart from poor Dad, knows she does!) Mum and our three cousins have never learned how to drive. Today our van is noisy with three of the grandchildren – Dad's favourites, and he spoils them rotten.

My sisters and their obedient husbands, who're all afraid of Dad, and the other six grandchildren are in their vans and cars in the street, waiting for us.

They follow us through the still empty streets of Mangere on to the Northern Motorway. A fine haze hangs over everything. Even though I'm not keen on this picnic, my stomach lifts as I gaze up into the immense summer sky, stretching up into God's head …

As we go over the Harbour Bridge, I imagine an endless line of our congregation's cars and vans trailing us, all of them chocka with large adults, large children and large amounts of food and drink. We're snaking merrily towards Long Bay; yeah, it's going to be another Hamo New Year's takeover of Long Bay Beach.

Twenty minutes later, after meandering through the wealthy, comfortable, all-Pālagi Eastern Bays suburbs, which are beyond the dreams of my parents, we drive down the hill to Long Bay. Over the heads of the houses and vegetation, the still sea glitters as it stretches out to the horizon with the blazing sun trapped in it. To our right and along the shore are the newest and most expensive homes and beach houses. Again, all Pālagi, but one day I'm going to have me one of those, just for the summers, just for the beach. A super-bach! Yes, my hero, the millionaire owner of the Warehouse and my boss, is quite right: you work hard for yourself and your community, plan and work out your proper place in the business world, get a good education, then go for it, and you can't miss. He's also encouraging us to apply for grants from his foundation to help us through varsity, promising to hire us for managerial training once we get our degrees. And I'm going for it, man! Already I've switched from law to a business degree, without my parents knowing.

The first three parking areas along the beach are almost full of vehicles; picnickers are spread out under the trees and along the dunes. As prearranged, many of our people are already parked in the last parking area when we arrive there, and ensconced already in the spacious pavilion under the line of trees across the field are Rev. Loa and his wife and many of the elders.

As usual, Dad and Mum and their grandchildren get out of the van and head for the pavilion, leaving Aunt Umi and me and my sisters and brothers-in-law to unload and carry our picnic eskys and bags to the shade beside the pavilion. Our congregation greet us as we do that.

For an amused while I observe Mum and Dad and their noisy brood waddling across the burnt grass. The annual FOB New Year's fashion parade is on! Our elders and recent FOB bros and sisters are parading the attire they got as Christmas presents. The public display is also to show how much (or how little) their children and relatives loved them.

Dad's wearing the thick sunglasses his favourite grandson gave him, the Chicago Bulls cap I got him after numerous hints, Levi's jeans from a daughter, the Nike sports shoes he told Mum to get, Nike sports socks from another daughter, a purple t-shirt with 'MANU SAMOA, THE BEAST' printed on the front and the black leather belt with the silver buckle and studs that he kept telling Aunt Umi she could buy at Victoria Market.

Mum's attired in Ray-Bans from me, a silvery Michael Jordan t-shirt, Levi's with a floral lavalava over them to try and hide her over-thick thighs and hips, black sandals with six inch platform soles and a Miami Dolphins cap sent by a sister in Los Angeles. Needless to say, most of their attire, like everything else in Kiwiland, is MADE IN CHINA. Again, I believe in the capitalist philosophy: use the cheapest labour and sell your products in first world markets. That provides a lot of work in poor countries, cheaper goods for the world and healthy profits for yourself.

My 'Au Talavou committee and I had planned everything for our picnic the Sunday before. So as soon as I go on to the field to start the kilikiti, all the players join me, put up the wickets and divide into their pre-chosen teams. The batting team retreats to the shade of the macrocarpas, and the fielders spread out over the field and around the edge of the dunes.

As the team of cooks follows me to the barbecues beside the pavilion, the batting team starts singing and clapping. The cooks are the team that came last in our annual 'Au Talavou kilikiti competition. They moan and gripe, but not too loudly, as they start the fires and prepare the lunch.

I go over to the pavilion and, politely, greet the Reverend and Mrs Loa and the elders. 'Is everything in order?' Rev. Loa asks.

'Yes everything is operating smoothly, sir,' I reply in Samoan. Shit, they like that – me still being able to speak Samoan, and correct respectful

Samoan at that, and being an obedient leader who will that day assume all their 'taxing' responsibilities.

'He's a good boy, a good boy!' I hear Uncle Makiva, the senior deacon, whispering to Rev. Loa, who nods sternly. My parents inflate visibly with pride.

'Let's play cards,' Rev. Loa suggests. The others agree, and start bringing out packs of cards. Uncle Makiva and a few other elders are already stretching out on the floor to sleep. I note that their grandchildren have been removed by others; taken away to the swings and beach along with their noise and incessant demands.

'May you have a good day,' I say in Samoan, then move back and away.

Non-Samoan groups, mainly Asian, continue arriving, and, unwilling to challenge our occupation of the main field and pavilion, stake their claims to the shrubbery and low trees at the end of the fields and dunes.

I try to be invisible as I inspect the cooks and their work. The sharp sound of sizzling is now the dominant noise in the cacophony. And the enticing smell of barbecuing meat and fat is waking hunger in my belly. I thank and encourage the cooks and then wander over and watch the kilikiti.

Every time a batter is bowled out, the Ta'ita'i of the fielders blows on his whistle, shrilly, and he and his team go into a mock slap-dance routine. Every time runs are scored, the batters sing and clap louder.

My resentment at having to be here is gone, I realise. I feel *rewarded*; yes, rewarded! All is well, everyone is happy and our Hamo tribe isn't going to disgrace us in front of the Pālagi and other people.

Robocop in Long Bay

I rub sunblock all over my body and, without the elders noticing, slip back through the trees to the dunes. The tide is out, well out, leaving the seabed exposed. Many people are walking, running, skipping out to where the water starts. Long Bay. Yes, it is long: as long and as round as my new feeling of freedom. I sink up to my ankles in the soft hot sand as I march down to the beach.

I stand where the wavelets pancake in and around my feet, gazing out at the cloudless horizon. Caroline, where are you? What are you doing? I met her when I started university, in a first-year course in anthropology, and though she looked Pālagi, I *knew* from her build and the shape of her face and eyes and mouth she was Samoan. I was right. Her father's a Pālagi, a well-off car salesman who wants nothing to do with the Samoan Catholic Church and the Samoan community. 'The way Samoans live will continue to keep them poor,' Caroline has reported him saying. I tend to agree with him, but I'm not going to tell Caroline that, because basically, crudely, her dad's a redneck who doesn't want Caroline and his other kids to have anything to do with Hamos. So Caroline hasn't told him about me and I haven't told Dad about her. Dad prefers to believe that, because of my very strict Christian upbringing and my 101 percent focus on my studies, I'm not interested in 'girls'.

As I've already said, I learned early from observing my elders' behaviour to always behave as a 'tama lelei' while under the severe scrutiny of those elders. So that while they believe you're the ideal, dutiful, loyal, generous, Samoan-church-God-loving son, you can go right ahead and be who you

Ancestry

feel like. It's not hypocrisy; it's what I'll describe as a 'practical schizophrenia' that allows you to survive and be admired by your community as a 'tama lelei' while, with a clear conscience, you also give expression to the side that they condemn as 'evil and sinful and of the flesh and un-Samoan' without hurting them. What they can't see won't hurt them, eh? Open rebellion or dropping out is not my way. I've seen too many mates wrecked doing that. So, while my elders were/are convinced I'm not interested in 'the temptations of the flesh', I've gone right ahead and revelled in them. Caroline is the latest in a long line of females and sex that stretches, exhilaratingly, back to when I was about ten.

The balmy sea air wraps its sensuously soft skin around me as I remember some of that line. I retreat to the dunes and, in a low hollow, wrap my beach towel round myself, lie back against the slope and, from behind my sunglasses, savour the flow and variety of women on the beach and in the water …

Webbed across my vision and plunging down swiftly as I glance up is a fine net. I cringe and try avoiding it, but it catches and spreads and tightens round me as I struggle. Gasping and slick with sweat and fear, I wake, remembering where I am. For a dead still moment, I don't recognise the three figures sitting two to my left and one on my right.

'Hi Robo!' one on my left greets me, smiling. Three gold front teeth. Leupega, known as Rube.

Robocop in Long Bay

'Long time no see, Robo!' Daniel, Rube's younger brother and nicknamed Den, adds. Haven't seen them for almost three years. I return their greetings and we shake hands.

We glance at their small lean-muscled companion, who is sitting with his back to me, gazing down at the beach. Fa'akali, nicknamed Wait, Rube and Den's cousin.

'Lotsa good looking keige, ā!' he says over his right shoulder, which is flying a tattooed eagle.

'Yeah, lotsa temptation, bro,' chortles Rube, who tries to hide the fact that he possesses the richest vocab among us – he gets it from the crime novels he loves reading. 'As sweet as honey-coloured velvet fudge.' His American accent and manner of talking comes straight out of Elmore Leonard's crime novels and Marlon Brando as the Godfather.

'Maka'ukia!' exclaims Den.

'I can kekega jus' watchin' 'em stroll sweetly by,' Rube continues poetically.

'Yeah, yeah,' laughs the usually laconic Wait.

They're three years older than I am, and I've known them since Ā'oga Samoa at our church and at primary and high school. It was Wait who nicknamed me Robo, after we saw *Robocop* and he concluded I was as bright as Robocop. Collectively, the three are known as 'the Makiva Boys'.

'When did ya come?' I try to appear relaxed being with them but I'm feeling awkward, uncomfortable, knowing what Rev. Loa and our elders and my parents and their Uncle Makiva think of them. As yet not many of our congregation have come to the beach to swim.

'We came with Uncle Makiva in the new truck we bought him,' says Den. After Wait's dad was killed in a pub brawl, his mother left Auckland with another man, and Wait shifted to live with his cousins at their Uncle Makiva's large and feared 'āiga.

'Ya lookin' great, Robo!' says Wait. 'Don't ya think so guys?' The others agree enthusiastically. 'Ya remember the times we us'ta sneak out of bed and go into Queen Street and play spacies, Robo?' Wait starts reminiscing. My awkwardness worsens, because I know he doesn't do this without another purpose in mind.

'Shit, yes!' I try to sound keen about it.

'Cos you've always been the brainbox among us, Robo – ya soon figured out those games and we started making lotsa bread, eh!' Den continues Wait's line of interrogation.

'Yeah, with your genius intelligence, Robo, ya also soon mastered the art of wiring cars so we could drive home in luxurious comfort …' Rube adds.

'Fuck, man, we could barely see over the steering wheel!' laughs Wait.

'Remember that time the cops chased us along the motorway and into Magele and we were crapping ourselves cos you were doin' 150 ks?' I enthuse, hoping the anecdotes and stories will circle away from me.

'Because it was so dangerous – some innocent motorists and pedestrians might get killed – the pigs called it off …' Rube continues.

'… and we escaped, got to the park, soaked the car and kafēfē – 'oi – kafēfē! – set it alight!' Wait's eyes blaze. 'Some fucking rich Pālagi lost an expensive Tranzam that dark night!'

We continue piling story upon story, one anecdote triggering off others, about our escapades as reckless fearless teenagers. When I see more and more of our congregation coming out to swim, I pull my towel over and around my head and face. Some of them wave to us but keep well away. The more Rev. Loa preached at them, and the more Uncle Makiva and the elders of their 'āiga beat them for their 'āmio leaga', bad behaviour, the more the Makiva Boys took to 'le olaga agasala lē pulea', the 'life of crime and without control and law' – Rev. Loa's description. But it wasn't until the fourth (or was it the fifth?) time they were sentenced to the boys' home that they dropped permanently out of high school and church and community. Uncle Makiva refused to let them continue 'disgracing me and our 'āiga in front of God, our church, our community and the Pālagi.' The Makiva Boys, so we heard soon after they shifted out of Mangere, graduated to burglary, robbery, protection and drugs.

You must be curious about why I didn't continue going off the rails with the Makiva Boys. I've often wondered myself. Recently I listened to a radio interview with the highly respected Maori Judge, Mick Brown. He was asked if over the years he'd observed some common reasons and causes why young people went off the rails. No, he replied sadly, but once they start, it is very very difficult getting them back on the straight and narrow. I think the metaphor of the straight and narrow rails as the 'good and righteous life' is too simplistic, too narrow!

I had enjoyed le olaga agasala with the Makiva Boys: the intimate trusting friendship, the adrenalin rush and sense of triumph and achievement that came with the risk and daring, the breaking of the rules and outwitting the cops and our elders, and of course the money and things we pinched. No matter what Uncle Makiva now claims, he accepted, without questions, all the money, food and property his enterprising nephews brought home. Yes, sir! My dad did the same at first, but I made the mistake of giving my ill-gotten gains to Mum, believing she'd react the same way. Well, she beat her face with her fists and wept as if I'd crushed her heart. Then after Aunt Umi and I dried her tears, she gazed at me with those frighteningly innocent brown eyes of hers and, in a whisper that cut like a scalpel, said 'I'll stop loving you if you continue being a kama leaga!' She scared me shitless. After that Dad threatened to do the same. But that's not really what stopped me being part of the Makiva Boys. A short time after my mates were committed to the boys' home for the fifth time, I had to ask myself why I'd never been sentenced with them for any of our crimes.

As I reviewed all the instances of our being caught, accused and interrogated, and my mates copping it, I discerned one obvious truth: Wait, Rube and Den hadn't conferred the heroic name of Robocop on me for nothing. They really believed I had great intelligence and ability and guts, and they respected me for that. Despite the fact that, like them, I am the son of an ignorant and loud-mouthed, hypocritical, unemployed FOB, I had the gifts to rise above that. When at school I topped everything except sports, they kept insisting, even when I argued against it, that I should finish high school and go to university and prove we weren't 'dumb coconuts'. And whenever we planned a hit, Wait, our leader, always valued and respected my views about it.

'It's bloody hot!' I announce. They agree. 'Let's go over there,' I say, pointing at the low tree-covered headland a few hundred metres up the beach to our left. I keep my face and head covered with my towel.

They look so out of place as we stroll the beach, in their thick leather boots, tight black leather trousers, black-and-red leather waistcoats and black t-shirts. Wait has his curly shoulder-length hair tied at the back in a ponytail. The other two have number two haircuts, and their skulls shine in the fierce light. Sleek black lizards strutting their stuff in the height of the summer.

Once in the shelter of the sprawling pōhutukawa on the headland, Rube lights a joint. The little moralistic creature inside me starts panicking. Not that the creature doesn't know I smoke and enjoy dope regularly. It's just too public and too anti with our congregation. I hurry up the gravel track; the others follow. I veer off the track and through the low vegetation and sit on a large boulder overlooking the beach and bay. Wait sits down beside me. Rube hands him the joint. He sucks on it nonchalantly and hands it to me. 'Sweet as.' I thank him, suck long and deep and hold it in. 'Great stuff, great,' I sigh.

'The best,' Den says. 'Our very own, grown by Māori mates up north. We go up, collect it and then distribute it here in Tāmaki Makaurau.'

'Bloody good prices at the moment,' says Wait.

'We brought ya some,' says Rube. Den pulls a plastic pouch from the inside pocket of his waistcoat. The creature panics some more, but my greed at the sight of such a fat pouch out-jumps it.

'Are you sure?' I ask as Den extends it to me.

'Shit, yeah. You're our best uō, Robo. And we haven't seen ya for a long time.' Wait smiles.

'Thanks, Wait, thanks a lot, mate.' I try to sound humble as I take their gift.

So for a long, slow, easy, becoming-more-relaxed while, in the cool healing shade, we pass one, then two, then three joints round. I think of the 'ava ceremony, when, through the ritual sharing of the 'ava, 'āiga, friendship and community ties are reaffirmed and reinforced. We're mellow, anchored in our friendship in the breezy air and light …

'Ya still bored with that stuff and our church?' Wait asks, slowly. From below us waft the sound of the tin drum, singing and dancing at the kilikiti, and the hungry smell of barbecued meat.

'I've learned to live with it,' I reply. 'Though I don't need it, like our FOB parents, to feel safe in Kiwiland.'

'Robo's one hundred percent correct,' says Rube. 'I mean if all us Kiwi-born Hamos ditched the Fa'a-Samoa and our fobby parents and kin, and opt out, what's goin' to happen to our culture?'

'So what are we doing outside it?' Den asks.

'Din't have a fuckin' choice,' Wait replied.

'We started pinching things cos our poor fucking parents were too bloody poor to get them for us,' offers Rube. 'We stole to help keep our 'āiga fed, mate.'

'Bullshit, mate,' Wait whispers. 'Only partly true. We also *loved* doing it, bro. Loved stickin' it to our teachers, the Man, the cops. Then we got to love the dough we made, especially that.'

'But why didn't we listen to our Faife'au and Uncle Makiva?' Dean asks, smiling.

'Cos they're hypocrites, bro, hypocrites,' I laugh.

'But they're still our elders and 'āiga, eh?' Wait declares. I look at my friends. A deep sadness has suddenly trapped us. I remember that their parents deserted them when they were kids and that they were raised by strict, severe guardians who abused them. I want to remind them of that, but don't. I mean, Wait is right. My dad is a narrow-minded, chauvinist, cruel bigot, but he's still my father. 'And we can't change that, ever!' Wait emphasises.

'Yeah, look at us,' Den continues. 'We can't keep away from our 'Āiga Sā-Makiva even when they don't want nothin' to do with us kama leaga!'

'Gotta admit that,' Rube choruses. 'There're no 'āiga out there, not even the gangs we've joined. So we keep comin' back to the Hamo 'Āiga Way …'

'… and keep wasting our hard-stolen dough on fa'alavelave and more fa'alavelave!' Wait continues.

We're all laughing uncontrollably – the vegetation, the air, the sea, the light, the sky reverberate with our laughter.

Ancestry

When Den declares he's bloody hungry and we should follow the rich smell of barbecued māmoe and pākua moa down into the heart of the Hamo Christian camp, I jump to my feet – my moralistic creature and wariness gone – feeling as if I'm hovering in a dancing ocean of love for my three mates. 'Yeah, let's go eat the generous Hamo Israelites out of their misery,' I remark, and start heading down towards the beach and the kilikiti and the barbecue. Robocop is scared of nothing. Not when he has the protection of the Makiva Boys.

When we hit the edge of the water, Rube starts stripping to his boxers. Den follows suit, and when Wait, who's usually prudish about exposing his tall, skinny body, hears I'm swimming too, he strips quickly. Boxer shorts are the latest craze, and the Makiva Boys are wearing the coolest most expensive silk ones: Rube's shimmer with luminous white skulls, Den has golden revolvers on his and, as Wait runs into the water, a sexy Madonna with bloody red lips pouts at me. And before the approving sky can say 'Cool man!' we're diving in and out of the refreshingly cold waves like we used to as kids on our first Long Bay picnics.

We don't stay in for long. Our invigorated bodies smarting from the cold, the sun lodged in the centre of our heads, we grab our clothes and run up and over the dunes to Uncle Makiva's new truck. The first game of kilikiti is over, all the players are having drinks under the macrocarpas, the kids and their minders are eating round the barbecue area, and the cooks and servers are distributing trays heaped with food among the elders in the pavilion.

Robocop in Long Bay

Laiga, Uncle Makiva's wife and my mates' aunt, is drying two of her grandchildren behind the truck. She smiles and greets me and ignores her nephews. We dry ourselves and hitch on floral 'ie lavalava. 'Don't do anything to shame us,' she reminds them in Samoan. 'Not in front of our Faife'au and congregation.' I avoid looking at them.

'Let's go,' I say.

We cross the field, the burnt grass feeling prickly under my bare feet, to the tables and benches under the trees. 'Bugger her!' Den says.

Most of the older men and all the women and girls under the trees greet me and ignore my friends as if they're invisible. Again I'm acutely aware of the silent disapproving scrutiny of our community. 'You know Leupega, Dan and Fa'akali.' I force my mates into their attention. A few of the older ones nod and say hello. Some of the mothers don't bother to hide their hostility.

Deliberately I sit down in the empty seat at the first long table and gesture to my mates to sit with me. There are no empty seats. They hesitate. Two of the girls and a boy get up and offer them their seats. I instruct the children to go and get us drinks from the barbecue area. Robocop is leader of the 'Au Talavou and he will be obeyed! 'Let's go and get some mea'ai,' I suggest to Den. Wait and Rube get up too, but I tell them Den and I will get their food. 'You're makai, man!' I laugh.

'Everything's fine,' one of my committee members reassures me in Samoan. The other cooks and servers echo him. We laugh and do fives. We're handed four large plates and paper serviettes.

'Lotsa great mea'ai!' I exclaim. Den and I go up to the food-laden table and fill our four plates almost to overflowing. 'Ese le māgaia o la kākou chow!' I thank the cooks.

We head back to Wait and Rube. Many of our 'Au Talavou join us. Soon they're all relaxed and joking with the Makiva Boys. I feel really good about that.

Later, after we help the servers clean up the pots and pans and other things, we string up the volleyball net and choose four teams. Because the Makiva Boys have always been good at sports, the others compete to be in their teams.

That afternoon as the elders play cards or sleep and the minders and young children go swimming, we play as if the Makiva Boys have never left us; as if we're all still heading towards a righteous boundless future on God's blessed rails.

Den's team, the White Mongrels, wins the play-offs against Wait's team, the Black Angels. In a noisy mock ceremony, I present the White Mongrels with the tournament prize: four dozen large Cokes and the sole right to clean up the grounds. And while they quench their thirst and start picking up the rubbish, we take off for another swim.

'There's something we wan' ya to do Robo,' Wait asks me as we're drying ourselves beside the sleek black truck they'd bought for their uncle.

'Anything mate!'

'I'll ring ya on Monday,' he says.

'Ring me at the Newmarket Warehouse, I'm working there.'

'It's been a really neat day,' Rube says. 'Thanks ta you, Robo …'

'… and all the other 'Au Talavou,' Den adds.

'Yeah, it's been like old times,' Wait says, smiling – and he doesn't do that often. The suspicious brooding gaze that's always in his eyes is gone.

Right then Uncle Makiva and Aunt Laiga and some of the other 'āiga elders arrive and, ignoring their nephews, thank me for having organised the picnic. 'Māgaia kele la kākou aso,' Uncle Makiva concludes, patting my shoulder.

'We're grateful our boys didn't spoil it,' Aunt Laiga remarks. I sense Wait, Den and Rube again withdrawing, quickly.

'Faigakā kele kama.' Uncle Makiva apologises for his nephews.

'Pack our things,' Aunt Laiga orders them.

I can't help it. 'You've got a beautiful new truck,' I congratulate Uncle Makiva. Rube winks at me.

'It cost us a lot,' Aunt Laiga lies. Uncle Makiva nods his extra-large head but avoids looking at me or his nephews.

I look across the park and notice that my aunt and cousins are packing our things into our van. 'Gotta go,' I tell my friends.

Wait walks with me. Once out of his guardians' hearing, he whispers, 'I'll ring ya on Monday, mate.'

'Don't forget.' I mean it.

On our way home, driving away from the blood-red sunset and the swift incoming tide, through suburbs that make me feel I don't belong here, and after my mother threatens to sew up her grandchildren's lips if they don't stop their noisy arguing, my fuming dad has to do it. 'Ya can't keep away from them, can you? Everyone saw it. God witnessed it too. What a disgrace! How do you think your mother and I felt in front of our Faife'au and congregation?'

I refuse to reply. My eyes fill with tears.

On Monday, I keep busy at the Warehouse while I wait eagerly for Wait's call.

He doesn't ring.

Three days later, after lunch, I get back to work to find Aunt Umi waiting for me near the front entrance. She avoids looking directly at me. I move back into the safety of the huge shelves of the shoe section. She follows me. The acrid smell of new leather clogs my nose and head. 'I thought I'd come and see if you'd heard,' she starts. I turn away. 'It was on the midday news.' I withdraw further between the shoe shelves. She holds my arm, gently. 'The announcer said two of them – two of them – died. Their car crashed while they were escaping …' I pull my arm out of her grip. '… they'd robbed a bank at Otahuhu …'

'It's not them!' I'm drowning in the slick stench of new shoes.

'Leupega is in intensive care at Middlemore Hospital …'

'It can't be them!'

'I rang Makiva, Robo,' she whispers. 'He told me.'

I watch them, their cool boxers flashing in all their silky brilliance, diving into the forgiving embracing waves of Long Bay.

Now I'll never know if they'd wanted me to rejoin Their Way or whether they'd again abandoned me to God's narrow and demanding schizophrenic rails.

INTERROGATION

I

Andrea, my wife, possesses this uncanny, wonderful, sometimes frightening gift of experiencing these uncanny, wonderful, sometimes frightening dreams and then recalling them for only me and Regina, our daughter, in multi-coloured detail and in what she calls 'the dream's language'.

So on that unusually cold December Saturday morning when she woke as usual at 6 am, and deliberately woke me by rolling against my side, and, out of the dim dark, said, with urgent excitement and awe, 'Although it sounded all the year round; although it rang out sometimes as early as half past six in the morning, sometimes as late as half past ten at night, it was in the spring, when Bengel's violet patch inside the gate was blue with flowers, that that piano … made the passers-by not only stop talking, but slow down, pause, look suddenly – if they were men – grave, even stern, and if they were women – dreamy, even sorrowful,' I knew we were again into another enthralling interrogation session. It was as if she was quoting from a story written by an experienced writer such as Katherine Mansfield, whose work I'd loved at high school. 'That's exactly how I *saw* that dream and how it wrote itself into my sight,' she insisted.

Our life together has been influenced intensely by the way we interrogate and read her dreams. Even the name of our daughter, Regina, came in a dream the night before Andrea gave birth to her. The dream had also said that the love between Regina and Andrea would be special and would never be broken.

'So shall we interrogate the text you've just described?' I asked, for that was our usual procedure after each dream she considered important. Gently she slid her leg over my stomach, and put her right arm around my chest, her warm nudity and the odour of dry sweat and Figiel perfume wrapping round me like a comforting second skin. The centre window curtains were parted down the middle and the summer light was pushing itself through that gap and lying protectively across our shoulders.

'I didn't recognise the street, the garden, the house,' she whispered, her warm slightly stale breath pulsing against the right side of my face. 'But I knew the street is here in Ponsonby.'

We married a few months after we completed our master's degrees – she in civil engineering and I in architecture – and then, with my parents' financial help, bought this villa, which was built in the 1910s, and which I've restored and enlarged, even having it lifted and a double garage constructed under it. Impressed with my restoration, many of

Interrogation

our architectural clients, over the years, have hired us to retore their villas.

'What about the Bengel?'

'A very striking name. Whatever its origins, I've never come across that name in my life.' I asked her if she'd seen any of the Bengels, and she replied, 'Almost. I think the father – yes, the father was prematurely old and had salt and pepper hair, and he wore a black double-breasted suit, like the ones men wore in the 1920s, and his son was the pianist but I wasn't that interested in his age and appearance.'

'What about the music he was playing?'

'It was that classical stuff that I've always found – difficult. But this time I found myself loving it and I wanted to tell you that. It just entered my welcoming eyes and shimmered, like the pianist's fingers, down my throat into my ravenous belly and other vital regions!' Her body trembled invitingly against me.

'Chopin or Mozart or Bach?' I tried the few classical composers I was familiar with.

'Yeah, the first one – Chopin, the music our nephew Rodney plays every time we go to your arrogant sister's house.' I ignored her denigration of my sister because her live twinkling fingers were now playing Chopin, as it were, across my belly just above my 'vital regions.'

'So what about the passers-by?'

'Yes, I saw two very thin middle-aged men wearing heavy woollen overcoats – dark blue their coats were – stopping in front of the front gate, and, putting their right hands to their right ears, listening intently to the playing, with smiles radiating across their pale faces, radiating and radiating until they were part of the exhilarating tide that was the music.'

'Any others?'

'Yes, an elderly rotund woman, with a court jester's multicoloured felt hat – I didn't find that strange – and a long blood-red scarf wrapped round and round her throat, its ends fluttering in the breeze that was funnelling down against her.' Andrea paused, pondering, and then, chortling almost inaudibly, she said, 'She stopped and gripped the front gate's handle, but, unable to unlock it, she shook it violently once, twice, three times, and said, "Fuck that!" – and that really shocked me because women shouldn't swear in public.' She paused and then said, 'You know, I don't care if women swear wherever and whenever, but in that dream that's how I felt about that woman swearing.' She paused. 'By the way, I think the dream is also sexist in pandering to the stereotypes that men assumed "grave, even stern" demeanours and women "dreamy, even sorrowful "ones when they heard that music.'

'Perhaps it was part of the time the dream is set in?'

'I suppose, so it's dated in that way, the wording of it coming out of the late nineteenth, early twentieth century, maybe.'

'And why do you think spring and blue violets in that garden?'

'Perhaps it's because I *love* blue and randy spring – you know that, darling.' Her fingers were now searching pleasurably through my garden, as it were.

Interrogation

'Do you want to continue this dream interrogation or not?' I insisted.

'Okay,' she said, taking her hand away. She turned onto her back, and, gazing into the blue ceiling across which the morning light was now pushing back the darkness, pondered and then said, 'The piano was a black lacquered grand.'

And so we continued that interrogation into the eternal question that whole civilisations have tried to answer: where do those strangers in your sleep life come from, and why do they come? A question that Andrea, well before we met, had started living with because of her gift and the circumstances of her life; a question which her grandmother had tried to answer years before; and a question that, over the years, has become a binding strand in our marriage.

Andrea was born in Samoa as Autasi Lagilua in the village of Gagaifo, Lefaga. (She changed her Christian name to Andrea, with my encouragement, not long after we met.) I was born in Malie and my parents brought me to New Zealand when I was only five, so I was raised here, while Andrea migrated here after she graduated from high school. When we first courted at Auckland University in the late 1970s, she told me that her parents had drowned at sea when she was a toddler and she had been raised by Faivai, her maternal grandmother, who'd believed profoundly in the *truth* of dreams being at the heart of all reality, and that because of that you had to learn not only how to live with them and facilitate their entry into your sleep, but how to read them and what they meant for your waking life. For instance, the first of her grandmother's *readings* that Andrea could remember and describe to me, in her grandmother's compellingly poetic story-telling manner, with which I was to become familiar as Andrea narrated her readings to me over the years, was this:

'In the centre of the silver dark, in the protecting feel of it, is a luminous ocean-green dragonfly, a variety I've not seen before – delicate, with darkly veined transparent wings beating quickly, keeping it hovering, defeating gravity. Then at the rim of the dark I sense a crowd of spectators, their hushed curiosity focused on the wondrous creature. When their faces are lit up by the dragonfly's luminosity I don't recognise any of them, and wonder why I don't, and am afraid because they aren't Samoan or Papālagi or Chinese or any other race I know. Before I can identify them, the dragonfly rises up suddenly to the height of our breath and sight. We all sigh, loudly in applause. It turns its head towards me and my heart sings with joy as the creature bows, yes, bows once, acknowledging my worth, my value, my existence. And I wake up, weeping, sobbing …'

Andrea first told me this on a Saturday night, on our second date after we had been to the movies – a forgettable thriller – and were eating at the Ponsonby KFC. (And I can still smell the acidic odour of the cooking oil.) I couldn't understand why she was telling me this and why it was important to her. I'd been raised by my deacon lay preacher father and scientifically trained mother to consider such things as irrational, even superstitious. But because I was extremely attracted to Andrea – and had been so since I'd first seen her at our MA anthropology class on Polynesia – I needed to indulge her. She went on relating her grandmother's narration:

'For the next few days I tried to decipher that dream. What puzzled me most was this question: how do people and creatures you've never known

Interrogation

become part of your dreams? Have we existed before, not only as peoples but as other creatures and things? My beloved, Autasi, that is one of the questions that will be at the centre of your life forever.'

Andrea stopped and, gazing skeptically at me, asked, 'You're not really interested in this stuff, are you?' She smiled when she caught my half nod. And immediately explained that her grandmother had believed that every one and every thing was connected through gafa/genealogy right back to the atua, and that gafa was intelligent, and when you maliu-ed – moved on – you became part of that intelligence and the inheritance of your descendants.

The rest of that fried chicken conversation amid that invasive cooking-oil smell I can't recall in detail, except that she had reached across the table and, grasping my hand firmly, had smiled – it was like a beautiful gardenia opening to fill all my sight – and said, 'Don't worry, I'm not crazy, I'm just strange, but you'll get used to that. And I hope you want to get used to it, right?'

I nodded, unreservedly, unconditionally, and meant it as a promise.

'Good,' she whispered, 'I want to know you too.'

When I drove her home that night, the dragonfly continued hovering with all its marvelous luminosity and gravity-defeating flight in my eyes. Holding onto my arm, she slid into my side as I drove.

II

Andrea jumped out of bed, arms wrapped round her chest. 'Fuck, for summer, its bloody cold!' she cried, and scrambled into the bathroom and the shower, as she did every morning. She was right; it was crisply cold out of bed, so I put on my favourite dressing gown – the blue-striped woollen one she had bought me for my fortieth birthday – and, scurrying down the cold passageway, turned on a few of the heaters. By the time she came out, according to the quick breakfast routine we'd established over our life together, I had the electric jug on, the coffee ground, the milk in the microwave for eighty seconds, a glass of orange juice for her, a glass of grapefruit for me, two whole-wheat slices in the toaster, and the table set – even with napkins.

'So how are you reading your dream?' I continued, as soon as she had sat down opposite me, smelling sweetly of McMullin soap and Daniell shampoo, and in her bright red dressing gown, which was open down the front. I took the first sip of my coffee, eagerly anticipating its hot, addictive taste sliding down my throat and warming up my chest, waking up all my nerves.

With both hands and a thick fluffy white towel, she continued kneading the wetness out of her hair, her face and exposed breasts glowing red from the heat of the shower. How she glowed!

'First thing is: I've never seen violets in any Ponsonby garden. So what does that mean?'

'Perhaps they represent how you felt while in that dream, as you observed the Bengels. So repeat the wording of the dream and we'll see.' After she repeated it, I asked, 'Don't you think there is some sadness in that?'

'Yes, maybe in the way it's worded, but I didn't feel any sadness in the scene while I was there.'

Interrogation

'The piano playing, you know. Doesn't that suggest strange compulsive behavior?'

'It may to someone who reads the wording, but wasn't in the dream. I accepted it as normal behaviour.'

'What did you think of the relationship between the father and the son, if you thought anything at all about it?'

'Normal. Now I'm awake, I could read something else into it, but I don't want to.'

'So, say you didn't wake up at the time you did, and the dream had continued for some length, what do you think would have unfolded, darling?'

'You know I never speculate outside the dream itself!' Her knife crunched across her piece of toast. 'I never unfold a dream outside the boundaries of sleep.'

I knew that, but for some inexplicable reason, for the past few weeks, ever since our daughter Regina had rung and told us she and Ralph were separating, I now wanted her to. 'Just indulge me, darling, just …'

'Because you're a lit freak who feeds on stories, you want me to do that, even though it's against the rules I've determined?' She took an impatient gulp of her coffee; thrust the piece of toast into her mouth. Her immaculately white teeth crunched down decisively on it and she started chewing rapidly. 'Okay, let me develop the story outside the dream.' She gulped down more coffee, took another massive bite of her toast, thumped down her mug and, gazing through me, back into her dream, said, 'The plot line would go something like this: Harold

Mansfield Bengel, the father, is a retired bank manager who, five years before, had lost his lifelong, devoted wife, Katherine, to a pulmonary haemorrhage, leaving him to care for their only child, Dyer Beauchamp, who is autistic and a savant.' She paused, deliberately challenging me: so, see what you can do with *that*!

We'd often discussed autism and savants, ever since Andrea had claimed, after excelling in three papers in psychology at university, that perhaps her grandmother had had a mild form of autism and was something of a savant in her incredible gift for remembering and re-singing any music you played or sang to her, and in her mesmerising ability to talk in the accents of the strangers in her dreams. 'Wasn't she feared, considered evil, by your village because of that?' I'd asked. Not feared, not evil, she'd replied. 'Hadn't the church condemned such – such behavior as being part of Samoa's evil and pagan past?' I pursued her. 'Yes, but when people learned that through her they could connect with their loved ones who'd passed on, and that through her the future could speak to them, they came to love her – but behind the church's back, of course! They especially loved her songs – the songs she fished out of her dreams, which, when I was old enough, she taught me and I taught our village choir. Some of those songs became national favourites and are still sung today.' She listed a whole swag of them, but because I was raised in New Zealand, I recognised only two.

III

'So to continue my Hollywood script: With the help of the best psychologists, Dyer Beauchamp is identified as a savant with an

Interrogation

insatiable talent for playing the piano. He is given the best teacher' – Andrea refused to slow down as she steered our shopping cart through the crowded entrance into Foodtown in Williamson Avenue, where we shopped every Saturday morning — 'As yet I can't think of a suitable name for that teacher. The teacher *has* to be a middle-aged woman – men are bloody useless at handling autistic kids. She could be a failed concert pianist with the relentless determination to become triumphant through her gifted pupil …' In hurrying to keep up with her, in a busy aisle, I bumped into a tall, solid man dressed in a dirty singlet and black shorts and mud-caked sports shoes, who exuded the foulest BO my nostrils had ever encountered.

'Watch where ya going, chief!' the BO objected as I stepped left and out of his way, catching red-veined eyes, a stubbled face and gaps in his front teeth. I refused to apologise as I hurried after Andrea, who hadn't noticed the incident and was still talking as if I was beside her.

'At the age of ten, Dyer gives his first public concert. It's a smash hit. People especially love his being autistic. Being a very experienced bank manager, Harold Mansfield becomes his son's fulltime manager …' We hit one of the coldest sections of the supermarket – the vegetable and fruit section. Dressed only in blue cotton longs and a black t-shirt with three red roses stitched boldly across the front, Andrea shivered and started rubbing her hands crisply up and down her goose-pimpled arms. Her long black hair was tied back in a ponytail and her skin glistened with health – she trained at the gym four days a week.

'Darling, how do you like the script so far?'

'It's like the one for *Shine*,' I tried to joke.

'And all the other Hollywood ones about autistic geniuses and other "challenged people".' She wasn't joking. 'But, darling, it's meant to be that. You're the one who wanted me to go outside the reality of the dream.'

'But not into corny plots!' I tried disguising my annoyance.

Thrusting a package of lettuce into the cart, then a large pumpkin, all the time avoiding my gaze, she said, 'Are there any other types of plots, darling? You should know; since high school when you fell in love with Mansfield, the only New Zealand author they taught then, you've continued reading all those *serious* novels and stories.' I didn't know how to take that accusation – yes, it *was* an accusation. 'Isn't there just one major plot line: the hero and heroine are born; they meet, fall in love and if they don't fall out of that, they live happily or otherwise, and then die?' Before I could react to that, she said, 'Another variation is: the fearless stranger rides into town, which evil villains have taken over; the citizens are too scared of the villains to help him, so, alone and with the fastest guns in the West he outguns the villains, and then rides off into the sunset.' She pointed at the potatoes and bananas and automatically, as I did every Saturday, I grabbed a small bag of potatoes and a hand of the ripest bananas and dumped them into the cart.

She started hurrying to the meat and fish section. 'You should know all that from reading Borges, who was once your favourite writer and who you introduced me to.' Why was she being so aggressive, deliberately belittling me? Why was she so bloody upset just because I asked her to go beyond the boundaries of a dream?

I hurried up to her back as she chose a rack of lamb and dropped it on top of the potatoes. She began again. 'So the plot line for Dyer Beauchamp is a variation of that: genius who uses his major handicap and gift, led by his mentor and manager and utterly devoted mother, to win the world's love for a while, but instead of riding off into the triumphant sunset, he's left with his dying but devoted father in their lonely family home in their lonely street, which he fills every day with his marvellous playing.'

Without waiting for me to answer, she strode to the fish counter, which was misted over with condensation, and, using a small light blue sheet of waxed paper, picked up a whole snapper with silver, bulbous eyes. She held it up to my face as it dripped, and asked, 'You want that for dinner?'

IV

Williamson Avenue was a glittering river of late morning sun over which heavy lines of traffic were running, separating us from Café Oceania across the street. Andrea wasn't deterred by the traffic: she simply stepped off the footpath and, with her charming smile and holding out her right arm, slowed down the next car. Then she stepped through the gap and, stopping at the middle line, again charmed the left-lane traffic to a halt and stepped through. I waited until the traffic lights stopped the vehicles and then hurried after her, my whole being taut with angry tension and trepidation at meeting Regina and her *problem*.

Regina was waiting for us when we entered the cafe. Most of the tables were occupied, and the fierce sizzling and smell of frying bacon and sausages and coffee saturated the air. She got up and waved us over to her table. It was one of our favourite eating places; we had taken Regina there ever since she was a child. Physically my daughter looked like me – a delicate, slighter, kinder, handsomer female version of me, or so her mother and everyone we knew kept telling her (and me) as she'd matured, as if I'd find that a hugely uplifting compliment. I didn't – in fact I've always felt anxiously uncomfortable about it. At first Regina had loved it, taking it as a sign she was 'Dad's girl'. But when – and I can still remember that cruel, painful happening at her fifteenth birthday party, when she was surrounded by all her awkwardly self-conscious friends – her best friend Tricia said, 'Gosh, Regina, you look just like your Dad!' and Regina declared, loud enough for everyone to hear, 'No, I don't!', a swiftly delivered stab into my heart wounded the cord of love that bound us.

When we reached her she embraced her mother, kissing her on the cheek. As Regina gazed at me over her mother's shoulder, I once again experienced the startling pain of that stab. 'Hi, Dad,' she said, stepping away from her mother and holding her hand out to me. I clutched it firmly, pulled her into me and kissed her on the cheek, and was hurt when she pulled away swiftly, smiling. 'How are you, Dad?'

'Good, good,' I said, and took my seat. We'd meant, with my parents' enthusiastic encouragement, to have three children but, after Regina, trying to raise her and at the same time working fulltime and building up our careers, the three children remained Regina, whom Andrea indulged beyond the limits I demanded of a respectful, dutiful daughter.

We ordered quickly and, when the waiter was gone, were left in awkward heated silence, because even though Andrea and Regina found it easy to make small talk between themselves, I've never found it so, and after Andrea's treatment of me in the supermarket I certainly wasn't feeling charitable and ready to lay myself open to a continuation of that abuse.

'Mother, you remember a few years ago you were into the Genome Project and read and talked about it all the time?' Regina asked. Andrea nodded, nonchalantly. 'Well, it's completed now – I read that in *Time* magazine.' I caught a short wounded pause in Andrea's manner – annoyance? I was surprised by this because I was usually the one who underrated our daughter's intelligence and, by trying to hide my attitude from Regina and Andrea, merely made it more obvious. Before Regina could continue, the waiter arrived with our drinks. I drained half my beer quickly, the stark cold of the liquid bursting up to the back of my eyes, stinging them.

'Dad, you shouldn't drink cold things so fast!' Regina said, watching the tears brimming from my eyes.

'Actually, darling, the Genome Project was completed three years ago, and their revolutionary findings are already being explored and used by hundreds of scientists and businesses,' Andrea corrected her. I was dismayed – in the past it would have been me saying that. At university and since, Andrea had learned all she could about cells, DNA, genomes, chromosones and the Genome Project, and had filled our dream reading with that knowledge, transforming her grandmother's belief in gafa with the whole connectedness of DNA and cells. She decided that our past lives and the people we knew then were all contained in and connected through the cells. It made sense to me, and she'd always been patient explaining it all to Regina, but here she was humiliating our daughter.

'How's work?' I asked Regina, and she looked relieved I'd saved her.

She picked up her knife and fork and, looking directly at me, said, 'Its good, Dad. I'm still enjoying it.' Regina was working as a law clerk, a job our company's lawyer had given her, with Andrea's encouragement. I've always been upset by our daughter's inability to hold down jobs for long.

'Darling, you really *have* to complete your law degree if you want to go any further in law,' Andrea interjected, and I caught the wince in Regina's facial muscles. Why was Andrea behaving in this awful way? Regina had spent three years at university but had dropped out after meeting Ralph, to my huge disappointment. Andrea had again defended our daughter by contending that perhaps Regina didn't have the ability to get a degree, which she didn't really need anyway. I'd reminded Andrea that she herself had come from a very poor 'āiga from a backward village in Samoa, but through relentless hard work and scrimping and saving every cent she had completed two degrees – and with first-class honours. I also took Regina's 'failure' as a reflection on us as parents and as high achievers. 'You're just a bloody snob and tight-arsed father,' Andrea had accused me. 'Loosen up!'

Interrogation

I took a mouthful of bacon and tomatoes. 'And are you still enjoying your karate classes?' I asked my daughter.

Dismayed by her mother's reversal of roles, Regina observed her warily from the corners of her eyes. 'Yeah, Dad, I should have my black belt by the end of this session.'

Andrea was now into her food, her head lowered, hiding from the inanities my daughter and I were exchanging. I was the one who usually did that.

'Congratulations, darling!' I replied, now deliberately enjoying seeing Andrea excluded. 'I never completed mine. Too much other work.' A foolish admission in front of Andrea. So I added, 'Your mother completed hers, of course.' We both expected a reaction from her, but she continued eating as if she'd not heard.

V

When Andrea had nearly finished her meal, she glanced up, blinked and then, deep black eyes focused on Regina, asked, 'And how is Ralph?' She'd always admired Ralph, and had quickly agreed with Regina's wish to marry him. I'd considered Ralph an unreliable, smooth-talking wastrel, and had opposed it. All these weeks since Regina had rung us about their separation, Andrea and I had carefully avoided discussing it, not even in our interrogation of her dreams.

Regina swallowed twice, avoiding our eyes. Trying to smile, she said softly, 'He's okay, he's fine. Yes, he's fine.'

'That's not what we're asking about, darling,' Andrea continued.

'Then what *are* you asking about?' Regina challenged her, and I was glad for her – if a little surprised. She'd never questioned me and her mother in this defiant way.

I saw the trace of a sly, sarcastic grin on Andrea's face as she turned to me. 'Your father didn't want you to marry him,' she said accusingly.

'No, he didn't, Mother. In fact he ordered me not to!' Regina retaliated – and was it satisfaction I was experiencing right then? I caught Andrea staring at me, but I maintained my silence, refusing to be party to her unexpected attack on our daughter.

'Yes, he ordered you and you took absolutely no notice of him and now look what's happened!' Controlled but utterly merciless, she stopped her voice from reaching the pitch at which those near us would hear.

Regina caught the encouragement in my demeanour and replied, in the same controlled manner as her mother, 'And what *has* happened, Mother?'

Her remaining piece of crisp bagel crunched as Andrea stabbed her fork into it. Carefully she placed her knife across her plate, straightened up and, rigid face and burning eyes snaring her daughter, declared, in barely a whisper, 'What has happened is, you're in the shit again!'

Incredible! How could she berate our daughter this way? But before I could react, Regina, tears tumbling down her cheeks, her body trembling, grasped at my aid. 'Dad, are you going to let her talk to me like – like that?'

I reached across, grasped her shoulders and said, 'Its okay, darling, your mother didn't mean it that way.'

Interrogation

'Yes, I did!' It was a slicing blow that cut my breath away and severed my daughter's windpipe, left her gasping. I jumped up and, holding her tightly round her shuddering shoulders, started steering her out of the restaurant, people trying not to scrutinise us too openly.

Once outside on the busy footpath I continued holding her; waited for her to swallow back her pain. I handed her my serviette, which she used to dry her tears. 'I'm sure your mother is already very sorry about her behaviour, darling,' I tried. 'I don't know why she's behaving the way she is this morning.'

Regina twisted out of my embrace, face distorted into a rage I'd never seen there before. Holding me at arm's length, with my reflection trapped in the centre of her eyes, she declared: 'Dad, she meant every cruel word of it. Yeah, she fucking well meant to hurt me!'

'No, she didn't,' I insisted. 'She's never treated you like this before.'

'So why's she hurting me now?' Then, focusing on me, she said, 'All our life together *you've* been the one who's put me down. To you I've been a dumb, ugly person unworthy of being your daughter.' I opened my mouth to protest but she said, 'Don't, Dad, don't. You know that's true!' As she wheeled to flee from me, I tried to hold her arm but she shrugged me off. She paused, and, holding the noonday world's full attention, said, 'And now you've got her treating me the same way. Yes, she came here from a poor 'āiga in a poor village in a poor country, but she married you and *you* turned her into a pretentious fiapālagi!' She waited and watched the truth gushing up from the unhealable wound in my heart and then said, 'Our 'āiga reckon you're so Pālagi you've only got temporary suntans!'

VI

Borges, I think, once claimed that we exist only in one another's dreams. As I waited for Andrea to come home I wanted my reality to be that: that Andrea's totally unexpected attack on our daughter had been true only in a dream that I'd wake from. After I'd watched Regina disappearing into Foodtown, I'd hurried to our car and driven home, without Andrea, unable to shake off the truth of Regina's accusation that I had never considered her a daughter worthy of me – and that I'd somehow persuaded her mother to believe that too.

'Thank you for leaving me stranded!' Andrea started as soon as she entered our kitchen, where I was sitting having my second coffee. 'I had to walk three bloody miles from the café.' She was always precise about distance.

'Good on ya!' I heard myself saying. 'In the dream we're in, it couldn't have been all that strenuous.'

She dumped her handbag on the table in front of me, her face flushed with anger. 'What the shit are you talking about?'

'You're the one who believes in dreams,' I said coolly. I sipped my coffee. It was turning cold.

She thumped herself down on the stool opposite me, her armpits and front of her t-shirt drenched with sweat. With both hands pressed against her face – a gesture I was so familiar with – she sighed deeply, as if everything was beyond exasperation, and recited through her spread fingers: '"Although it sounded all the year round; although it rang out

Interrogation

sometimes as early as half past six in the morning, sometimes as late as half past ten …"'

'Why re-quote me that?' I deliberately interrupted her, continuing the interrogation.

As she took her hands away from her face, I knew there would be a superior smile there. 'Because, my darling, you and your daughter *need* to be reminded you can never read dreams.'

'So why are the Bengels and their savant son's music important to us?' I wasn't going to relent this time. 'And why is Dyer Beauchamp's playing so, so sad?'

FRIENDSHIP

Laura needed one more stage one paper to complete the BA section of her BA LLB, so she enrolled in Anthropology I: An Introduction to Pacific Cultures. She'd heard it was an easy option – besides, she'd always been fascinated with things Māori and Polynesian, inheriting that, she now believed, from her grandmother Nettie, who she and her mother had stayed with and who had cared for her whenever her mother had suffered 'another bad spell of her illness' and checked herself into the 'hospital', sometimes for weeks, with Laura praying that her stay would be permanent. As time had passed, she'd ceased feeling guilty about it. Her grandfather had died before she was born, and she knew little about him because Nettie and her mother had erased him from the family history they fed her. Grandma hadn't remarried, preferring raising her daughter (and later Laura) on her own in her comfortable home on Ngāmotu Beach in New Plymouth, living off her salary as a teacher and the small but careful inheritance her farming parents had left her. Laura preferred Grandma Nettie to her mother not because Nettie played to the stereotype of the grey-haired, loving, overindulgent grandmother who spoilt her grandchild but simply because her mother – and she'd always found it difficult to remember her name – was insane, and her illness was worsening with every year, and she was in precarious jeopardy of her mother's blazing demons, who spilled out of her visions and tried to invade her heart. With Grandma and in her house she was safe from them; they daren't invade her dreams because she was protected by the Māori artifacts, especially the ferociously faced carvings, which Grandma had strategically placed around their house. When she asked Grandma about the carvings, she'd admitted she knew little – and didn't want to know more – about those 'pagan idols your grandfather collected, using up most of his salary each month.'

Winter was cold and damp, the brisk wind cutting into her face, so she was relieved to get into the large lecture theatre that was almost full, and she squeezed into the second to last row. She unwound and folded her long woollen scarf, took off her black beanie and shoved them into her satchel. The theatre was noisy and already smelling obnoxiously of damp sweaters, wet shoes and bad body odour; row after row of students appeared in semicircles below her, where there were a long desk, a moveable lectern and blackboards. There were about 200 students, and she didn't know any of them, although in her three years at Auckland University she did not come to know and befriend many students: she'd never felt safe, comfortable, secure in large groups, or with a large network of friends who expected you to adhere to a group code of behaviour. She *loved* people – certain people anyway – but every time she really worked to become a loyal, trusting, self-giving member of a group of friends, she just couldn't go all the way; some inexplicable dark distrust lodged in her core adamantly refused to allow her to contribute herself, unconditionally, to the pool of selves that comprised the group. As far back as she could remember, she'd not had more than three friends at any given time. Three; why three? Or, as her driven mother would have challenged, why not four or five or two hundred? To her mother, numbers had magical properties that, if not interpreted and used correctly, would harm you, even cause velvety dragon-like creatures from the Great Wall of China to erupt into your bowels and devour all your succulent family secrets, which had been stored there since the blazing instance of your conception …

She broke from her thoughts when the lecturer – and she was pleasantly surprised he was Māori/Polynesian and in his thirties at the most – walked self-consciously past her and down the aisle, while most of the students watched and wondered about him. Suited in navy blue, white shirt and red tie, with abundant kinky black hair, finely chiselled face and tight fatless body, she imagined him coming straight out of Rousseau's and the European Enlightenment's visions of the Noble Savage. Yeah, and she was ready to pay him her full attention. But right then someone, who was standing above her in the aisle, pressed her bony knee against hers, and nudged her twice, rudely. She glanced up and saw another Noble Savage, who, in her height and immaculate black sweater and jeans and bearing and arrogance, couldn't be denied entry into the seat next to her. So Laura slid over to that seat and allowed the 'beautiful

Polynesian maiden' – a princess? – to *ease* into her seat. This was the closest she'd ever been to a Māori, and she realised – and was intrigued about it – that she *wanted* to be that close.

'Tēnā koutou, good morning, my name is Doctor Maurice Matangi, and I'm Ngāti Whātua!' their lecturer started. Laura turned her attention to him.

'Yeah, and I hope you know a lot about that, *doctor*,' the Noble Princess beside her challenged under her breath, and so Laura's attention, on her left, focused on her, while her attention to her right remained with the handsome, fearless one in the front.

'For most of you – and I can't see many Polynesians among you – this will be your introduction to Māori and other Pacific cultures …'

'I like that reference, doctor, I hope your suntan goes all the way into your ihi!' … Laura continued her pretence she was not listening to any of her neighbour's bold challenges to their permanently suntanned lecturer, but was enjoying and savouring and admiring, fully, all of it.

Dr Matangi, after distributing copies of the course description, a list of prescribed texts and a detailed and lengthy reading list, spent most of that session explaining that material and answering a few questions from the first-year students who were still intimidated by the indifferent, hostile, threatening atmosphere of the university. While he was doing that, the princess continued voicing her 'hopes for and expectations of Dr Matangi of the Ngāti Whātua and his course', skillfully and poetically. Why Laura did it and why at that junction, and with someone who obviously didn't give a shit about her or any other unsuntanned member of their class, she was never able to figure out. But she took out her pad and, with her black ballpoint, printed a note: 'HI, MY NAME IS LAURA + I DON'T KNOW ANYONE IN THIS COURSE,' and pushed it, cautiously, towards her neighbour, feeling absolutely vulnerable exposing herself like that and expecting to be trampled on for doing so. She dared not look up at her possible tormenter, her ears ringing, her belly thumping. A long, slender-fingered hand with a silver ring on the middle finger eased into her view, fingers closing round her pen, which it withdrew, and, in quick circular movements, scrawled beneath her note: 'Hi, Laura, my ingoa is Mere, and I don't want to know anyone on this course, except you because you're not scared of me.' Laura's masochistic dread drained away rapidly, to be replaced by upsurging, healing relief, and she wanted to *know* Mere, know her as a friend without boundaries, hesitations and conditions.

'... You going to pay for the coffee?' Mere said, voice tingling with mischief, as they hurried out of the theatre before the other students got up.

'Suppose I should, since I introduced my pale self to you first,' she replied. They laughed, on and off, as they headed for the café in the Student Union building. Blocked momentarily by a surge of students rushing towards them, Laura took another risk. 'Mere, when you first demanded the seat next to me, I thought you'd come straight out of Europe's dream of the Noble Savage.'

'No, not savage – savageress!' They laughed some more. 'And I'm not going to miss a session with our handsome Ngāti Whātua doctor of the suntanned body – and heart.'

'Me neither!'

There were not many customers in the café yet, and it was overly warm, so they took off their coats and draped them over the backs of their seats before going to the counter, Laura sensing acutely – she'd acquired that extra sensitivity (or was it ESP?) while surviving in the cupboard – that Mere, who wasn't aware of it, *wore* an almost visible aura of what her mother had called *magical and dangerous emanations,* which immediately attracted the inquisitive attention, respect and admiration of most people in her presence, and sometimes caused fear, envy, wariness and suspicion among others. For instance, at the counter, the bony young waitress, with spiked black Mohawk hair, automatically ignored Laura and, beaming as if she was fortunate to be in Mere's presence, asked her politely what she wanted to order. 'Flat white and a tomato and ham toasted sandwich, please,' Mere replied.

'Single latte, not too much froth, and a blueberry muffin,' Laura added. 'And I'm paying.'

'Yeah, my Pākehā mate is paying,' Mere said, and the young waitress thanked her, and, without looking at Laura, accepted the money from her.

Walking back to their table, Laura reconfirmed, to herself, that it had little to do with Mere's commanding height and physical beauty and haughty manner. She just *had* it and wasn't aware of it – and that added to her 'mystique'.

She'd anticipated – and was anxious about it – that Mere would not be *accessible* but, as soon as they were seated, Mere, with elbows on the table and long woven hands bridged under her chin, gazed directly at her and admitted, 'I was annoyed by your intrusive move because I don't normally mix with – with other students.'

'You mean, Pākehā, eh?' Laura interrupted her, but she continued.

'… but you were so open …'

'You mean, rude and foolish?'

'… I had to reply,' Mere ended. 'And you're now paying for being so open.' Right then their order arrived and the Mohawked waitress smiled at Mere and ignored Laura altogether. 'Besides, I sense you're different.'

'In what way different?' Laura immediately asked.

'Are you always *that* direct?' Mere asked. Surprised, puzzled by Mere's question, Laura struggled to accept Mere's description of her. 'See, you don't even *know* you're direct.'

'I suppose you're right. I've always thought of myself as being timidly diplomatic and guarded, afraid of people.'

'You're like my mother. She has no sense of diplomacy or guile, and *sees* into people. Scary sometimes what she comes out with.' She paused, and then informed Laura that she was Mere Handsend and lived with her mother and brother and sister in Freeman's Bay, labelled 'a slum' by the media. But where did they expect poor people to live – in Remuera? They laughed about that.

Laura then informed her – and she'd realise later it was the first time she'd ever told anyone about her childhood – she was from New Plymouth, where she'd been raised by her grandmother and mother who, suffering from mental illness, had been driven ultimately by her relentless dragon demons into an asylum, where she'd committed suicide. Her grandmother had died two years later from lung cancer – she smoked forty a day – and Laura found herself a 'ward of the state', an orphan; and so began her battle to survive her many foster families.

'See what I mean, Laura? I'm a stranger and you've just told me the secrets of your childhood.'

'Yes, I wanted to; I meant to,' Laura said. 'You're the first person I've told.'

'Thank you, Laura,' Mere said softly. For a quiet, contented while they drank and ate their food.

The café filled quickly; a male student came over and asked Mere for the two empty seats at their table. Mere glanced at Laura and said to the student, 'Ask my friend here: the seats are for her dragon demons.' The puzzled, annoyed student turned to Laura.

'Yes, and they're invisible, and will be ferocious if you try to remove them from their thrones,' Laura said, seriously, and meaning it. The student straightened up, his large frame looming threateningly over Laura. 'If ya don't believe me, try and take the chairs, mate.'

'Just try, they'll bite ya valuables off!' For a burning instant, he stared down at Mere, who returned his violent gaze, then he wavered, his eyes sliding away in defeat, and he lumbered off.

Laura held the backs of the two chairs and, through the crowd, dragged them over to the defeated student's table, where she bowed to him and his friends, and said, 'My dragons don't need them any more.'

'Thanks,' the student said, relieved she'd saved his face.

Friendship

'You're a tough orphan,' Mere whispered, when she returned, and they chortled, but tried to hide that from the student and his friends.

'Yeah, tougher than Oliver Twist!' Laura said.

They each had lectures at 11 am, so when they got out of the café, they agreed to meet at their next lecture and sit together and then have coffee afterwards.

Laura had not had a sister, so she couldn't say if her feelings for Mere were like those between loving sisters; she'd not had similar relations with other women before Mere, so she didn't know what that was like; she'd had crushes on two boys at primary school and then, at high school, on her handsome maths teacher, but this was nothing like that. Beginning at high school, she'd had very sexual, sometimes unbelievably lust-filled and mind-blowing relationships with many men and a few women – she'd been celibate for the last year. But there was none of that here, though she found Mere physically the most beautiful human being she'd ever known; and, in the language of her mother, this wasn't 'a spell' Mere or some trickster shaman had cast over her. This was new, exhilaratingly new, and she trusted it and would let herself go with it to wherever it led her.

Three weeks later, after their late Thursday afternoon lecture, when she was suffering a slight cold and cough, Mere invited her to have 'a whiskey or two to cure her cold' with some of her friends at Shadows, the bar in the top floor of the Student Union Building, and she agreed readily. She'd been to Shadows a few times before with John, a member of her previous year's history class, who was obviously vying for more than a drink with her. At first she'd been interested, but had, with definitive finality, ended it when he'd emailed her and, with pornographic aggression, detailed his 'dimensions' and how he could therefore give her the greatest multiple orgasms she'd ever had.

A torrent of cigarette smoke and the heavy smell of beer and alcohol rushed against them as soon as they entered the dimly lit bar. Her eyes adjusted quickly as she followed Mere across the room, weaving their way through tables noisy with groups of students, Mere ignoring all the suggestive greetings and obvious lascivious examination of her body. They dared not touch her though, Laura noted.

There were four of them, one giant Pākehā man and three Polynesians, at the corner of the room around a raised table. One of them, who wore the face of a young Al Pacino and a stained green corduroy shirt and worn Levi's jeans, jumped to his feet, and bowing, greeted them, 'Hail, Mary, Mother of Māui!' Mere hongi-ed him.

'Yeah, Mary, Mother of Māui, Mighty is thy Beauty!' the other three chorused.

'Fuck you, guys, for that blasphemy, you're buying Laura and me some whiskey to cure our colds,' Mere greeted them.

'You got a swish looking friend there,' the giant Pākehā said, reaching over and shaking Laura's hand, gently. 'Keith's ma name.'

'And her name's Laura,' Mere said. 'And Laura, this silly guy is Aaron'. Laura reached forward and shook hands with the Al Pacino double. 'Watch him all the time, Laura, he thinks he's irresistible to women.'

Friendship

'Not irresistible, sis, just a harmless bachelor who just wants to hold a caring wahine's hand!' In one quick illuminating instant, Laura *glimpsed* Aaron's scary depths of intelligence and cunning and ability to *read* people and situations in all their complexities and frailty – and that he was expert at disguising that, and she decided (and there was no fear) she had to be wary of him.

Mere then introduced Paul and Daniel, who shook her hand politely and then fenced her out at the edge of their circle and talked to Mere. She was pleased when she didn't suffer any feelings of rejection; in fact, as they joked and laughed and drank after getting her a whiskey, she preferred to stay at the edge, observing their circle, with Mere at the centre, and every time Mere pulled her into the circle she stayed until they forgot her – and that didn't take long, and then she moved to the edge again, a position she valued after adjusting her whole self to it in order to survive her foster families and institutions. Not seen, not felt, not heard, forgotten, you were out of reach of their abusive attention, safe at the edge. And because she didn't yet know Mere's four male friends well, it was best to be at the edge. She *knew* Mere would bring her more and more into their circle when she knew it was safe, welcoming.

As they talked and drank and then, surreptitiously, lit and passed round a joint, one of Laura's favourite 'relaxations', she gathered they were all finishing bachelor's degrees in various fields: Aaron in chemistry, Keith in education, Paul in history and Daniel in English. They also lived near one another in Freeman's Bay, and their families had known one another since the five of them had met on their first day at primary school. Terrific achievement, she sighed, sucking the joint; how many people can maintain that length of friendship and loyalty? She had no idea what large families were like – she'd not been part of one or known any. And this was not a biological family or a group of one ethnicity; no, this was a combination of Māori, Niuean, Samoan and Pākehā, and that was also new to her.

'Hey, Laura, you having a good time curing your cold?' Aaron broke into her thoughts.

She nodded and couldn't stop grinning, which made them laugh.

Mere offered her another joint; she shook her head furiously, but Mere said: 'Don't worry; there's plenty more where that came from.'

'Yeah, mate, Aaron's the King of Dope in this bar.' Daniel, for the first time, spoke to her.

'And I'll take ya home if ya get too fucked up,' Mere whispered.

Laura's eyes clicked open and her panicking consciousness was again snared in the black featureless darkness of her childhood; automatically she gulped back the scream surging up from her gullet, and clenched her eyes shut, again. Don't panic; breath slowly, in, out, in, out … All of her started feeling safe. Now, open your eyes again. The darkness, the feel and look and smell of it, was definitely not her bedroom, not her flat. The sheet and soft blanket not hers. She'd not been here before. She was wearing a white t-shirt much too big for her and one of those floral things PIs wore round their waists. Quietly she searched for the switch of the lamp on her bedside table. Click, the light rolled like a wave across the room and brought into view the bed opposite, and a sleeping face jutting above the blankets and

Friendship

contoured by long black hair, facing her. Mere. She realised she'd drunk and smoked too much, recalled her eyelids feeling heavier and heavier, her speech slurring against her wishes, her body disobeying her instructions, Mere catching and holding her up, then – was it Daniel? – holding her other arm. 'Sorry, sorry, sorry,' she kept saying as they carried her … She switched off the bedside lamp, snuggled deeper into the bedding and, facing Mere across the room, let the darkness draw her into its healing, welcoming embrace. Thank you, Mere, thank you.

When she woke again, she sensed it was mid-morning, and Mere wasn't there – her bed was remade neatly – but she'd left her a towel and flannel, a clean black sweatshirt and sports trousers, which she put on; she had to roll up the sleeves and trouser legs but she felt at home in them, in Mere's clothes; their shape and odour and friendship. Cold and damp in the mildewed corridor as she hurried to the bathroom, she switched on the cold shower, shoved her head under the hard punishing water and held it there until the fuzziness was shocked out of her head. She wrapped the towel round her wet hair and, with toothpaste and cold water, loudly gargled the stench out of her mouth, promising herself she'd never again consume so much whiskey and dope.

She opened the kitchen door, shyly, and was immediately swamped by the smell of fried bacon and eggs, toast and coffee. 'Kia ora,' the woman at the stove, with her back to her, greeted her.

'Good morning,' she replied.

'Come in and take a seat,' the woman said, and turned, smiling. 'Mere's at her waitressing job: been gone for a couple of hours. I'm her mum.' About fifty, hair streaked with grey, deep wrinkles round her sad, inquisitive eyes, which were hard to hide from, solid body that anchored her firmly to the earth.

Laura slipped into the nearest seat. 'I'm Laura,' she said hesitantly.

Mere's mother came over and, tonging strips of bacon onto her plate, said, 'You two were really plastered when you came home last night. Dan had to help both of you into the house.' Nothing judgmental in her remarks. She scooped two fried eggs onto Laura's plate, then some fried tomatoes. 'It's good Mere doesn't get hangovers. Do you?'

'Sometimes,' Laura replied. 'Not this morning though.'

'Lucky, eh?' Mere's mother said. 'I've given up the booze because my poor head can't take any more of the hangovers. I get awful migraines too.' She put some food onto her plate and sat down opposite Laura. 'By the way, my name's Mahina, but all Mere's friends call me Hina or Auntie. You choose which one. Okay?' Laura nodded eagerly. 'I don't believe in the Christian bullshit but, in my whānau, we still say karakia.' She stopped and looked quizzically, amused, at Laura.

'Yes, I'm an atheist,' Laura admitted for the first time to anyone.

Mahina closed her eyes and, in a measured, mellifluous and dramatic way, said the karakia in Māori, then opened her eyes and invited Laura to eat. 'Mere didn't know where you live so she – or should I say, Dan – brought you (and her) here.'

'Mere and I met only a few weeks ago; we take anthropology together.'

'I thought so,' Mahina said. 'I know all her other friends.' Paused. 'My choosy daughter doesn't have many friends.'

Friendship

'Last night I met Keith and Daniel and ...' She couldn't remember the others.

'Paul and Aaron,' Mahina filled in. 'Yes, they're joined by the hip, all of them. And through them we, their lucky parents, are joined hip to hip.'

So for Laura began an utterly open confessional exchange of information about their lives, and when they finished eating, Laura washed the dishes and Mahina dried them, while they continued that exchange, and then Laura put on the huge laundry, following Mahina's instructions about the quirks and idiosyncrasies of the ancient washing machine, and helped her host clean the kitchen, the bedrooms and bathroom. They were happily cleaning the sitting room when Mere returned with their lunch of restaurant food. As if Laura had always been a member of their whānau, they lunched and continued the captivating, thrilling exchange of information, and Laura listened in on the latest gossip about the neighbourhood, which Mahina referred to affectionately as their 'tūrangawaewae'. It was late afternoon when Mere reminded her mother of the time.

'Gotta go to work,' Mahina sighed. She hugged Laura and said, 'You come any time. No good living on your own all the time, Laura.' She left for her cleaning job.

'Thanks for the clothes,' Laura said to Mere.

'That's okay; sorry I didn't have anything better and they're not your size.'

'And thank you for getting us here safely last night.'

'Thank Dan. I thought I was fine until we got into the bloody cold of the car park, and then I collapsed. You were too bloody high to tell us your address.' She laughed and then added, 'Daniel is always there when you need him.' Eyes twinkling, she said, 'You'd like him; he's your type.'

'And what type is that?' she asked.

'Frighteningly intelligent, shy, reserved, annoyingly reticent when he wants to be, and a fucking good poet and writer …'

'I'm not like that,' Laura interrupted, 'and I can't write for nuts and I'm as dumb as nails …'

'Pull me other leg, girl! You may be reticent, but you're articulate enough to ring and thank him and maybe teach him not to be so reticent.'

Later, as Mere drove her to her flat in Mt Eden, Laura said to her, 'Your mother's the greatest, Mere. She wants me to choose between Hina and Auntie. I'll call her Auntie. I've never had an aunt.'

'She'd like that, and she *is* the greatest. It takes great character to overcome the shit she's been through. Or you can say, her battle through the shit has turned her into a mighty mum.' She stopped, and Laura sensed Mere didn't want to continue in that direction.

Heavy sweeping rain buffeted their car as they drove up Mt Eden Road, the front window wipers, at their highest speed, screeching as they struggled to keep the window clear, and Mere clutching the steering wheel and concentrating keenly on the road ahead, which was busy with traffic that swished by like large sea creatures. Up the driveway, they stopped in front of a two-storied block of apartments that was barely visible through the torrential rain. Mere sighed audibly and said, 'Fuck that!'

Friendship

'You want to come in and see my place?' Laura invited her, again feeling exposed, vulnerable, in case Mere refused.

'I can't drive back in this shit.'

'Better wait till the rain's over,' Laura said, elated. She'd moved into the two-bedroom apartment three years before when she'd turned eighteen and, for the first time, was entitled to the trust fund her grandmother had left her. The trust was mainly the money from the sale of her grandmother's house and the collection of Māori artifacts after her death; the value of that had increased hugely over the years. Laura had survived the foster homes until she was sixteen and then went out on her own.

They both flung their car doors open, slammed them shut and, in the cold dark deluge, scrambled up the steps onto the front veranda, along it and up the stairs to the second storey.

They were soaking wet and shivering when Laura unlocked the front door and they rushed into the apartment. 'Bloody cold!' Laura ran and switched on the heaters, pulled two beach towels out of the linen cupboard and flung one at Mere, who caught it as she was stripping off her drenched clothes. Laura wrapped her towel round herself and, under it, stripped off her wet clothes. She got out two more towels, which they wound round their wet hair, and then, wrapped up to their necks in the beach towels, they knelt and huddled round the large central heater in the fireplace, rubbing their hands together, shivering.

They warmed quickly and Laura put on the electric jug and made some instant mushroom soup, which they sipped in front of the heater.

'Nice apartment,' Mere remarked as she looked up and around the sitting room.

Awkward, with a rising sense of guilt, Laura said, 'I was able to move into a place like this after I got some money from my grandmother.' She paused and, avoiding Mere's scrutiny, added, 'Before this I had to live in skungy, awful places.'

'You're lucky, Laura.'

'You want to look around?' Laura invited. Mere jumped up and, with her towel parted down the front, exposing part of her breasts, belly and navel, she followed Laura. 'I haven't got much,' Laura apologised.

'But they're your things, Laura, they're yours, and you've furnished and made this flat your own.'

'I suppose you can say that,' Laura replied, pleased. 'Because I've never had much, I've reduced my life to essentials; to what a poet once described as the "Zen of things".' Mere was silent as they moved from room to room, and Laura hoped she was liking what she was seeing: she'd painted all the walls in cream and hung just a few framed photographs of her favourite trees on them; there were Pacific blue window curtains in all the rooms, and three large posters she'd framed with discarded rimu timber of her favourite actor, Marlon Brando, in shiny black leather motorcycle gear and wicked sexual smile, her favourite philosopher, Simone de Beauvoir, and her favourite animal, the rat.

'Why the rat?' Mere asked. 'That *is* strange, Laura.'

Friendship

'Rats taught me how to survive.' She suddenly didn't want to talk about it.

'But your life couldn't have been all *that* terrible.'

'Because I'm Pākehā?'

'No, because your family had money,' Mere countered, and Laura knew she was trying to evade her stereotyping.

'One day I'll tell you about it,' she murmured, and immediately sensed Mere wasn't going to pursue that any further.

In her spacious bedroom, where everything, except the books in the bookcases, was in various shades of blue, Mere whooped and swept her long arms over everything. 'You must dream in blue, Laura!'

'No, I just like blue bedrooms. None of the other rooms are in blue, right?'

'Right, but this is a blue womb …'

'Guess you can say that,' Laura said. 'Mere, that's the best description I've ever had of it.'

'And it's so Zen!' And then Mere whooped again. 'Now I understand why you describe your apartment that way: it's stripped down to the essentials: no waste, no decadence, no overindulgence.'

This time, Laura considered Mere's philosophical description too fanciful and unnecessary. She just wanted to live in a place that fitted her shape, suited her simple needs and kept out the demons who'd killed her mother. But she wasn't going to offend Mere by telling her that; no, Mere and her friends and her mother were her friends, her family, she hoped with all her belief and courage.

ABSENCES

It had rained heavily all night and the dull, steady, drum roll of it on the roof had made Fale sleep soundly until dawn. Now, the breeze weaving in through his half-opened bedroom window was heady with the odour of wet vegetation, compost and the soaked earth of the newly turned vegetable beds that he and his dad had planted last week with three types of lettuce, capsicums, carrots, tomatoes, cabbages, leeks, string beans, and two types of potatoes and kūmara – before his dad had gone away again. They had also replanted the plot of taro with a new variety that was supposed to grow well in New Zealand's temperate climate.

They've done it every spring since Fale could remember, and everyone kept telling him he had green fingers like his dad. As he smelled their garden in the breeze, his whole body warmed with pride. Nothing like digging up the black soil – he was no longer afraid of the hordes of earth worms that wriggled out of it, because they were his fertilising friends – and turning it soft and pliant with a hoe, and then, after mixing plant food into it, smoothing it down with his bare hands.

'I don't use gloves,' his dad told him at the start, 'because I want to *feel* the earth, be close to it, feel it flowing through my hands. You know the Samoan names for soil?' His dad held up a large fistful of it. 'Ele'ele, palapala. And those are the names for blood also. So, when you're planting things in the soil, you are planting them in the blood of the earth.'

Over the spring and into the summer, Fale *loved* watching the astonishing miracle of the seeds sprouting and breaking up into plants and those maturing and him caring for them, protecting them from pests and diseases. He loved it because all that lush green growth belonged to him. He and his dad had given birth to it.

Fale rolled out of bed, pulled his dad's Auckland Blues rugby jersey over his t-shirt, and, careful not to wake his family, crept down the dark corridor, through the kitchen that still smelled of the pisupo and fa'alifu kalo he'd helped his mum cook for dinner, out the back door and onto the porch, where he stood with folded arms – it was still chilly – gazing across their garden and up into the dawn that was flooding the eastern sky. On the back steps, his dad's black jandals lay at the top of the pile of family work footwear. He shoved his feet into the jandals – still a bit too big – and went down the three steps and across the narrow back lawn, the flapping jandals leaving squishy footprints in the wet grass.

There was a tightness in his groin, so he walked quickly between the vegetable plots to the corner of their back fence, well away from the garden and compost boxes, and pissed noisily against the fence, shivering occasionally.

Absences

His mother had told him the history of their section and home. Theirs was a large, original Ponsonby section that his mother's parents, who'd died before he was born, had bought cheaply in the late 1950s, when Ponsonby had been considered a working class slum. Over the years, they'd renovated and enlarged the original house, and made his mother promise she'd never sell it. When she married his dad, they'd continued to honour that promise, despite the lean times they sometimes experienced, especially whenever his dad was unemployed or away and the real estate agents offered them huge sums of money that most of the other Māori and Pacific Island families couldn't resist. One way or another, his parents kept them clothed and well fed and defiantly proud – and it was easier now that his mother had a good job. Dad was a wizard fix-it man, doing all the painting, plumbing, electrical and carpentry repairs on their house and to their property. Now the property was worth well over a million, he'd heard Mum telling Dad last Christmas.

While dawn changed into morning, Fale inspected the vegetables, squatting down and brushing the dirt or insects off them and picking up bits of rubbish. When he heard his mother clattering round the kitchen he knew it was time to water the plants, so he connected the hose and, after pulling it out into the garden, started watering them with a fine spray. All this he'd learned from watching and imitating his dad.

The back door swung open. 'Fale, you've got to get ready for school!' He sensed his mother watching him and knew what was coming next: 'Are you going today?' The pleading tone (and hope) in her question stirred his guilt.

Fale squirmed, finally calling over his shoulder, 'Okay, I'll go!' He'd missed a few days each week when his dad had been home.

'You have only a few weeks till your NCEA exams, Fale.' Now it was no longer a plea but an accusation. 'And you *have* to pass them if you want –'

'Okay, you don' hav'ta remind me!'

He switched off the hose and rolled it back on its roller. The vegetables, border shrubs and flowers glistened lushly, the water dripping off them. He felt them gazing gratefully up at him. You lucky bastards, you've got me taking care of you.

Fale shaved quickly, using his dad's shaving cream and razor, wincing as he dabbed his dad's expensive aftershave into his face. He loved the smell of it and the knowledge that his friends envied him for having such flash aftershave and deodorant. The girls loved it too! Yeah, especially Rochelle. And Rochelle was there wrapped round him, and he was wrapped round her in her bed with her parents away at work, and they were shagging slowly, slowly because that's how she liked it until she was heaving up wildly ... Hard-on, here it comes! And he reached down and wrapped his hand around it. Hot, hot, hot! God, god, he loved the lemony scent of her hot skin and her clutching heat and her mouth and tongue ...

'C'mon, Fale, I'm going to be late for work!' Fou, his older sister, cut him off from the explosion that always made the back of his head feel like it was going to blow open. 'C'mon!'

He pulled up his pyjama pants and stuffed his dad's toiletries back into his sponge bag. 'Just bloody well wait a minute!' He unlatched the

Absences

bathroom door and pulled it back violently, but before he could leave, Fou pushed past him.

'Christ, Fale, look at this mess,' she snapped. Fale was already out the door, running back to his room. 'Bloody lazy shit,' she cursed after him. But there was that special love in her voice, the love she'd forged with him back when he was five and she was eleven and they'd watched their father leaving for the first time. That time, he was away for eight long, long months.

Like his dad, Fale didn't allow anyone else to get him his breakfast. Like his dad, when he found the foods he really liked, he stuck to those. This morning, when he got to the kitchen and got out his usual, his mum and Fou were already having their breakfast. Fou said, 'Hell, you're a bloody creature of habit, Fale, and you're still without hairs!' His mum laughed.

'Betcha I've got more than those peanut-muscled boyfriends of yours,' he answered, sitting down with his heaped dish of cornflakes, tinned peaches and milk.

'Betcha they have jungles of it,' Fou retorted, reaching over and jabbing her forefinger into his right bicep. 'And they certainly have mountains of those compared to your molehills!' She was six feet tall and ever since they were children she'd been mad on sports, getting into her school's netball, swimming, aerobics and weightlifting teams with their mum's dedicated support. She'd graduated from university two years before with a degree in sports management and was now a personal trainer at one of the leading gyms.

'Yeah, but I betcha their brains are so microscopic you can't find them in all those mountains,' he quipped. They laughed together, Fou ruffling his hair and wrecking his spiky hairdo.

'We've got another big order for uniforms so I'll be late home tonight,' his mum said. She was branch supervisor for a large clothing company. 'Fale, you cook whatever you like.' Automatically, Fale started objecting, but she caressed the side of his face. 'You're a great cook, son,' she said.

'Not as good as Dad,' he heard himself saying. He regretted it at once.

Fou jumped up, reached across, hugged him, and plastered a huge kiss on his forehead and another on their mother. 'Love ya. Fa!' She rushed out.

Later, when he came out of his room with the blue haversack his dad had bought for him and which was now bulging with his books and other school things, his mother (who as usual at that time of day looked smart and strikingly beautiful) stopped him and inspected his appearance. 'Fale, you look tidy today; keep it up, son.' She unzipped his bag and shoved his lunch into it. 'Your favourite: ham and cucumber and mayonnaise sandwiches, and a blackberry muffin.' He shuffled uncomfortably but then hugged her and kissed her on the cheek.

'Thanks, Mum.' Fale could feel her melting into tears. 'Don't worry, Mum, Dad'll be okay – he's always okay.'

Their street was empty of people when he came out of their house. He stopped in their gateway and texted his friend Richard with the mobile phone Fou had given him for his sixteenth birthday. As he walked down towards John Street, some Ponsonby Intermediate students approached

Absences

him. He recognised most of them from his street, and nodded at the ones who smiled and nodded at him. 'Hi, bro,' a skinny kid with cut-off jeans, a holey t-shirt and bare feet said, raising his eyebrows. 'Hi, bro,' he replied, feeling good with the brother-acknowledging-brother routine.

Richard was waiting for him in front of his two-storeyed house at the top of John Street near the junction with Richmond Road. With a shock of red hair and heavily freckled white skin that burned with the slightest kiss of the sun, Richard was one of the few Pālagi still going to St Paul's, street-tough and skilled enough to survive and navigate the Tongan-Samoan domination of their school.

He was the only one Richard allowed to call him Rick; one of the few Richard invited home to play electronic games and watch porno and go into the chat rooms and chat up girls on the elaborate system his computer-programming dad had helped him build. Richard – who was at his house at least twice a week, who had a crush on Fou, and who his mum and dad treated like their second son – was the only friend Fale allowed to help him with his garden.

'How's your dad?' Richard asked, after they made fives. Bony, angular and frail-looking, he only came up to Fale's shoulder.

'Gone back.' He didn't want to go there. 'And Fou's as beautiful as when you last saw her a few days ago.'

Richard grinned. 'How's the garden?'

'Growing like mad. Fucking growing like, like …'

'Like Miss Timble's pubic jungle?' Richard interrupted. Miss Timble was their maths teacher.

'Dunno Rick, cos I haven't seen that!' They strolled towards their school.

On the other side of the street, many of their fellow students were milling round the Busy Oven Bakery, buying and eating meat pies and other pastries.

Guilt and worry and distress about his studies started clogging Fale's attention and churning up his stomach as soon as they entered the front gate of the school. He saw some of his teachers getting out of their cars in the parking lot.

He was so far behind, all his course assessments – except for art – were *unsatisfactory*, and Fale knew he was lucky that his mother didn't know how to read the complicated assessment system, letting him read his reports for her. For last semester's report, he told her he got *excellents* in art and physics, *merits* in phys-ed and maths, and *satisfactorys* for the rest. He felt like shit when she hugged him and congratulated him for doing so well. His dad never asked him about his studies, but Fale knew his dad got his information about it from Mum. Fuck, she was going to die when she found out he'd been lying his head off! And when she found out he'd been ducking a hell of a lot of classes, she was going to kill him!

Form period. Their class of fifteen and their form teacher, Gregory Marshall, were already seated. 'Good to see you at school today, Fale. You too, Richard!' Mr Marshall singled them out even as they were trying to hide at the back of the room. 'But I'm sad to tell you, the deputy principal wants to see you. Now.' They shuffled forward, heads bowed, trying to ignore their classmates' muffled laughter and Mr Marshall's searching

Absences

look from under his bushy eyebrows. 'Sorry, guys, but it's about your absences and abysmal grades,' he whispered as they went past.

In the empty corridor Richard mumbled, 'Fuck it, I'm not going to see that shit-face.' Whenever one of them wanted to duck school, the other went too, and they'd been doing that ever since Year Nine. 'What do you expect when everything here is so fucking boring, man?'

'I can't piss off my mother again, Rick. Especially with my dad – you know …'

'Sorry, mate, I forgot,' Richard said. 'My father doesn't give a shit how I do at school, you know that.' Ever since Richard's mother had died when Richard was six, Richard had been raised by a workaholic but sex-crazy dad. He was still bringing home a series of pathetic women who didn't last longer than a few months each and who ranged from druggies who gave his dad any variety of sex he desired in return for support of their habits to the latest one, who, according to Richard, was addicted to watching animal-fucking videos while she and his dad imitated them.

'That's bullshit, Rick, your dad *does* care!'

'Whatever,' Richard said finally. 'But I sure wish the prick would stop letting his prick rule his bloody life – and mine.'

'So what are we going to do?'

Richard shrugged his shoulders. 'I'm so sick and bored with school.'

'So let's go and see Mr Bell, deputy principal and god of our champion league team, and tell him just that: that we're bored with school and see no bloody use in it.'

'You do the talking then, mate!'

Ancestry

'You know I'm not good at that, Rick.' In the past, Richard had always done their talking whenever they were in trouble or wanted to con things from others.

'Not this time, mate,' Richard chortled. 'Not this time. It was your idea, so you bullshit Mr Bell.'

They straightened up and started marching down the corridor, utterly united in their friendship. It had started in Year Nine. Richard was one of only three Pālagi in their class and someone Fale didn't even really care about. After a day of watching him being bullied by a trio of large Samoans, he'd inexplicably experienced the urge to help Richard, but was too scared to do so.

He went home that day and told his dad about it, who explained, 'If you're afraid of something, you've got to face it straight up in order to overcome it.'

'But there are three of them and they're bigger!'

'Then you have to even the odds,' his dad replied, smiling. 'There are two of you: you and the boy being bullied. So you need a third helper.' He looked at Fale, waiting. 'Got it?'

The next morning, Fale wrapped up his baseball bat and hockey stick in 'ie lavalava. Before form period he found Richard, who at first refused to believe him when he said, 'I'll help you fix those bastards.'

During lunch time, Fale went up to Mat, the leader of the three bullies, and told him that Mr Bell wanted to see him and the other two in the gym straight after school. Something to do with Mr Bell wanting them to play for his second league team, he'd flattered him.

Absences

When the trio stepped through the front door of the deserted gymnasium, Richard stepped out from the side and, confronting Mat head-on, whacked the baseball bat into Mat's right knee. As Mat collapsed to the floor screaming in pain, Richard brought the bat down on his left shoulder. One of Mat's mates sprang forward to his aid, but Fale drove his hockey stick into the boy's belly. As the victim grasped at the hockey stick, Fale pulled it out and up and down with a whipping tthhwwaacckk! across his head. The third bully turned and fled.

One clutching at his knee, the other at his bleeding head, Mat and his cohort sobbed in pain. 'You threaten us again, and we'll kill you!' Richard promised.

'And if you tell anyone it was us, we'll kill you, you got that?' Fale leered into Mat's face. 'You got that?' Through his stream of tears and snot and excruciating pain, Mat nodded and nodded.

The next day the *official* story – that Mat and his friend had suffered severe injuries falling off the pummel horse and parallel bars in the gym, where they had been messing around unsupervised – which all the staff believed, spread quickly throughout the school. The true and mesmerising *unofficial* story, which all the students believed, resulted in the school's students acquiring a massive fear of – and respect and admiration for – Fale and Richard. Richard was a Year Nine lover of the TV series *The Fresh Prince of Bel-Air*. He nicknamed himself and Fale 'The Magnificent Duo of Ponsonby', a name that was later adopted by many others, including staff, at St Paul's.

Ancestry

Now, Fale steered Richard ahead of him when Mr Bell called, 'Come in!'

After the many times they'd been summoned to Mr Bell's office, they thought they'd be used to it being the untidiest office on the planet, but they were again shocked – or was it disgusted? – by its wild tangle of sports gear, books and files and papers, framed photographs of his wife and three children and the many rugby league teams Mr Bell had coached over the years, which had made their school the most famous rugby league school in the country, and piles of *National Geographic* magazines, which everyone at the school knew was Mr Bell's favourite reading.

They stood shoulder to shoulder on the only unoccupied space in front of Mr Bell's desk, trying not to breathe in the stink of stale sweat that emanated from the tangle. 'Be with you in a minute, gentlemen!' Mr Bell said, without looking up from the school reports he was reading. Fale peered across the deputy principal's desk. Fuck, the bastard's reading ours! 'Very interesting, very,' Mr Bell murmured. They both tried not to look into Mr Bell's expansive bald spot or at the long grey hairs sticking out of his large ears. Once, when Fale had mentioned Mr Bell's name to his parents they'd told him that Clarence 'the Shoe' Bell was an ex-priest who'd left the church and married a former nun. His nickname came from the time when corporal punishment had been the main method of discipline in schools. Instead of using the cane, he'd used one of his old shoes. The name had stuck, long after corporal punishment had been abolished.

Absences

'So, Mister Feao and Mister Scown, we meet again.' The Shoe began his clever shuffle. 'I know I have many important things to do today and I know you two have *very* important things to do, such as studying and trying to catch up on all the work you *haven't* done this year, so I'll get to the point.' The Shoe ran his tongue over his dry lips. 'You, my handsome friends, are going to leave this marvellous institution without – yes, *without* – your NCEAs. You, Mister Feao, are going to join that staggering statistic of Pacific Island students who leave high-school without *any* qualifications, and you, Mister Scown, will do the same and thoroughly disappoint your brilliant, highly qualified father.' Fale felt the pressure of Richard's elbow on his left arm. He moved his arm away but Richard's elbow followed. 'Your reports are absolutely disgraceful.' The Shoe's voice was now more decisive, demanding. 'Not one single merit, not one single satisfactory, and there are two of you.' He paused and raised up his offended eyes, and Fale felt as if he were going to topple into them. 'Which is to say in the more honest language of the past: you two are failing, yes, *failing*, everything.' He paused again, screwed up his face dramatically and asked, 'By the way, can you tell me why you've been absent for thirty-one days each this school year, and on the same days? Are you Siamese twins – or should I use the simpler term, conjoint twins?'

'Sir!' Fale heard his voice squeaking. 'Sir, my dad is very ill in hospital and I don't feel too good.' Immediately the Shoe was on his feet and offering them chairs. 'I haven't been sleeping well,' Fale added.

'Sit, sit.' The Shoe seemed concerned about his welfare. 'Is your dad going to be okay?'

Fale nodded slowly and bowed his head.

'Mr Feao's been really crook.' Richard joined the play. 'Might be prostate cancer.'

Fuck, that's too big a lie for the Shoe to swallow! Fale thought. But he did. 'My dad died of that: a terrible, terrible way to go,' the Shoe said, his voice trembling with sadness.

'The doctors got it early,' Fale continued their attack, 'so they've got it under control, *sir*.'

Gazing at him with sympathy, the Shoe murmured, 'I hope his recovery is swift. Please give him my best wishes when you see him next, Fale.'

'We're sorry about your father, sir,' Richard said, injecting sorrow into his voice.

'My dad had a good innings,' the Shoe answered. 'He was in the Auckland league team, was a front rower.' That explained the Shoe's wide shoulders, short massive legs and squat build. 'You know, Fale, I've never understood why you stopped playing league at the end of the third form. You've got the build, the speed, the –'

'Intelligence, sir?' Richard found the word for him. Fale looked away. Why can't Rick stop his suicidal shit?

'Thank you, Richard,' the Shoe said, nodding. 'Yes, Fale, the intelligence. You could be in our champion team right now.'

Absences

'Sir, as you know, in Samoan families you have to always obey your grandparents, and mine have absolutely refused to let me play any sport after I suffered a seizure in Year Nine and the doctors diagnosed a faulty heart valve.' He observed the Shoe's face closely and, when he recognised total belief there, experienced a warm sea of elation lapping at his heart. He'd decided in Year Nine that league meant too much training and giving up too many nights out, afternoons for practice and Saturdays for games, as well as suffering the bullying of coaches like the Shoe.

Blinking repeatedly, the Shoe said, 'How is it now, son?'

No hesitation. 'My last annual check-up showed I won't need a valve replacement until I'm in my fifties at least, sir.'

'Wonderful news, son, wonderful!' the Shoe exclaimed. 'You should have told us that years ago, and I wouldn't have pestered you about playing league.' Surreptitiously Fale glanced at Richard, who refused to look back at him. 'Now, for that other matter of not performing to capacity, gentlemen,' the Shoe said, clearing his throat. 'All your teachers know, I know, and you know that you have extremely high intelligence.' No threat or sarcasm in his remark. 'So why are you not performing?'

Fale felt Richard's gaze, urging him to answer, so he lowered his head, and confessed, 'Sir, I have lost interest in studying, yes. I keep trying and trying but I can't seem to …' The right word wouldn't come.

'Connect?' the Shoe offered.

'Yes, sir, connect with my studies. I just can't!'

'Neither can I, sir,' Richard chorused, screwing up his face in painful regret. 'I try, sir, really try, but my studies don't feel relevant any more.'

The Shoe sighed. Sitting up, he said, 'You're not the only boys over the years who've felt that, but most of them have kept trying, really trying, and gone on to have very successful careers.' The Shoe sounded just like Fale's mother, and he had to resist that, stop it from churning up his guilt and remorse again. 'So do you want to leave school and get jobs?' the Shoe asked. 'Without qualifications and during this recession you're not going to get anything, and if you do they'll only be shit jobs with little pay.'

'I don't know about Richard, sir, but I'm going to really settle down and try and get my NCEA,' Fale vowed.

'Me too, sir!' came Richard's agreement, with military-like commitment. 'I'll get my dad to help me.'

'As you know, sir, my dad's a science-maths graduate, so I'll get him to help me, too.' Fale was proud of that embellishment.

'I'll talk to all your other teachers and get them to help you as well.' The Shoe shuffled to a triumphant stop. 'You must promise me you won't be absent from school again, though. If you are, I won't bother to have another confessional session like this with you.' He paused. 'I'll just release you from this terrible prison called St Paul's!'

'Thank you, sir,' Richard said. 'I'll really do my best, and I'll get my NCEA if it kills me!'

'Me too, sir.' Fale felt like snapping to attention and saluting the forgiving, understanding Mr Bell.

Absences

The Shoe rose slowly to his large feet. He extended his hand to Fale and declared, 'Son, I hear you're a marvellous gardener, so get your NCEA and go to Massey and be a horticulturist or a scientist.' He had a crushing handshake, but Fale didn't flinch. He was so stoked with the deputy principal's reference to him being a great gardener. Really stoked!

'How did he know about your gardening?' Richard asked as they walked back down the hallway.

'Cos the Shoe is shuffling to God's tune and knows everything.'

After school that day – and they didn't skip any of their classes – they went to Richard's house, changed, walked down to the Richmond Road supermarket and, like they'd done many times before, bought two coconut milky bars, a packet of barbecue chips and some golden kiwifruit, and shoplifted a six-pack of Coke, three packets of condoms and the Aveeno body lotion that was popular with the girls. However, when they got back to Richard's home, the promise they'd made to Mr Bell jabbed into Fale's insides and revived his guilt about failing, so he told a disappointed Richard he was going home.

His mother had given up telling him to clean up in his room, so it was the untidiest one in the house, with his clothes, empty food wrappers and packets and bottles, sports equipment and other possessions strewn everywhere. 'Go ahead and kill yourself with your own filth and stink!' his mother told him. She continued to do Fale's laundry though. When he returned to his room that afternoon he realised it was as bad as Mr Bell's office, and he *did* see the filth and smell the stink for the first time, so he stripped his bed and put on clean sheets and pillowcases, piled all his dirty clothes into the laundry bag, collected the other rubbish – including three filthy pairs of underpants and socks (what a pong!) he found under his bed – stuffed it into a large rubbish bag and dumped that in the green rubbish bin. He dusted his bookcase, books, DVDs and CDs and put them back into the bookcase, lined his shoes along the bottom of his wardrobe, straightened his clothes on their hangers and, with even more care, sprayed his desk top and computer with anti-bacterial fluid and wiped them clean, then placed his textbooks, exercise books and writing utensils on his desk. Quickly he vacuumed the floor. Then, as he dripped with sweat, he stood and admired his work. Whew, he ponged! He peeled off his sweat-drenched shirt, dried his body with a hand towel and sprayed himself with deodorant. Now he was ready! Fale sat down at his desk to start his revision, his catching up.

Apart from art and maybe physics, Fale knew he had to start almost from scratch with every subject. He only had the required textbooks for physics and maths, so he started with maths. He opened the massive textbook and tried concentrating. Tried. Tried and tried. Couldn't. Fuck!

Then the insight came. Just like Einstein *seeing* that equation for relativity. Yeah, think of the textbook as a rich garden, and he was entering it to study all the plants in it: how they got to be what they were, their relationships to one another … Soon he was in the zone, deeply in the zone, as the sports-mad Fou would have described it.

When Fou's car pulled into the garage, Fale broke from the spell and remembered he had to cook. 'I'm bloody tired,' Fou said. 'So I'm going to have a sleep. I can't help you with the cooking.' He was glad of that

Absences

because she was a hopeless cook. She also messed up the kitchen and used up all the pots and pans and left him to clean up.

He had a main course of fried pork chops and thick mushroom sauce, steamed green beans in butter and mashed potatoes, and a desert of fresh fruit salad and plain yoghurt ready when their mother got home just after the six o'clock news. Before she came into the dining room, he withdrew his father's chair from around the dining table and rearranged the others so there was no gap. He also opened a cold Heineken stubby and put it with a long beer glass by her placemat. For his sister, who treated any form of alcohol as poison, he put ice cubes in a glass and filled it with water. Mango juice for himself.

Straight after their meal, while Fou washed the dishes, he went out and inspected the garden, plucking out the new weeds and collecting the rubbish.

At about eleven, his mother took him a cup of drinking chocolate. He could hear her opening his door quietly and he knew she was wary she might not be welcome. Out of the corner of his eye he could see her looking around his spick and span, healthy-smelling room, and shaking her head in disbelief.

'Don't say it, Mum,' he cautioned, not wanting her congratulations.

'I won't, then,' she said, putting his cocoa beside his maths textbook. He continued pretending he was totally preoccupied with his work. Gently she put her arm round his shoulders. 'What are you studying?' she asked.

'Maths,' he replied.

'I was bloody hopeless at maths,' she said. 'Have your cocoa before it gets cold.' She bent down and kissed him on the cheek. 'Don't work too late.' She turned and was going out the door when he called, 'Thanks Mum.'

Next morning his mother insisted he take an umbrella because it was drizzling outside. Reluctantly he took it, but he was glad he did because, as he hurried up John Street, the rain got heavier. 'Man, I tried ringing you most of last night,' Richard protested as soon as he reached him. 'So did the other guys – and Rochelle.'

'My battery ran out,' he lied, extending his umbrella over his friend. 'Got to get my phone recharged.' Everything was sleek with rain.

'Need something to eat,' Richard said, so they manoeuvred their way through the splashing, swishing morning traffic to the Busy Oven Bakery. 'Tried to study last night but I just couldn't concentrate …'

'Same here,' Fale lied again. They returned the greetings of some of their friends inside the bakery, which smelled enticingly of hot bread and pies and other baked treats. Richard bought two mince and cheese pies.

'Shit, you should have stayed yesterday. I got bored with trying to study and trying to get you so I rang Manu and he came round with some great videos he *borrowed* from the video shop,' Richard said. 'We sucked up all the liquor we got from the supermarket yesterday while we watched them. Man, hot, hot stuff!'

That's it, Fale realised. That's the stuff that blocks us from our studies! Since his first shag – and the luscious, hypnotising memories of that were even now threatening to clog out everything else – sex and sex and sex dominated most of his waking life (and much of his dreaming), and he knew it was also true for Richard and his other friends. Ever since that first shag, his grades and interest in school had plummeted like a sad sack of stones. When they added alcohol and dope to that, using them until they blottoed out, doing well at school and getting a good job went out the fucking window. Last night he had been in the study-revision zone until midnight, then sex and sex and sex infiltrated his concentration again and he'd given into it willingly, heatedly, with a naked Rochelle sitting facing him while he was in his desk chair, her legs around him as she pumped and –

He broke from those delicious thoughts as they left the bakery. Richard handed him one of the pies; it was hot. Absolutely nothing can compete with – what did Richard's father call them? Yes, their 'natural addictions' as teenagers. He bit into his pie and with his tongue juggled the piece that was burning the inside of his mouth. Hot but bloody tasty!

That day, when Richard tried to persuade Fale to skip their last three classes and go to the movies with a couple of girls he'd met over the internet, he refused, and was confused as to why and hated himself for refusing. Feeling bad about turning down Richard, he agreed to bus down to the New World at Victoria Park after school, where they shoplifted two six-packs of Coke, a packet of potato chips and two peanut slabs, before stopping by the bottle shop next door and lifting two bottles of Jack Daniel's.

But he declined Richard's offer of a party at his house. He told Richard he had promised Fou he'd come to her gym that afternoon so she could start him on a fitness programme, knowing the Fou-struck Richard would never doubt that. They divided their loot and Fale went home and straight into his revision. When sex and sex and sex threatened again, he escaped into the garden and raked and turned over the compost many times, the powerful acrid stench of it driving up through his nostrils and cleaning out the sex and sex and sex in his head. When Fou and their mother came home, Fale could tell they were surprised to find his bedroom door open for the first time, and even more surprised that he was sitting at his desk, studying.

Friday night, they had the fish and chips Fou brought home, and then his mother and Fou went off to a hen's party for one of their cousins. He showered, sprayed himself with deodorant with a wild exuberance and rubbed some of the Aveeno lotion that he'd meant to give Rochelle all over his body and, with swooning care, into his genitals until his erection threatened to burst and he stopped, saving that for the lucky girl he would surely meet at the party he and Richard and Manu were going to. He plastered gel into his hair and then, for a long, narcissistic while, admired his face while he spiked and respiked his hair. You look great, dude!

An hour later, after dressing and changing and redressing and changing in front of his wardrobe mirror until his outfit was right, yes, the latest shit, man, Fale shoved his comb and wallet, with the twenty dollars from Fou and the forty from his mother in it, into his back pocket. He put on the brand new Bron James boots that he and Richard had lifted from The Flying Shoes at St Luke's the Saturday before, got out the bottle of

Absences

Jack Daniel's and the six-pack of Coke, checked that all the windows and back door were locked and then headed for Richard's, feeling as if he was made of helium and floating a few miraculous inches off the ground.

Richard had persuaded his father to let him stay in their garage, and it had been renovated according to Richard's specifications: a bedroom with three bunk beds for his friends to use, a small toilet and shower, a small fridge, a large flat-screen TV and, most important of all, a computer-music-video-party studio. Fale envied Richard's palatial pad.

They never went to the clubs or parties until after ten because that was when the real action began, so when Fale got to Richard's they ribbed and congratulated one another about the ways they were dressed, mixed a large jug of Jack Daniel's and coke, which they sucked back while they watched *The Fresh Prince of Bel-Air* reruns and waited for Manu and ten o'clock.

Manu lived with his parents, strict deacons in the Tongan Wesleyan Church, and eight sisters and brothers in Westmere. He arrived at Richard's dressed in a plain blue shirt, tailor-made charcoal 'ie lavalava, and thick black scandals, his hair combed conservatively. He was allowed out by his parents to supposedly stay at a Tongan friend's house for the weekend so he could attend a church choir competition in Otara. Manu had his parents and school conned. His proud parents swallowed everything their angelic Manu said or did because he always got high grades, was a prefect and in Mr Bell's champion league team, and outperformed all other Tongan youth in being 'truly Tongan'.

'Shit, bro, you look just like a FOB!' Richard greeted Manu.

'Yeah, just like Manu Vatuvei on his way to church, bro!' teased Fale.

Laughing, Manu disappeared into Richard's bedroom, where he kept clothes and possessions for his other life. He strode out half an hour later in his unlaced, thick-soled Air Nikes, his hair curled and glowing with gel, wearing an oversized black t-shirt with the golden profile of Bron James on the front, his beltless jeans with the dropped backside barely clinging to his lower flanks and showing off his multi-coloured silk shorts.

'Now do I look like a FOB?'

'Wow, you look just like the poncy Prince of Tonga!'

'Yeah, man, the fags are gonna love you, Manu!'

'You guys are jus' jealous, eh,' Manu retorted. Richard handed him a mug of Jack Daniel's and coke. 'So what party are we going to?'

'A girl's birthday party down off Jervois Road,' Richard explained. 'A girl I know texted me the address and said it'll be okay for us to come.'

'Are you sure?' Manu asked.

'Too right,' Fale intervened. 'Anyway, doesn't matter if it isn't; there'll be other uninvited guests.' They laughed and drank some more, knowing this was only one of the many parties happening around Auckland that weekend, particularly in Pālagi suburbs where wealthy parents indulged their children.

'Got two others I know of,' Richard offered. 'And if we don't like this one, we'll trip over to those.'

A persistent ringing, far away but coming closer, was seeping into the core of her ears and head. Her heart was thumping wildly in her gullet

Absences

when she awoke with that stark fear she experienced every time one of these early morning calls broke into her life. She scrambled for control and stopped her hand from grabbing the phone on her bedside table. Slow down. She swallowed repeatedly while the phone continued to ring. Her husband was now right in the centre of her vision, right there again as he always was whenever these calls came. Six times now, in the twenty years of their marriage, and each time meant the beginning of another long period of the unbearable fusion of police and lawyers and court and suffering victims and pain and humiliation and his absences … She cut that off by picking up the phone.

'Hello?' She tried to control the shaking in her voice.

'Is this Mrs Feeaou, Mrs Victoria Feeaou?' The speaker struggled with their name.

Her dread turned to suspicion, to guardedness, knowing automatically it was a policeman. 'Yes,' she answered slowly.

'Do you have a son by the name of Farlee?' The policeman mispronounced Fale's name, too.

She swung her legs out of bed and was on her feet, phone clutched to her ear with all her strength, as if she was shielding Fale, trying not to cry aloud. She nodded and nodded and said, 'Yes, yes, yes, he's my son! What's happened to him?'

'We have him here at Auckland Central,' the voice said, 'with a friend. They were involved in a fight –'

'Is he all right?' she interrupted, starting to undress. 'Is he?'

'Yes, Mrs Feeaou, but one of his friends was killed –'

'I'm coming down!' She dropped the phone onto the stand, and dressed quickly, swallowing back her tears. Calm down, calm down, you have to save him. Like you've had to save his father all these years.

She hurried into Fou's room and woke her, and while a panicking Fou dressed, she used her mobile phone to ring her husband's lawyer on his unlisted number – he wasn't happy about being rung up at that hour – and tell him what had happened and that she was going to the police station. Again, the pattern of defence she'd learned and followed over the years was taking over.

As Fou drove them down through the empty streets, she reached over and, holding Fou's trembling arm, said, 'Darling, we have to be calm and in control of our emotions, otherwise we won't be able to help your brother.' She paused and reached over and kissed her on the cheek. 'We're used to it after all these years. And your brother is used to it too.'

Fou nodded once, knowing her mother was referring to her father and the life that had evolved to enable them to cope with him and his lifestyle. Now they had to save her beloved brother.

HOUR OF THE WOLF

Often, after a confusing time of trying to analyse, understand and untangle your most demanding and immediate relationships, you may finally see them clearly, and that clarity usually allows you to believe you can sort your way through them or live 'comfortably' with them and not cause too much rancour or pain for those involved. That's how you now feel about your relationships to Annette, your former wife, Earl, your eleven-year-old son, and Paula, your partner of seven months, the second one since Annette ended your marriage four years ago. Besides, you've never been one for 'over-worrying and over-analysing' relationships: you usually allow them to happen, evolve and develop according to circumstances.

You can say that's how Simon found himself married to Annette: it all began when her advertising firm hired him to make a series of television advertisements for a big poultry company, and, as the scriptwriter for the ads, she joined his team.

He didn't notice her at first: being of slight build, with short auburn hair, grey eyes and a soft voice, she kept a low profile, only breaking her *reticence* – that's how he would come to describe it – when she needed to correct the direction of the filming. He and his crew also found her unattractive physically. After filming each day, Simon and most of his crew hit the Blue Tide, their favourite bar in Ponsonby. He was intrigued when some of the crew informed him Annette wasn't joining in, so after shooting on Friday he deliberately invited her to join them. She looked relieved more than grateful at his invitation, and that intrigued him more. She wasn't into drugs, she declared when they were seated at the bar. Surprised (cynical) silence, the crew looking at him. 'So what are you into?' he heard himself asking on their behalf. A slow, challenging smile, then, gazing mischievously at him, she said, 'Oral sex, God and Obama!' Unbelievable; 'what the hell?' was everyone's reaction. She started laughing, deeply, from the pit of her belly, and when it reached her throat and then her mouth it was a shrill satirical declaration of accepting them as equals. He joined her laughter, and so did the others soon after.

The next night he wasn't surprised when she accompanied him to his apartment, where she refused his offer of drugs but accepted, with incredible enthusiasm, his offer of oral sex, during which, as she mounted towards her climax, she repeatedly evoked God's and Obama's names.

Before Annette, only three women had lasted more than three weeks in sexual relationships with him. One of them had even lived with him for that period. Sometimes he even believed – but it never lasted – he was 'in love'. He found his inability to forge lasting relationships with women 'strange' and 'worrying', because his parents had stayed together for fifty-five years and he believed their annual declarations that they were 'in love'.

After a few nights of leaving in the early hours of the morning, Annette shifted some toiletries and clothes into his apartment and stayed whole nights; by the time they finished the shooting, she'd shifted everything into his apartment and was selling her apartment with his encouragement; a month or so later, when her father asked when they were getting married, they decided 'why not?' and, with her parents' financial encouragement, they had the white wedding (in St Mary's Cathedral) that her mother insisted her beautiful daughter and only child had always wanted. Annette's best friend, Wilma, a well-known chef, and her restaurant catered a reception for two hundred guests round the theme of 'Kiwi fusion', enjoying the most expensive New Zealand wines and Wilma's fusion cooking of New Zealand lamb, seafood and produce.

It is a balmy Saturday morning of bright sun and slow traffic as Simon drives past Mercy Hospital and then past the Governor General's official residence into the heart of Epsom and Exeter Street, stopping in front of an impressive double-storied house with spacious gardens and grounds and an exuberant spread of indigenous trees. He and Annette had bought the property soon after they married: her wealthy lawyer parents had paid the hefty deposit and they'd gone into an even heftier mortgage unconcerned about it because, at that time, he was making lots of money producing lucrative television commercials and documentaries, and Annette was earning heaps as an advertising executive. Besides, like all

Ancestry

their friends in the advertising/film/entertainment business, their credit seemed limitless in a booming share market.

He gets out of his car, noting that the grounds and gardens need attention, badly. Nothing to do with him now; Annette had bought his half of the property in their marital settlement. He's never liked gardening, and while they were together they were both busy with their careers, so they'd hired a gardening firm to tend the gardens once a month.

Before he can press the buzzer, he hears Earl running towards the front door. After months of a bitter custody battle, he'd reluctantly agreed to his having Earl the last weekend of every month. Why he'd fought for custody he didn't understand because he's never felt that close to his son – to him children aren't that interesting and take up too much of your time and energy. However, over Earl's subsequent stays with him, he's grown protectively fond of him; uncanny how he observes so much of himself in his son, not only physically but in his mannerisms, and he likes that: good for his ego and their bonding.

'Hi, Dad!' the red-haired teenage boy says, awkwardly, avoiding his eyes. 'I'm ready!' Earl is dressed in his favourite Breakers cap, dark blue and white Adidas track suit and Puma sports shoes, and is carrying on his back his red rucksack that is bulging with what Simon knows are his sci-fi fantasy books and electronic games. Under his arm is his Dolphin Racer skateboard. Simon has bought all those for him.

Annette is down at the end of the corridor. Dishevelled, pale and utterly distant in her red silk bathrobe, she nods once. He waves to her.

Out of the kitchen door steps Robert, Annette's partner, who, in the heady young days when they were establishing themselves, was one of Simon's best friends. Simon raises his arm and nods. Now it feels so unreal that he was once married to her – and for seven years. Even more incredibly, she is with Robert, who they all considered a 'loser' unable to hold down a job for long because of his drug habit. 'C'mon, Dad, let's go!' Earl urges. 'See ya, Mum,' Earl calls over his shoulder.

As they drive away from the house, into the brightening day and the thickening traffic, Earl declares, 'Robert's a fucking dope-head!' Startled by his son's directness, Simon fumbles for an answer as he gazes straight ahead. 'He's a dickhead!' Earl attacks him again. Simon continues fumbling. 'And now she's doing it too, Dad!'

'Lots of adults do that, you know that,' he tries to counter.

'I know that, but when you and Mum were together, she never touched any drugs except alcohol,' Earl reminds him. 'And they're having lots of rows – and she bashes him.' Simon doesn't want to hear any more but Earl continues, 'Last week, I had to ring Granddad and he rushed over and stopped them …'

'Sorry, son …'

'I want to come and live with you.' And there it is: the demand Simon's been dreading ever since he and Paula started living together. 'Can I, Dad?' Though Earl isn't looking at him, the penetrating intensity of his demand is inescapable.

'I'll have to discuss it with Paula.' He hears his evasion. 'Besides, your mother may not agree to it. Legally she …'

Ancestry

'Fuck her!' Earl snaps, hugging himself and turning his back to him. 'You shouldn't talk like that about your mother!'

Paula is ready and is dressed in her usual summer wear – brightly coloured aloha shirt, black jeans, and sandals – when they reach the house, Earl webbed in sullen silence and Simon desperately hoping for understanding from Paula, who is much younger than him and who he'd hired as the sound recordist for a BBC-commissioned documentary he was making, and who is now totally meshed into his 'sinews, heart and desire'; so he described it to his friends a few days before. 'What's the bloody problem?' she asks Simon when she slides into the back seat, behind Earl. No reply. She reaches over the seat and, caressing Earl's hair, says, 'Hey, how are ya, man?' He winces away from her hand.

'He wants to come and live with us,' Simon hears his trembling voice pleading.

'So, what's wrong with that?' Her statement is so unexpected Simon can't believe it for a moment. 'Is that what you want, Earl?' she asks, thrusting her face over the car seat. Earl squirms away. 'If you want to come and live with us, then you have to leave all your shitty behaviour with your mother, man! Right?' Again, Simon can't believe she can be so frank, and expects Earl to react angrily. 'Right?' she demands in the boy's ear. Earl nods once. 'Good, man,' she says. The tension in the car deflates immediately, and Simon is joyously relieved – and surprised, because over the past five months, since they met, Paula and Earl have been moving around each other as if they are treading on eggshells, Paula trying not to interfere with Simon's and Earl's relationship and the boy communicating with her only through his father. Is she now trying another strategy?

His producer had recommended her as 'a most innovative and talented recordist,' and Simon discovered that to be true as soon as they started filming. 'As far back as I can recall,' she said that first evening at the Blue Tide, 'I've been into sound, all sound, all sorts of sound.'

'Like it's your blood,' he'd cynically tried to put her down.

'Yeah, like the blood in my veins,' she said, unaware of his cynicism.

During the next few days, while they worked together, he had to tell himself she was like blood, like sound, flowing into his veins, especially when she declared that her ambition was to be chief recordist for a New Zealand feature film, and he confessed that the main reason he'd gone into film-making was to make feature films telling New Zealand stories. 'Why haven't you?' she'd asked in all innocence. He'd changed the topic, but during the rest of the filming she'd drawn the details from him that after graduating from film school he'd worked, unpaid, for Geoff Murphy and then Ian Mune so he could learn the trade of making feature films. He'd even completed a full-length feature film script, titled *Noses*, but had failed miserably to get a producer and money for it. To stay alive, he'd worked as a producer's assistant in a small advertising company, and within a couple of years was directing commercials for it and enjoying the money that came with it. And he soon found he couldn't do without that.

Just before they finished the documentary, he confessed – and he didn't understand why he was doing it – he was ending 'a row-ridden relationship with an ambitious, arrogant, conceited film studies lecturer at Auckland University'. Paula simply gazed back at him and asked, head askance, 'So you now want to start an affair with me?'

'No!' came his automatic denial. How could she be so – so brutal, so confrontational?

'Don't you find me attractive? Sexy?' She smiled, her ebony gaze capturing him. He started shaking his head then stopped. She straightened up. He is almost six feet tall but she is taller by at least two inches, and larger – not fat, but long-limbed, strong-boned, sleekly muscled and exuding a presence that, for the first time, wrapped around him like a healing embrace. For the first revelatory time, he realised she was 'beautiful' – a word he hated using, considering it cliché-ish and therefore meaningless, but now the most apt description of her and how he felt about her.

As is now their practice at the end of every month, Earl rings Simon on Friday night to remind him to pick him up and tell him what he wants to do in the weekend. 'So, Earl, first in the programme today is the eleven o'clock session of *Hour of the Wolf*.' Paula pauses and then adds, 'Good choice, man, I've been wanting to see that. Supposed to have great sound and special effects.'

'Then we go to Burger King for lunch,' Simon itemises, catching Paula's reflection in the rear-view mirror, expecting a negative reaction.

But she smiles and says, 'I haven't had a burger for ages.' She rolls her eyes at Simon. Placing her hand on Earl's shoulder, she asks, 'Then what, man?'

Hour of the Wolf

'I'm meeting some of my friends at the skateboard park in Victoria Park,' Earl explains.

Paula's eyes light up hugely. 'May I come too? I haven't done it for a while but I used to be quite good at it.' Simon senses Earl's reluctance. She clutches Earl's shoulder and urges, 'May I? I promise I won't let you down in front of your mates.' Earl nods and smiles, but Simon still senses his reluctance. Since he met her, there have been many surprising and mostly marvellous revelations about her. This claim to being a skilled skateboarder is the most surprising – the least believable; after all he has never seen her doing anything athletically demanding, or displaying any exceptional physical coordination.

'Bloody good, eh?' Paula says through a bulging mouthful of cheeseburger. They have just walked from the Metro Theatre complex across Queen Street to the Burger King, after seeing *Hour of the Wolf*. There aren't many customers, and they're seated at the central front table looking out into the bustling, noisy, sun-drenched street.

'Eh, it's great!' Simon lies, smiling and gently digging his elbow into his son's arm. 'Great choice, son.' Earl looks pleased: he'd chosen the burgers, French fries, bean salad and Lemon and Paeroa drinks for them.

'So you didn't think much of *Hour of the Wolf*?' Paula asks Earl as soon as they're settled into their eating.

The boy squirms and says, 'Crappy story – and the special effects, uggh, aren't anywhere near as good as *Avatar*.' Simon agrees with his son but is enjoying the other two's conversation too much to intrude into it. Up until this outing, Earl's conversation with Paula has been limited to an infuriating grunt-and-monosyllabic language.

'Okay. What did you think of the acting?' she continues. Immediately they're into an animated, very intelligent and perceptive discussion of the film (and many other horror films about wolves), Paula keeping it flowing with relevant questions. Occasionally, Earl includes Simon by prompting him with questions, usually to support his views. It is obvious to Simon that Paula knows children and teenagers well – and how to cope with them. Simon for the first time wonders what sort of family she has: parents, sisters, brothers? Early in their relationship, he'd heard that Paula is 'part-Samoan' and hadn't considered it important. Now, that is conjuring up all kinds of answers to his curiosity about her family: struggling new migrant parents, large family with lots of siblings in a state house in Mangere probably, close to church …

'Dad, what was the name of the special effects guy?' Earl's voice severs his thoughts.

'… In *Hour of the Wolf*?' he asks automatically. Earl nods. He tells him.

'Your dad's got a great memory!' Paula exclaims, then she and Earl continue discussing the quality of the special effects and sound, and gorging down their meals.

Simon observes that the restaurant is filling quickly, mainly with people from the Metro Theatre complex across the street. Most of them are Paula's and Earl's ages and dressed in similar clothes, and for the first time in his life Simon identifies many of them as Māori or Polynesian, and he compares Paula to them, trying to see if she *is* Polynesian. In hindsight, from his primary school days until now Māori have always been present in his life – most recently he'd hired three Māori/PI technicians – but he now admits to himself that they've always been at the periphery. He can't identify any Māori or PI he has known as a 'close friend', and he has never had an affair with any Polynesian woman. Racial prejudice on his part? No, no. It's just that he's never considered them important to his life. And unlike many of his friends and colleagues he doesn't get upset and angry and frustrated by continuing Māori protests and demands, the most recent being the abolition of the Foreshore and Seabed Act. As long as they don't interfere with his work and the enjoyment of his life, Māoris and PIs are – he struggles for the most apt word, and finds *unimportant.*

'… Darling?' Paula's voice breaks into his attention. Simon blinks and nods. 'Are you with us?' She smiles. He laughs softly. 'I don't have a skateboard or pads, and Earl doesn't have any spare ones, so we have to go and buy some,' she tells him.

'Did you two come to an agreed-to conclusion about *Hour of the Wolf?*' he asks them, as they leave the restaurant.

Earl's eyes light up and he glances at Paula, who nods, so he declares, 'Too bloody slow, special effects are too ancient, and the sound was too loud.' Paula nods repeatedly in agreement.

In the past, whenever Earl and Simon were in public, Earl has simply refused to be identified as Simon's son. The few times Simon has tried to put his arm round his son's shoulders as they've walked along the street, Earl has simply moved away from under it. This time as they stroll down Queen Street towards the Rebel Sports shop, Earl walking between Simon and Paula, Simon tries again and Earl doesn't move away, glancing up at Paula and smiling as if to say, 'he belongs to me!' Simon feels joyously light with what he will later describe to himself as *love*, the love between son and father. Paula reaches down and caresses the back of Simon's hand, which is clutching Earl's shoulder. The lightness swells to fill all of him, and he gazes across at her.

As soon as they reach the Rebel Sports shop, Earl weaves his way through the customers at the entrance and heads for the section containing skateboards, surfboards and similar sports equipment. Simon puts his arm round Paula's waist and, pulling her into his side, kisses her on the side of her face and whispers, 'Thank you for agreeing to let him come and stay with us.'

'No problem,' she says. 'He's good fun – and intelligent.' As she pulls away to hurry to Earl, who is waving her over to the skateboard display, she adds, 'I hope his mother agrees to it.' And he's back in the stressful complicated realities of Annette.

There are no other customers at the skateboard section. The short, tightly muscled young shop assistant comes and stands quietly beside Paula and Earl. There is a thickly padded bench in front of the skateboard display, so Simon sits down on that. Earl is taking down different skateboards. Showing them to Paula, he tells her what each brand is and its history. Simon is impressed with the boy's detailed knowledge. '… That's my brand; my Dolphin skateboard belongs to the Victory Skateboards

Brand, which was started by Bill Hanson, a Kiwi champion in the 1990s …' It is also the first time he's seen his son showing a passion – yes, that's the word – for anything. Earl takes down a skateboard just like his own and slides it along the floor to Paula, who stops it with her sandalled right foot and, expertly mounting it, crouches on the deck and balances herself.

'Choice. Feels good!' she exclaims.

'Ya look cool,' Earl says. 'How does it feel? Not too small for you?' Simon looks again at Paula; the over six-feet size of her *looks* too big, too precarious for that skateboard. Paula puts her right foot down and pushes off, heading down the floor, arms outspread, crouching low, steadying herself on the board. She stops and, turning round, says, 'Yeah, I'll try a heavier one.' Earl takes down another Victory board – a sleek black one with white stripes and silver-black trucks and wheels – and pushes it along the floor to her. It's evident to Simon that she knows what she's doing.

'That's the fucking Black Dolphin!' Earl tells her. 'So it's pricey.'

Without hesitation, Paula steps with her left foot on it and, her right foot pushing down, propels herself towards Earl. 'Wow, wow, it feels right, just right!' she cries.

'Yeah, ya riding the Great Black Dolphin!' Earl exclaims, and steps aside as Paula glides by, the shop assistant stepping forward to try and slow her down.

'You can't do that in here,' the shop assistant cautions her. She slams her back foot down and, stopping the board, swivels round to face the shop assistant; she stamps down on the back of the board, flipping it up into her hands. She knows her stuff all right, Simon concludes, his centre leaping with admiration.

'So where can I try it out, mate?' she asks the shop assistant.

A few minutes later she and Earl have convinced the shop assistant to let her try it out on the footpath. 'Hell, mate, I may lose my job!' he insists.

'You don't need to worry, mate,' Paula assures him. 'Ah'll make it up to you.'

Immediately she skates through the aisles, Earl and the shop assistant running beside her, skilfully avoiding the other customers, who stop and watch her. Though inflated with admiration, Simon is now also worried about her damaging property, others and herself, as he hurries after them.

It is hot, the sun at mid-afternoon burning behind a thin screen of clouds. On their right on the cricket grounds, a couple of matches are in progress — not many spectators, the players glowing in their white uniforms. The park echoes with the click and clack of wooden bats on ball. Simon is sweating even though he is seated on a bench in the shade of a tree. He has bottles of water and hand towels for Paula and Earl.

In front stretching away from him is the skateboard park: a spacious arrangement of concrete curved banks, a central inverted dome-shaped arena, rinks that circle and slope down and around and joining flat levels, and wide steel railings and steps. Apart from Earl and his three friends (two of them Polynesian) and Paula, there are only a few other boarders. Immediately on arriving at the park, Earl had slid out of the car, clutching his board. 'Wish me luck, darling,' Paula had whispered, kissing Simon quickly on the cheek, and then hurrying after Earl. Her long hair gathered up and hidden in a red beanie, and dressed only in a white t-shirt and long khaki shorts, elbow and knee pads and Nike Air sports shoes, she looks thinner, more vulnerable, a Paula he's never seen before, Simon thinks.

Being much older and taller than the others, Paula stands out from them. The leader is a chunky, already heavily muscled Polynesian boy who Earl and other three boys immediately gather around, leaving Paula at the edge. With belly-churning concern about her and Earl's safety, Simon observes them closely.

The leader sets the moves. For the first fifteen minutes or so, the leader takes the group through what appears to Simon to be a warming up session, adjusting to their skateboards and the lay of the park. Both Earl and Paula adjust well, Simon observes.

Then the leader skates along the flat path, gathering speed. Earl and other boys follow him, then Paula; from that flat level the leader swerves down the path to the next level and the others follow, with Paula holding back; then the leader leaps down over three steps and, landing with a sharp thud, balances, arms outstretched. Whooping loudly, he continues along the next level. Fear is now threatening to burst Simon's throat as he watches Earl crouched on his board leaping off the step. He lands, almost stumbling forward onto his face, but catches his balance, and laughs as he steadies himself and follows the leader. The other boys leap one after the other. The last one loses his board and lands painfully on his side. Paula leaps high and lands beside him, swerving and stopping dead-still to help the boy, who is squirming in silent pain and clutching at his side. The others gather round their fallen comrade. Paula squats down and gently massages the pain from the boy's side. They help him up and take him to sit on the bench beside the track. Paula and the others gather round the leader, and Simon can't hear what they're saying.

They move to the edge of the round, steeply sided arena. The leader, on his board, steps off the edge and runs down with gathering speed, the wheels swishing metallically over the concrete, and then across the bottom and up the opposite side right up to the edge; he flattens out, lands and stops at the edge, gazing triumphantly (and with relief) across at them as they cheer and applaud his successful run. Simon is relieved when Earl and one of the other boys withdraw. He wishes and wishes for Paula not to do it.

But she is away before Simon can stop wishing, swiftly down, crouched low, arms out to keep her balance, eyes wide with adrenalin, speeding, speeding safely down to the bottom, then gathering momentum across the straight, and then she is up and up the opposite slope, and is in the air at the edge (with Simon's desperate hope) longer than the leader had been before she lands on the level and swerves to a stop, laughing freely as she raises her arms in victory over her fears. Even from that distance Simon can see the drops of sweat glittering, like black pearls, on her face and arms. Such courage and grace and daring! Her comrades cheer. The leader bows once towards her, grinning. Then they both slide down the slope and wait at the bottom for Earl and the others to join them. They take fives, with Paula now at the centre of their group.

In the next act of the game, she performs successfully all the moves that the leader sets, the younger boys dropping out as the level of difficulty and danger increases. She stumbles twice, landing once with a pain-crunching ahhh on her right hip and grazing it. Simon stops himself from rushing to her aid. She jumps up, brushes her sides with her hands and waves to Simon that she's okay.

For the rest of the session they get her to teach them some of her moves. Such grace, such mastery, such daring; no wonder *they* filled the All Blacks, the Silver Ferns, the Kiwis, and many of the other national teams! Simon thinks.

As they head towards him, the boys walk on both her sides, talking with brilliant animation. It is obvious to Simon that Paula is now their admired leader and that she is feeling awkward about that.

'I now believe the stereotype of you Polynesians being natural at sports!' Simon jokes, handing her the hand towel, which she starts wiping her face and arms with. She reacts with only a smile, saying nothing. The bottom of her t-shirt on her right hip is red with blood from the fall.

'It's okay.' She stops him from referring to it.

'Dad, Paula's the best!' Earl says.

'Yeah, really cool!' the others echo, and nod eagerly. Paula fishes fruit bars out of her sports bag and tosses them to the boys, who rip open the packaging and start biting hungrily into the bars. Simon hands them bottles of water.

Ancestry

While Earl and Paula are having showers, Simon boils some new potatoes, makes his favourite salad of tomatoes, beans, mixed leafy lettuce, pine nuts and capsicum and mixes a French dressing to go with it and the cold ham and salami he'd bought at Nosh. He's never enjoyed cooking but loves preparing summer meals of this kind. He opens a bottle of chardonnay and starts drinking.

He is puzzled when Paula appears dressed in jeans and a light sweater and sandals, her hair gathered under her Lightning Bolt beanie, ready to go out somewhere. Her face, without make-up, and arms glow with health, vigour and what he now admits is a magnificent beauty. 'Wow, that cold shower really shocked me back to earth!' she remarks. 'Looks good,' she compliments him. 'My dad's not well – got a text message from my mother. So after our meal I'll go and see him. He's the one who taught me how to skateboard.' Simon hopes she'll reveal more about her parents; she doesn't as she sets the table. His breath catches in his throat when he suddenly senses she is avoiding looking at him – but he dismisses that revelation, excusing her inattention as her being worried about her father. Right then, Earl enters and, without being asked – which, in the past, Simon has had to do – he helps Paula, all the time reminiscing, with boastful delight, about their skateboarding that afternoon.

When they sit down for their meal, Simon expects Earl to start eating without waiting for them, but he doesn't: he sits looking across at Paula, who bows her head. Earl bows his head too, and surprises his father. This is the first time she has behaved like this, Simon observes, as he feels a deep reverence emanating from her, a respect for things beyond them.

Hour of the Wolf

Previously he'd always scoffed at religion, boasting he is an atheist, but he now finds himself bowing his head.

'Our Heavenly Father, thank you for this marvellous day and for protecting Earl and me and our new friends from accidents, for granting us strength to express and fulfil the gifts of our bodies and spirit and courage.' As she prays, Simon acknowledges that she is using skating as a metaphor for life, for challenging death and injury, testing your courage and ability and daring at the edge, along the razor-sharp borderline between injury and death and continuing to breathe. '… Please help Earl become the boarder he wants to be; give him the courage and strength and agility and grace that he needs to achieve that,' she continues. 'And heal my dad, and help Simon and me in our work and life together.' As she blesses their food, Simon's cynicism about religion and Samoan people's overly heavy commitment to Christianity eases away.

'I'm bloody hungry!' Earl declares. Paula hands him the salad first. He hesitates, with scepticism.

'All champions eat lots of vegies, Earl. This is not the *Hour of the Meat-Eating Wolf*,' she tells him, smiling. Merriment dances in Earl's eyes as he uses the tongs and heaps salad onto his plate. 'Good, man,' she congratulates him.

'It's the *Hour of the Vegetarian Skater*,' Earl offers. She laughs softly and he joins her.

Because he isn't hungry, Simon takes a small helping and, while picking at it, sips his wine and watches, with envious wonder, the other ravenous two quickly devouring the salad and meat and potatoes and drinking heaps of water, and then cutting up more ham and salami and, with thick slices of wholemeal bread and mayonnaise, devouring those, ending with huge satiated belching and Earl exclaiming, 'Thanks, Dad, thanks!'

'Yeah, we needed that; skaters need fuel, heaps of fuel to live,' Paula adds.

Shortly after, when she starts clearing the table, Earl, again to Simon's pleasant surprise, orders her not to; that he'll do it and wash the dishes as well.

She brushes her hand in gratitude through his admiring hair, and says, 'Thanks, Earl. I've got to visit my dad. He's not well.' She embraces Simon from the back while he is still seated at the table, kisses the back of his neck, picks up her handbag and heads for the door.

'You want me to come with you?' Simon calls, wanting her to say yes, but she just waves her hand above her head. 'Ring me if you need anything,' he calls, his desire for her to need his help more demanding. She turns, and before he can catch her smile, she is out the door, and he is left with his now unquenchable *need* for her, of her.

FIRST VISIT

Laura slips out of bed, quietly, believing Dan is still asleep. After tying her hair in a ponytail and slipping on an 'ie lavalava and blue t-shirt, she glances at him and then opens the bedroom door and disappears down the corridor, her burnt skin still stinging from spending the previous afternoon in the hot sun. No one in their family is awake.

Outside she pulls a bush-knife out of the thatching of the kitchen fale, in which a few chickens are foraging, and then heads for the mangroves. There isn't yet any trace of sunlight in the transparent greyness of the dawn light that encompasses everything and into which she moves quickly towards the shore, her light auburn hair shimmering in the tangy breeze blowing in from the dark sea and the waves breaking on the reef, her bare feet, now toughened by a week of living in Malie, stepping fearlessly on the sharp rocks, bitsy sand and roots, and soon she is following the narrow leaf-covered track through the stand of palms and into the powerful smell of sea mud and the thick tangled area of mangrove trees whose long crablike roots are now covered by the high tide, her lungs and pores and head and nerves more alive than she's experienced for many years. Everything is so strange, so new, yet so invigorating, so challenging, like a perpetual injection of self-renewing adrenalin. So contrary to the ways Daniel and she had expected. Life is so *basic* and difficult and *different* in Malie, and there's little privacy, he'd warned her. As for the mozzies and flies and cockroaches, they are humungous! All that is certainly true, she'd concluded after their first two days, but instead of alienating her from Dan's 'āiga and village, those aspects had drawn her compulsively deeper and deeper into them. She hadn't expected herself to react this way, and she is euphorically surprised by it, and in congratulating herself in reacting like that, desires more of it.

For instance, yesterday, against Dan's, Lemu's and Fa'alua's caution that she'd get sunburn and hurt herself – besides, Pālagi shouldn't do such work – she'd spent most of the afternoon in the mangroves, with Teva and Ma'amusa, two of Dan's young female cousins who are finishing high school at Samoa College, gathering and stacking firewood. Hot, hard, dirty, smelly work, and, in her ineptitude, she'd been relentlessly determined to learn from her new-found cousins how to identify the right wood, use a bush-knife to hack it from the trees, slash the small twigs and leaves off the branches and then cut those into short lengths and stack them. And she hadn't minded her cousins laughing and giggling and wondering why Dan's very pale and delicate Pālagi wife would want to do such menial work unworthy of her. She could've stayed in their house, which had all the comforts of a Pālagi home. Why voluntarily choose to do this? And to enjoy it – they've

First Visit

never enjoyed it – was even more puzzling, strange; what's wrong with her? After they'd made the first stack and they'd told her that was enough wood and, without replying, she'd continued a second stack, and they then *had* to continue working, their puzzlement turned automatically to resentment. The Pālagi woman didn't even mind being covered with sweat-soaked dirt, mud and mosquito bites, and getting her hands blistered and cut and her soft skin burnt to the reddest red they'd ever seen! Serves her right for making them work and work and work and then, when she'd mastered the bush-knife and the techniques of cutting the firewood and stacking it neatly, correctly, outworking them in speed and skill and neatness. They didn't like that, no; no weak Palagi was going to do that to them! All that soon changed when, unexpectedly, she'd plunged fully clothed into the water and, like a dolphin, had swum into and around the mangrove roots, obviously loving it, and had then, in her hilariously inept Samoan, invited them to join her, and when they hadn't she'd scooped up handfuls of mud, rounded them into balls, and belted them with the balls, shrieking and laughing and laughing like a Samoan. They'd leapt in and, within seconds, a furious mud fight ensued, until they were all covered with stinking, healing mud and they'd looked at one another and, seeing only their eyes twinkling in their cloaks of mud, had stopped and laughed and laughed some more, with her out-laughing them in the way adults (and Pālagi), like her, shouldn't, and, in their growing, loving admiration of her, they promised themselves never to tell the elders of their 'āiga that Laura, *their* Laura, had behaved like a Samoan and a child while they'd been gathering firewood. They'd joked and laughed some more on their way back to the house. Lemu and Fa'alua, Daniel's stepmother, had rushed out, shocked by Laura being covered with mud and sunburn and bites and cuts and had started blaming them for her condition, but she'd laughed and told them she'd had a wonderful time. And again, they were surprised when she'd insisted on showering with them in their outdoors shower (in full view of everyone) and not in the one in the house.

A quivering sense of achievement radiates through her as she arrives at the stacks of firewood. She has to take the firewood home before others find it. She notes that no one has done that during the night. The problem is, short of carrying the wood home using her arms – that would take hours – how is she going to do it? Her delighted questing mind finds the solution in Albert Wendt's novel, *Leaves of the Banyan Tree*, which she'd studied in one of her undergraduate English courses. One of the characters had cut the firewood, stripped the bark from the branches of fau trees and used that to tie the wood in a tight bundle, then, using more bark strips round his shoulders to tie the bundle to his upper back, had carried the huge weight home, looking like 'a beast of burden'. She's vigorously eager to see how much weight she can manage and over what distance. She should be superbly fit after two hours of gym training, in Auckland, four days a week. Daniel, after years of training for rugby, now detested it and jogged only once a week on his own because she found jogging monotonous and boring.

Using the bush-knife she quickly cuts down long young fau branches, then with her teeth she grips the end of a bark strip at the end of one

First Visit

branch, grasps the branch firmly with her hands, and, triumphantly surprised at how easily the bark comes off and how well her teeth survive the ordeal, pulls it off with her teeth. She does that to two more branches. Still thinking of the passage in the novel, she takes two strips and places them parallel to each other on the ground. Across those she neatly stacks a layer of firewood, considers whether she can carry it and decides to place another layer on top, then another and, now almost bursting with her own self-belief, yet another. There!

With all her strength, and using her knowledge of knots acquired at Girl Guides, she ties the strips around the firewood, firmly, tests how well they are holding, steps back and admires her handiwork. No, she isn't romanticising the South Seas and the outdoors subsistence life, close to nature and using your ingenuity and the sheer strength of your body to survive. No, no noble-savage-thriving-in-a-South-Seas-paradise bullshit for this badly sunburnt Kiwi Amazon, who is revelling in her ability and strength and desire to overcome all the challenges in this different way of life, Samoa's, and through that learning other ways of doing and seeing and being, a compulsive continuation of a lifelong exploration of her own possibilities and testing the limits of her courage and body.

Around her the heat and light are intensifying rapidly, and her clothes are already soaked through with sweat and, like Tauilopepe – that's the name of the character in the novel – she stands above the large bundle of firewood, her muscles tightening with pulsing blood, her courage thudding in her throat, visualising, step by step, how she has to lift her load. She's relieved her teenage companions aren't there to see her crumpling under it. Now, one step forward, right above the bundle, turn your back to it, squat, reach down and back, grip the bark handles, first the left, uupp! Shove your arm through the handle now that is almost to your shoulder. Right! Now squat again, your right hand gripping the handle. Uuuppp! Yeah, sshhiittt! Got it! Hold the handles steady round your shoulders. Your whole body trembles with the weight of the bundle, your knees threaten to break; you stagger forward, stop and steady yourself. For a moment you doubt your ability to carry this weight. Just like Tauilopepe! Your saliva tastes suddenly of blood; you've bitten the corner of your tongue – yes, but it's proof of your stoic refusal to break under the weight. You take another step. The handles are cutting into your shoulders. You can bloody well do it! You take another step, then your feet start following each other, determined step by determined step, over the track through the mangrove trees now glittering with sun snared in their dew-covered leaves, through the fertile fetid smell of mud drying in the heat, through your easy comfortable, pampered, smug life of material and physical comfort back into the terrible, terrible cupboard darkness in which your increasingly insane mother had shut you whenever the fiery demons of her inevitable visions threatened to abduct you and where, in your desperate fear, you'd learned the feel and depth and geography of that darkness and had used that to live with it, overcoming it so you could confront any fear …

As she steps over a large puddle in the track, she hesitates and gazes down into her reflection: yes, you *do* look like a beast of burden, but a grinning victorious one ….

First Visit

Within a few demanding minutes she is outside the kitchen fale, trembling uncontrollably after bearing the weight all that way. She drops her shoulders, releasing the handles, and her load plunges with a resounding thud into the ground behind her. She flexes her arms, easing the pain from them.

She looks warily at the house, at the back veranda, and is relieved no one has been watching her. Swiftly she turns and, with firm steps, hurries back to the stacks, her whole being singing. Since meeting Daniel she's been learning Samoan and reading everything he's written and everything she can find on Samoa, including the poetry, and has loved it. Now she is testing *that* reality against the *real* Samoa; or is that read reality shaping how she is seeing and being in Samoa? Fuck that dry intellectual wanking, just live it and enjoy it – and she admits to herself that she *is* loving it. Besides, Albert Wendt's and Daniel's versions of Samoa are too bloody dark and bleak and distressing for her. She's never told Daniel that. Yes, her mind, body, everything that is her is thriving in the reality of Samoa as she lunges headlong into it …

After her fourth load, her body is a quivering bundle of wracked, pain-clogged muscles and bone, but she's heady with excitement at her refusal to give in. Fifth load. As she staggers towards the kitchen fale, she senses people on the back veranda, but she deliberately stops herself from glancing in that direction, not wanting any of them to interfere with her struggle by rushing forward and offering to take her load. Her sweat-soaked clothes flap round her. She turns her back to them. 'What are you doing?' Daniel's concerned voice slides over her left shoulder. She releases, her load cracks loudly as it hits the ground and, with her back still turned to them, she jogs back down the track. No, not even her crazy mother and the mainly abusive foster homes the welfare department had farmed her out to were able to destroy her. Daniel knows nothing about that – she hasn't allowed him into that past. Not because she's ashamed of it or doesn't want to shock him or win his love with it. No, she wants her whole triumph over the brutal, violent circumstances of her childhood to remain hers and hers alone.

Her astonished 'āiga is now on the veranda and in and behind the kitchen fale, observing her with her last load; her two cousins have already neatly stacked her previous loads and are now rushing to help her, but she holds her hands up and waves them away. When she falters, they rush forward again. 'Fuck off!' she orders. Astounded, shocked, the two look at their elders and Daniel. She pushes past them, stops beside the stacked firewood, throws back her shoulders wildly as if she's finally conquered the task that she'd set for herself, releasing her last load, turns, squats, pushes her arms under the bundle and, rising to her feet quickly, lifts it and hurls it onto the stack. Wheeling defiantly, she heads for the shower under the breadfruit trees. 'Mālō, galue!' Lemu congratulates her.

'Terrific work, Laura!' Dan calls.

Wonderful, wonderful! she sighs as the thick, bone-healing shower of cold water pours down over her; fucking wonderful! From the cupboard darkness, she'd learned to cherish even her mother, and after her mother had hanged herself in the asylum, Laura had, over the years, fashioned

First Visit

her memories into the tragic story of an innocent heroine whose insane demons had driven to her death.

Teva brings her a large towel, which, conscious that they're all watching, Laura wraps around her body. Under that, she copies how she's seen Dan doing it and carefully slips off her wet 'ie lavalava and t-shirt, squeezes most of the wetness out of them and, refusing Teva's offer, takes them and hangs them on the line. There, another achievement: undressing in public and not allowing others to treat you like a permanent guest. Teva and Ma'amusa are starting the fire in the kitchen fale to boil the kettle, as she hurries past and onto the veranda. 'Having a good time killing yourself?' Dan asks, eyes twinkling.

'Fuck yes,' she whispers so Lemu and Fa'alua, who are sitting on the veranda railing, won't hear, and sweeps past him and into the house.

In the bedroom, she gingerly spreads calamine lotion over the mosquito bites and sunburnt areas of her body, wincing and shutting her eyes in relief as the coolness of the lotion eases out the pain. She's amused by her appearance when she looks at herself in the dresser mirror: red blistered skin with large expanses of white calamine lotion.

Reluctantly and carefully she puts on some light panties and a clean 'ie lavalava, dries her hair with the hairdryer and tells herself she is succeeding superbly in achieving the aim of her first visit to Samoa and Dan's 'aiga: to learn everything about everything so she can *see* Dan in his complexity and depth and failings – and he has many of those – and thereby be able to cope better with the boundless, frightening love she's had for him ever since she'd helped him survive the breakup of his parents' marriage. Before Dan she'd not experienced such a love – and it is, at times, terrifying because she knows but doesn't want to know that she would even sacrifice her life for it.

She meets Dan in the corridor, embraces him tightly, kisses him, before he can caution her again, sweeps out and over the veranda and, almost running, is in the kitchen fale, in the thick smoke of the fire, with Teva and Ma'amusa, who are fanning the smoke away from their choking faces with large breadfruit leaves.

'You strong,' Teva says in English.

'Yes, you very strong,' Ma'amusa echoes.

'Yeah, tough!' She laughs. She knows her cousins are quite fluent in English after spending four years at Samoa College, where English is the medium of instruction.

'You not need to do all this,' Teva says.

'No, this work for Hamo people not Pālagi,' Ma'amusa elaborates.

'I'm not Pālagi or Hamo, I just want to learn,' she counters. When Teva laughs and Ma'amusa joins her, Laura joins them too, and the smoke and fale and surroundings vibrate with their laughter. 'I don't even know how to make a fire,' she admits.

'But there is electric stove in the Pālagi kitchen in the house,' Teva points out.

'But I'm not a Pālagi, I just want to learn.'

'What is the use of open fires in New Zealand?' Ma'amusa asks.

'Good bloody question,' she replies, 'but I just want to know how to make a fire like this.'

First Visit

'What about the electric kettle in the kitchen?' Teva tests her. 'It is quicker and no smoke.'

'Don't care, just teach me how to make a fire,' she ends it, her eyes and nose now choking with smoke-induced tears. 'You teach me Samoan too, okay?' They nod eagerly. 'From now on you talk only in Samoan to me, all right?'

'What if you don't understand?' Teva asks.

'Never mind, only Samoan, okay?'

'Okay!' They chorus. 'We use the "t" or "k"?'

'I'm not a faife'au,' she jokes, 'so use the "k".' She struggles up, swallows back the tears and phlegm, catches it at the back of her throat and then, with a loud swacking sound, spits it out of the fale, like she's seen Lemu do. She takes the end of her clean 'ie lavalava and wipes her mouth and the choking tears from her eyes. Her companions try not to laugh when they see the black charcoal streaks she leaves on her face and 'ie lavalava. Yes, their strange friend is *learning,* they decide.

'Laura, 'o 'oe 'o le lōia, ā?' Ma'amusa asks. They wait as she struggles to figure out the question.

Teva starts interpreting but Laura says, like a real Samoan: 'Se, 'aua!' So they wait, knowing lawyers aren't dumb: only very smart and intelligent people go to university and graduate as lawyers, Lemu has told them repeatedly, and every 'āiga in Samoa wants their sons to be lawyers, so to be a woman and a lawyer, Laura is doubly intelligent. 'Koe fai … fai mai lau … fesili,' she requests.

'Māgaia lau fa'a-Samoa, Laura!' Ma'amusa congratulates her. So Teva repeats her question.

Ancestry

Laura's face glows, her eyes alight with discovery. "Ī, 'o a'u o le lōia e lē iloa – e lē iloa kafu se afi!' Her companions clap, and she claps with them. The smoke has cleared, and the fire is now flaming freely under and around the soot-caked kettle.

She's suffered a week of Pālagi breakfasts of cornflakes, fried eggs, toast, butter, marmalade and coffee because she doesn't want to offend their hosts by asking for Samoan meals. When she told Dan that the previous night, he'd hedged, and she knew he too didn't want to cause offence. Dan in New Zealand, where he'd grown up, is more difficult to understand because he's 'at home' there, blending in easily with everything. But in the past week of their first visit together to Malie, where she's expecting him to be even more part of everything, she is seeing him more clearly, because he is definitely *not* fitting into what is expected of him. Being a Samoan, Malie is expecting him to *know* about what that is and behave accordingly. And the Dan she loves has never wanted to conform to what the majority of people want in most things; not in New Zealand anyway. Here he is caught between being that and being 'a proper Samoan', which, she's now convinced, he doesn't really know much about. She's deriving enormous enjoyment out of observing him wriggling and squirming as he tries to walk that endless tight rope. Here, the people have accorded her what she calls pre-forgiveness: being a naive, manner-less Pālagi, they *expect* her to break and trespass and be ignorant of every feature of civilised Samoan behaviour, and when she trespasses, forgiveness is automatic. Poor Dan, though! My beautiful,

First Visit

tortuously introspective darling is caught in the quagmire of identity and his people's demanding expectations.

'O le ā le breakfast fa'a-Samoa?' she asks her companions, after struggling to formulate the question.

'O le fa'alifu, le koko Samoa ...', Ma'amusa starts.

'... Ma se i'a falai po'o se pisupo,' Teva ends the menu.

Laura remembers and looks at the basket of taro and bunch of green bananas, which she and Dan had fetched from the plantation two days before and had put on the far rafters of the kitchen fale. Beside those is a large black pot. Dry coconuts lie outside by the firewood, and, getting up quickly, she hurries over, takes down the pot and goes to the outside tap. "O le ā le mea 'ua kupu?' Teva calls. Ma'amusa gets up to go and help her, but Laura waves her back down to her seat of coconut husks.

They watch her as she staggers back with the pot now full of water, thumps it down next to the kettle on the fire and goes over to the rafters. Teva brings the pot's silver lid and puts it on the pot. Laura – and they marvel at her strength – pulls down the hefty basket of taro, and with one hand and on well-muscled legs carries it over to the valusaga outside and dumps it there. Again, more work, Teva and Ma'amusa sigh and look at each other, and they get up stoically and go to fetch the basins, other ingredients and implements needed for making the Samoan breakfast their Pālagi lawyer friend obviously wants.

'Why not make your Samoan breakfast in the kitchen?' Dan suggests hesitantly when he comes out and finds Teva teaching Laura how to husk coconuts using the dangerously sharp mele'i. One wrong move and you can impale yourself on it.

'Kaukala in Samoan,' Laura demands. She jabs the coconut down onto the sharp point of the mele'i. Dan jumps over and stops her. "Ou ke fia iloa fai!' she insists. So he steps behind her, his body tight against her back, his jaw pressing down over her right shoulder, grips her hands from behind and, pressing down on the impaled coconut, twists, and levers part of the husk off the coconut shell; then once again jabs the nut down on the point and twists and levers up, and another strip of husk peels off, and so on until the whole shell is bare of the husk. All the time she's breathlessly aware of his warm body, his slightly musky odour and his bulge against her buttocks. 'Sexy, too, darling,' she whispers. 'You've never been *closer*!'

'Fa'aaogā le gagaga Samoa,' Ma'amusa reminds her, and they all laugh.

So for the next hour or so, they teach Laura how to split open the nuts, scrape the meat out of them using a tuai and squeeze the milk out of the meat; and to scrape the skin off the taro and, using the heavy machete, cut them into pieces and lower the pieces into the boiling water; they then help her roast the cacao beans, peel off the hard skins and pound the beans into a paste in the wooden pestle; and when their breakfast is almost ready, her cousins congratulate her on being 'the best lawyer cooker of Samoan food in the world!'

'In Samoan', she reminds them. So they look at Dan who, grinning widely, interprets:

First Visit

'Laura, 'o 'oe 'o le lōia e gumela kasi i le makā'upu kau kuka i le lalolagi.' Dan and Ma'amusa and Teva bow to her, and she curtsies to them. When she looks round, the rest of their 'āiga are on the veranda and in the faleo'o, grinning and applauding.

She prefers to serve their Samoan breakfast the Samoan way, but when she hurries to the dining room to prepare for that, Fa'alua has already set the table the Pālagi way, with cutlery and crockery and even serviettes.

Since arriving she has felt uncomfortable being treated as a special guest, eating in the Pālagi house's dining room, with only Lemu and Fa'alua and Dan, while the rest of their 'āiga ate afterwards in the faleo'o. There are some things in the fa'a-Samoa that she will never conform to, and one of them is the strict division between class and age groups, the matai and elders receiving all the respect and preferential treatment while the untitled men, women and children serve them and then eat separately, afterwards. This time, she sets places for Teva and Ma'amusa at the table, and, when her cousins refuse that, she gazes heatedly at Dan, who orders them to sit down at the table.

In tense silence, the others take their places, with Lemu at the head of the table, as usual, and for the first time Laura experiences not one twitch of guilt about offending her hosts.

'Good morning,' Lemu greets them, in English. 'Laura, will you please say our grace for the breakfast that you have prepared?' What? She stops herself just in time from declining automatically, and for a lost moment she doesn't know how to react to Lemu's request, and everyone, especially Dan, experiences a tense awkwardness. Finally, she banishes her qualms about being an atheist, convincing herself that, from what she's observed of Samoan behaviour, religion is more a social custom than anything else.

'In Samoan,' Dan says, and she can feel him enjoying that.

She clears her throat, softly, and then, hesitantly but deliberately, she prays using the 'k': 'Le Akua e, fa'amolemole fa'amaguia mai iā Lemu ma – ma lo mākou 'āiga 'ākoa.' She pauses; now more sure of herself, she continues, 'Ku'u mai iā Kanielu se loko fa'amaualalo 'auā e lē iloa e ia oga fai se kuka magogi pei oga mākou kukaiga ma Keva ma Ma'amusa. Fa'afekai mo mea'ai 'ua e foa'i mai mo mākou kino. I le suafa o Iesu, Amege!'

Lemu chuckles and thanks her. 'You speak better Samoan than your husband,' he adds.

'Hear that, Kanielu in the lion's den?' Laura laughs.

'That'll be the day!' Daniel counters.

NEIGHBOURS

Apart from his lawyers, no one, including Anne, needed to know, Eric decided. It was overcast, with the heavy mattress of grey cloud hanging low, keeping the humid heat trapped in the city, and the nine o'clock sun hidden from view. He increased the pace of his walking, his thick-soled tramping sandals crunching mutedly over the footpath, sweat dripping down his body and soaking his t-shirt and shorts. He walked four times each week, for forty-five minutes, round the streets of Ponsonby, and had done so since he and Anne had shifted into Lincoln Street three years before. On the week days, if he had a full schedule of lectures and appointments, he walked early in the mornings. Otherwise, in summer, he preferred to walk just before evening when it was cool, and during winter at midday when it was less cold.

He turned into John Street and started uphill, on the last stretch of the walk before turning into his street. Hardly any traffic and only a young couple coming downhill, dragged along at a brisk pace by their magnificent husky. The couple glanced up at him as they hurried past, the young man raising his eyebrows in greeting. Eric acknowledged him with a nod. For a brisk moment, he inhaled the strong smell of dog.

His double-storied home was halfway up Lincoln Street, on the left-hand side. Just before it was the large white house, with the dark grey roof, that belonged to Jim and Mata Mein, a retired Samoan couple in their seventies – he'd been an executive in a supermarket chain, and she'd worked for Social Welfare. They'd been living there for over forty years. The Meins were the best gardeners Eric had ever known. Along the front of the house was a lush garden of ponga, nīkau and Tahitian pōhutukawa, with an undercover of ground ferns and grasses. Behind the house, taking up the second half of the back yard, was an even more enviable vegetable garden, which Jim was proud of showing them whenever they were over there. Bordered by feijoas, a couple of lemon trees and an avocado tree, the garden contained potatoes, tomatoes, green beans, carrots, different types of lettuce and other vegetables and herbs. Throughout much of the year, most of the street benefitted from that garden's abundant harvest.

Dressed in his usual gardening clothes – worn jeans, a faded Manu Samoa rugby jersey and Adidas cap, working boots and grey gardening cloves – Jim was in the front garden, weeding and pruning. He saw Eric and waved.

Eric stopped. 'How's the gardening?' Eric greeted Jim, going up to the white fence and into the fierce odour of freshly uprooted weeds and cut branches.

Neighbours

Smiling widely, Jim replied, 'Bloody difficult to maintain the gardens at our age and in this heat.' Ever since he and Mata had gone over, with a gift of vegetables, to welcome Eric and Anne the first week they'd shifted in, he'd grown to trust them, despite his wish, during the first year, to maintain a wary aloofness. Anne was the openly trusting one, and she and Mata soon became friends. Eric followed Anne into their affections. Now Jim and Mata considered them generous neighbours; the first Pālagi neighbours they'd allowed to be that.

'Looks great to me, Jim,' Eric said. 'And you're younger and fitter than anyone in our street!' He meant that: Jim looked as if he was only fifty-five at the most: Eric's age. On their second visit to the Meins' house, Eric had discovered that the Meins had a bench press and a full set of weights, on the back veranda, which they used five days a week in strenuous one-hour sessions. 'One weight-training session a day keeps osteoporosis away!' Mata had declared, jokingly. And they'd been doing it for over thirty years.

The strong enticing smell of coffee greeted him as he entered the house, bent down, pulled off his sandals and lined them along the wall. 'Hi!' he called as he headed upstairs to the bathroom.

'Coffee's ready,' Anne replied.

In the bathroom, he stripped off his drenched t-shirt and dried his face and upper body with a hand towel. On his way down and to the kitchen, he shoved on a clean t-shirt, combed down his long bristly hair with his fingers and suddenly realised he was hungry.

Ancestry

Dressed only in her blue bathrobe, Anne sat at the dining table, drinking her coffee out of her favourite mug and reading that morning's *Herald*. She'd just showered and washed her hair, so a white towel was wrapped round her head, and her face and arms were still red from the shower's heat. The coffee plunger, the small jug of hot milk, honey and his mug were in the middle of the table. He poured his coffee, put milk in it and, after honeying it, sat down opposite her.

She always looked neat, tidy and clean, an outward manifestation of her devotion to keeping the world around her in order, in logical symmetry and design and therefore easier to understand and manage. When he'd first met her, six years before, she'd just left her marriage and her lucrative partnership in the successful advertising company that she and her husband Bill had established, and was trying to establish a new company. The recession had stopped that, so for the past year, while working as a consultant, she'd been researching the financial feasibility of various business possibilities.

'Would you like some scrambled eggs, darling?' he asked.

'No thanks,' she replied without looking up from the paper. He waited but she didn't offer, so he went to the stove, pulled out the small iron frying pan, got out three eggs and, within a few minutes, was cooking scrambled eggs and some sliced tomatoes. 'Got any lectures today?' she asked.

'Just one at four,' he replied. He started laying out his breakfast on the table.

Neighbours

She got up and, unwinding the towel from her head, started drying her hair with it. 'Mata and I are picking up Jeannie later and going for lunch at the Fish Market,' she told him. Jeannie was Mata's only daughter and Anne's age. Anne and Mata loved seafood, especially fresh oysters and ota, and lunched at the Fish Market on the waterfront once a week. He and Jim, who didn't like any raw seafood, sometimes went with them. She paused and asked, 'Would you like to join us?'

'I've got to prepare my lecture and mark some essays,' he lied, sensing that Anne really wanted only females there. She was gone swiftly.

From the windows of his study he could see into the Meins' backyard garden. His whole body tingled healthily from the pummelling heat of the fast shower and the hard towelling he'd given it. He sat down in front of his computer and switched it on. Jim was now hoeing round the potatoes, sweat dripping off his face and arms. Such dedication and care, he thought with envy. Before they'd bought the house, which they'd both liked on their first inspection, he'd hesitated when he'd found out that their neighbours were Samoan and retired, but when he'd raised his reservations with Anne, she'd confronted him with, 'What's wrong with Samoans and superannuitants?' Immediate affronted defensiveness on his part; he'd been lost for what to say. 'Eric, I don't give a damn about the racist stereotypes. I love the house and what we can do with it.' This was their first confrontation, his first glimpse of her frankness and intolerance of anything that appeared to be discriminatory on grounds of race, gender, age and so forth. 'And going on the huge price they're asking for this house, the Meins, being Samoans, haven't brought the property values down in this street!'

When Eric looked down again, Jim was leaning on his hoe and drying his forehead and arms with a dirt-stained hand towel. Jim glanced up and, seeing him, waved. He waved back. He was so glad that they'd bought the house, and the Mein family was one of the main reasons for him feeling that way. They'd even built a gate between their backyards the year before, and Eric had paid for all of it. You live and learn. People were what they were, not what prejudice dictated or predetermined.

He opened his email. The third email was a lengthy one from his lawyers detailing their dealings with his father's lawyers and the contents of his father's will. He emailed them back, instructing them not to let anyone, including Anne and his surviving relatives on his father's side, know anything about the will or that his father had died.

For a long contemplative while, he sat watching Jim working, and remembering his parents with deepening sadness and regret. Even with his first wife, Pamela, in their ten-year marriage, he'd deliberately not told her the truth about his father (and his mother). For Pamela, he'd *created* parents with a brief history: at high school, his mother became pregnant – she never told anyone who the father was – and, after giving birth to him in a family and society that totally condemned birth out of wedlock and adopting him out, she'd died of incurable leukaemia. Later, when he'd realised that telling such lies – well, not really lies – only led to you telling more to make the first ones credible, and you had to remember those lies for the rest of your life in order not to contradict yourself and be exposed, he panicked every time someone asked about his parents. He broke from his recollections and noticed that Jim wasn't in the garden any more and the newly hoed soil round the potatoes was a wet, glittering black.

That evening when he got home from work, Anne told him that the Meins wanted them to come over that Sunday for lunch. 'When I asked Mata about what we could bring, she said, "Bring only a large appetite!"' She added. This was the first time they'd been invited for lunch; until now it had only been for morning or afternoon tea, or a casual drink, and they'd reciprocated in that way.

Throughout most of his life, he could never remember his dreams; not in detail anyway. However, ever since his lawyers rang him to inform him of his father's death, his dreams had become more detailed and they felt starkly accusing, threatening, because at their centre was a ferocious presence – a creature? – that was creating itself slowly and, when it was complete, would spring into his awareness. He and Anne slept in separate bedrooms; her choice because sometimes he snored badly and she said she preferred to 'spread out'. As his dreams worsened he wished she was there to wake him when the creature was whole, and save him from it.

Tonight, the presence – first a featureless swirling darkness – suddenly assumed the face of a young man he'd never seen before but he felt he knew. Penetrating black eyes under a high forehead, black hair shaved almost to the scalp, hollow cheeks, thin sharp nose, thin pale lips; a cocky, cynical, know-it-all face, with the assuming shape of a sneer rippling across it. Unexpectedly there was a close-up of his glistening eyes, of his silver black retinas, in which were reflected the face of a young woman with long wavy auburn hair framing a face that was shaped in a predetermined look of fear that was worsening, worsening, and in her eyes, in her retinas, was the enlarging reflection of the young man, clench-fisted right hand upraised, momentarily, and then lunging down at her, into the utterly exposed centre of her …

'… It's okay, darling, it's okay,' Anne was whispering into his ear, and he felt her reassuring arms around him. He buried his face between her breasts and sighed his fear into her warmth. 'I could hear you from my room, darling,' she said. He tightened his embrace. 'You were – were screaming, well, in a suppressed sort of way …'

'… Had a terrible dream …'

'About what?' she asked.

He hesitated and then lied, 'About a presence sliding into my room and into my bed, becoming the bed, which then enveloped me, wrapping itself around me, and pulling me down, down …'

In a short while she fell asleep holding him.

The dreadful fear he'd experienced and his mind's refusal to release him from admitting to himself that the young protagonists were his parents kept him awake for a long time.

Mata had told Anne not to bring anything but Eric made a large mixed vegetable salad and French dressing and Anne roasted a shoulder of pork. They also had four bottles of champagne to take. Though, as they showered and dressed, they continued to feel apprehensive about what they anticipated was going to be a large gathering in which they wouldn't know how to behave correctly, that eased away when Jeannie came through the back gate and into the kitchen, exclaiming, 'Wow, guys, that pork smells absolutely delicious!' She hugged and kissed them on the cheeks. 'Dad wants you to come over now cos he wants someone to drink with – most of our 'āiga don't drink alcohol on Sunday,' she said. Early in Anne's life, she'd realised she had the knack of winning other people's trust and affection easily – not that she worked at it deliberately. Her father had said 'my beautiful daughter loves people and animals and they reciprocate that automatically'. When she first met Jeannie, she sensed immediately that Jeannie possessed the same gift, and, though they were very different in other ways, Jeannie became the sister she'd always wanted. 'Champagne; wow!' Jeannie said as Eric pulled the bottles out of the fridge and packed them into an esky. 'Now I'm certainly going to have a drink!'

As they followed each other through the gate and up the path between the vegetable beds, carrying the food and esky, Anne saw that the wide back veranda was now the reception area, with all the sofas and armchairs from the sitting room arranged neatly across it. Each table had a large bouquet of flowers on it. And she knew this was more than a lunch.

Sitting alone on the central sofa was a thin old man with wispy white hair, dressed in a bright red floral shirt and black 'ie lavalava. Two elderly women, obviously sisters, sat in the sofa next to his. Jim and Mata occupied the armchairs opposite them. A young woman, with a yellow flower in her ear, was serving them snacks. On the corner on the ground was a hefty wooden table under a wide beach umbrella. On it were glasses and bottles – obviously the bar. Behind the bar was a young man who looked like Jeannie. A few men and women were coming in and out of the kitchen and house. Anne noticed that most of the people resembled one another, all sharing the prominent forehead of the old man on the sofa.

As soon and Jim and Mata saw them they waved them onto the veranda, but Anne and Jeanie veered off into the kitchen with the food, while Eric took the esky to the bar. 'What's this lunch for, Jeannie?' Anne asked, concerned.

'It's Dad's seventy-fifth birthday – and you're the only non-family guests,' Jeannie replied. 'Dad didn't want a party but we talked him into it.' She laughed. 'He didn't want anyone to know this lunch was his birthday party, so you don't need to worry about presents or anything.' She placed her hand on Anne's shoulder in reassurance, and Anne's anxiety eased away.

When Eric went onto the veranda, he walked round introducing himself, shaking hands first with the old man, then the women, and finally with Jim and Mata, who introduced the old man as Hans, Jim's older and only surviving brother, and the women as Renata and Effi, Jim's only surviving sisters. Such German names, yet so Samoan-looking, Eric observed.

When Anne and Jeannie and the young barman brought an opened champagne bottle and some champagne glasses, Anne kissed all the guests and offered them the champagne, which, shyly, they turned down. 'All the more for us,' Mata laughed as she took a glass.

Neighbours

'Eric and Anne, thank you for this!' Jim said, holding up his glass.

Jeannie quickly gathered everyone from inside the house. The five older men and women were Jim's sisters' children and Mata's cousins, the two teenagers and the barman were Jeanie's children, and the others were various nephews, nieces and cousins. None of them accepted Anne's offer of champagne or the young barman's offer of other alcohol. A young woman brought them mango juice. After they'd all been introduced to Anne and Eric, only the four oldest stayed with the elders; the rest returned to the kitchen and dining room to prepare the lunch.

'Like all true fundamentalist Christians and Samoans, most of our 'āiga do not drink the devil's water,' Jeannie remarked. Most of the elders laughed, the old man wheezing his laughter as if he was choking.

'You can laugh,' Jim accused Hans. 'You used to outdrink all of us until your heart started packing up!'

'And before I returned to God,' Hans continued. 'You know of course,' he turned to Eric and Anne, 'that Jim and Mata are the only atheists – or is it agnostics? – in our Christian 'āiga?'

In the conversation that ensued Anne and Eric gathered that the Meins' surname had come from a German sea captain who'd settled in Samoa in the mid-nineteenth century, marrying into one of the prominent families in a village called Malie. Because of his European surname, the original Mein's oldest grandson was the first of the family to be allowed to settle in New Zealand, and he had worked and saved and sent for the next Meins. That pattern continued to Hans, who migrated to New Zealand after the Second World War; he had saved money and sent for

Jim and another brother. Over the years, all of Jim's eleven brothers and sisters had settled in New Zealand, and mainly in Auckland.

'In case you're wondering why Jim's name is Jim and not a really hefty German one like all of ours,' Hans said, his body shaking visibly with mirth, 'it's because our father was apprenticed to a Kiwi plumber called Jim Katten, who he admired enormously.'

'Yes, Jim Katten Mein,' Renata echoed.

'What a handle!' laughed Effi. The two sisters were built slender and slim like Hans, and looked like twins.

'Better than Hans Bruno, Renata Eva, and Effi Johanna!' laughed Jim.

As this light-hearted banter about ancestry and naming continued, Eric grew aware that he was feeling more and more defensive. He was most alarmed when Renata asked Anne about her family, and Anne, without hesitation, explained that she'd been born in New Plymouth and, like Mata, was an only child. 'Well, I became an only child when my sister Ethel, who was born prematurely, died after only five months. My parents were both GPs who, after Ethel's death, never referred to her again; well, not in my presence. Beyond my parents, I know only vaguely of my grandparents and other ancestors before them. My parents seemed uninterested in any of that. They were more devoted to their patients and investing in property and getting me to do a business degree …' As she detailed her family history, Eric realised this was the first time he was learning a lot about Anne's family; a subject that, in their relationship, he'd avoided meticulously in case she asked after his family. And because he'd spent much of his life manufacturing a family history, he knew

Anne, like the Meins, was presenting a censored, heavily edited version of her family. Despite that, he knew she was telling 'the truth'. He tried to remember what he'd told Anne about his parents, and grew more afraid when he started doubting his recollections. '… Like many GPs, my parents, while caring wholeheartedly for their patients, neglected their own health badly. My mother, a heavy smoker, died of pancreatic cancer when I was finishing my degree, and my father of a heart attack about three years later.' Anne stopped, traces of tears in her eyes. Mata came over and held her. 'This is the first time I've talked about them in such a long time,' she admitted. Jeannie refilled her glass. 'Thank you for making me do that.'

'Here's to Anne's parents and 'āiga,' Hans toasted, raising his glass of mango juice.

"Ia manuia!' Jim and Renata and Effi toasted.

And they all clinked glasses and drank. Eric reached across and held Anne's arm and, after clinking glasses with her, he again drank his champagne until his glass was empty. Now he needed to divert the conversation away from himself, so he got up and offered to get drinks for everyone, but Mata told him he was a guest. The young barman came and took their orders.

Over the three years he had known them, Jim had gathered much detail about Anne's life and work – she was always forthcoming about those – and much about Eric's career and work, but very little about his parents and his childhood. Now, as the alcohol eased throughout his body and head and he felt even closer to Anne and Eric, he *needed* to know. All autobiographies that individuals and families made public were heavily edited versions. No one wanted their so-called skeletons to come clacking out of the cupboard. If they did, they dressed them up to bolster their reputation or they laughed them away. 'So, my friend, Eric, what's your whakapapa?' Jim asked, and tried to sound casual about it.

Eric took a sip of his refilled glass, smiled, and stated, 'Nothing really as long and as interesting as the Meins'. No adventurous sea captain from a cold Europe and the start of a huge and illustrious 'āiga – did I say that correctly?' The elders nodded and grinned. 'I never knew my parents; well – only for the first five or so years of my life, and I can't remember much about that. The information I have about them, and my ancestors before them, I've gathered from my Aunt Sybil and Uncle Roger, who raised me, and from other people and the little research I've done. My Pākehā ancestors, poverty-stricken, migrated here from England. What they did and how they fared here in those tough settler days I don't know anything about.' He paused, now feeling *comfortable* and safe with that narration. 'My parents came along after the Second World War. Dad was born in Blenheim; Mum in Hawera. They met in their twenties while she was working in the railway café in Wellington and he was a railway mechanic. Fell in love, had me, and five years later she died in a car accident …' He had to stop; sorrow was filling his throat. He swallowed it back and then continued, 'Dad was driving and he blamed himself. He gave me to his sister Sybil to care for while he retreated into the interior, to Taihape, to work in the railway gangs constructing new lines. A few months later, he fell off a new bridge they were building across a river.'

Neighbours

He paused again. Anne reached over and held his hand, tightly. 'My Aunt Sybil and Uncle Roger raised me. They were marvellous parents. They had no children, so when they died in the 1970s, I had no other relatives left. And here I am, fortunate to be married to this beautiful woman and being with neighbours we respect and' – he hesitated and then said it – 'love and admire.' He knew he had them believing utterly.

'Mālō, mālō!' Hans and Jim congratulated him.

'Here's a toast to Eric and his 'āiga,' Renata announced, raising her glass.

'To Eric and his 'āiga!' All the elders toasted.

Jim went over to Eric, embraced him and pulled him up to his feet. Mata pulled up Anne. 'To the best neighbours we've ever had,' Jim declared, and the whole veranda and neighbourhood resounded with another toast.

'Careful with the champagne!' Jeannie cautioned. 'We're going to run out of it before we can toast the birthday boy.'

Soon after, a woman came and whispered in Jeannie's ear, and Jeannie announced that lunch was ready.

They followed Hans and Jim into the spacious dining room. The heavy round rimu dining table was fatly laden with food, crockery and cutlery; at the centre of it was a small chocolate birthday cake with one candle in the middle. Anne had not seen such a magnificent feast before. She clutched Eric's hand. 'Wow,' Eric whispered.

'We know the birthday boy and Eric are not fond of raw seafood, Anne, but we made sure our favourite oysters and oka found their way onto this table,' Mata said. 'And there's more in the fridge because I know Hans, Renata and Effi are addicts too.' Some of the elders laughed.

'Good for the *muscles*!' Hans remarked.

'Speak for yourself!' Jim improved on the joke. Louder laughter.

Everyone came into the room, and those who were serving lined up behind the circle of elders. Anne realised that her appetite had been sharpened greatly by the champagne, the emotional happiness she was experiencing, the hypnotic aromas of the various dishes and not having had breakfast, but she knew she had to wait.

Hans stepped up and stood in front of the birthday cake. He looked round at everyone and then started speaking in Samoan in what was obviously oratory. Up until then, because all the elders had spoken only English, Anne had assumed their knowledge of Samoan was limited. But, as Hans spoke, and his whole being and voice assumed a charismatic strength that held her even though she didn't understand Samoan, she concluded that there was profound respect and love of the language – and other things Samoan – there. Hans was obviously welcoming everyone, acknowledging all the members of his 'āiga and Anne and Eric. He then wished Jim happy birthday: 'To our beloved brother Jim Katten, a happy seventy-fifth birthday,' he broke into English. Hurriedly, Jeannie and the barman refilled their glasses and they drank a toast to Jim.

'Jim Katten, may you live for as long as you want!' Renata called.

'Yes, as long as the Atua Tagaloaalagi allows!' Effi added.

Mata lit the candle, Jim blew it out and they cheered and then sang happy birthday. The singing was in four-part harmony, Anne identified.

Obviously the result of family and communal singing over generations. The stereotype of Polynesians being superb singers was *accurate* in this case!

In Samoan, Jim thanked Hans and his sisters and Mata and everyone for the party, and then said in English, 'For the benefit of Jeannie and all the other younger ones who don't know, Tagaloaalagi is Samoa's supreme god and creator.'

'Of course I know, Dad,' Jeannie protested. 'You told me years ago.'

'Apart from Jim Katten and a few other pagan Samoans, no other Samoan believes in Tagaloa any more!' Hans tried to joke, but Anne detected a deep regretful tone in his voice.

'Time for overeating and adding on the calories!' Mata declared, handing Hans a plate.

Hans bowed his head and said grace in English.

About two hours after lunch, Hans, Renata and Effi and their children left, saying they had to go to a church function, taking with them a share of the leftover food. The barman and the other servers cleaned up and then left, with their share of the food. Jim, Mata, Jeannie, Anne and Eric continued drinking wine and beer that Mata kept producing from the freezer in the store room under the house. Though they were feeling woozy and bloated from eating and drinking too much, their absolute contentment at sharing the Mein 'āiga's love and hospitality kept them lucidly buoyant and aware and wanting that time to continue. Anne discerned her speech was slurred, and her limbs were not moving smartly to her instructions, but she was enjoying that too.

'The birthday boy's asleep,' Jeannie laughed, pointing at her father, who was half-slumped in his armchair, his chin resting on his chest, purring audibly.

'At seventy-five, he's earned it,' Eric exclaimed. 'He deserves it.'

'And the birthday boy's girlfriend is falling asleep too, from too much eating, drinking and old age!' Mata staggered up to her unsteady feet. Jeannie held her up. Anne rushed over and hugged them both.

Eric went over to Jim and, taking the empty beer glass out of his hand, bent down and kissed him on the forehead. 'Thank you for inviting us, Jim Katten.'

… This time, the sneering young man's upraised fist was coming down in slow motion into his eyes as he was gazing up at him. And he could hear himself screaming at the edge of his hearing, screaming, and he was belching up the vile burning taste of his acidy stomach, and desperately hoping for Anne to save him … Thankfully he was awake, out of the recurring dream, but Anne wasn't there holding him, consoling him. He rolled onto his back and sat up, shaking and drenched with sweat, and wanting to rush into Anne's bedroom, but he forced himself not to.

Stripping off his pyjama pants, he staggered into the bathroom and into the shower, and switched it on. The cold water stung his body and head awake, and the dregs of the dream were gone, but the cold suddenly felt icy and he started shivering. He switched off the shower, rushed out and towelled himself with fierce ferocity until his body was warm again.

Neighbours

A short while later, dressed in the yukata Anne had bought him on a business trip to Japan, he sat in the computer chair in his study, gazing down into the shifting, murmuring darkness that now filled the Meins' backyard, at the bright reflection his study windows were casting across the vegetable beds. Such a happy, fulfilling family day; one that he'd never really experienced before and would not forget ever. And as his parents had once again insisted on intruding, he welcomed them, without reservation, for the first time in years.

Because he'd created so many lies, a whole mythology of them, about his parents, it took him a long painful time to sift through those to find 'the truth' about them.

The night deepened and heightened the brightness of his windows' reflection across the vegetables and made them look like black steel sculptures. Aunt Sybil and Uncle Roger were real, and they'd raised him after his father had killed his mother accidentally during a quarrel and was found guilty of manslaughter and sentenced to ten years in prison. He was nine when that had happened, and he couldn't remember much about any of it and had had to rely on his aunt and uncle to provide him with that information. As a teenager, he'd grown hugely ashamed of it, and had insisted that his guardians change his surname to theirs. (He would carry that shame and anger, he believed, forever.) When he went to university in Auckland he never returned to Blenheim. He kept in touch with his guardians until Aunt Sybil died unexpectedly of heart failure, and then, because Uncle Roger wasn't a very good correspondent, he'd let the connection lapse. Throughout his life, he'd kept well away from his father, but always ensured he knew where his father was and what he was doing, so he would never have to meet him.

Now, in death, his father was with him again, and with that returned his beautiful, beautiful mother. In the windows' reflection below he saw – coming into focus – the wedding portrait of his parents that had occupied the central position on his aunt's and uncle's fireplace.

ANCESTRY

Late morning, a dull Anzac Day, as I drove through largely empty streets to Foodtown. I parked my car in the almost empty parking lot, found the supermarket wasn't opening until 1 pm, and strolled across Williamson Avenue to the Café Oceania, where Andrea and I often brunched. I was relieved even more to find a hungry heater gobbling up the cold in that place. I've lived in New Zealand for over forty years, but I've always found it difficult to live with the cold. When Andrea gets impatient with my annual early winter complaints about the cold, she usually says, curtly, 'Go back to your village then and see what you think of the humid heat there. You'll soon be saying you're a winter lover!' Admittedly when our small family firm started doing well, I'd tried to persuade her we should build a house in her village and spend the New Zealand winters there. She'd been supportive then but, over the years, after the deaths of her beloved family elders in Samoa, especially her grandmother Faivai, who'd raised her, had stopped discussing it.

Ancestry

I sat down at the double table near the heater by the front windows, unbuttoned my jacket, stretched out my legs under the table and looked forward to being warmed.

For the first time I started analysing Andrea's surprising actions that morning. She'd risen early, showered quickly and, after dressing for the cold, had mumbled she was going with Regina and our grandson Amataga to the Anzac Dawn Parade. I hadn't thought it unusual then. Now, as the warmth eased into my limbs, I considered her actions extremely puzzling – and hurtful. It was the first time she'd ever done that; also she and Regina hadn't consulted me or asked me to come. Why? She knew I didn't hold strong views about war and Anzac Day. She was the one who was cynical about 'colonised people and the poor' sacrificing themselves for their colonial mother country; she was the one who at least twice a year suffered what she called 'terrible anti-war dreams', which, in our usual practice, she storied to me when she woke and we interrogated in order to fit them into the meaning of our life. And here she was going to the memorial service for the thousands of colonials who'd died in Gallipoli. Why? As far as I knew, none of our relatives had 'fallen' there. She was also leaving me out of something she considered important; if I did that to her, she would come down on me like a tonne of bricks!

There were only three other customers in the café: an elderly man with unruly grey hair and dressed in a black overcoat sat in front of the heater, sipping his coffee, while, to his right, a young couple sat elbow to elbow reading the newspaper. Overtly thin, the young man had spiky

Ancestry

red-tipped hair, and wore a see-through navy blue t-shirt, long pounamu earrings, a thick black leather belt spiked with silver triangles and red sandals. I assumed the Polynesian woman with him was his girlfriend. She was just as extrovert in her clothes and appearance: pale make-up, blood-red lipstick, black pearl earrings that dangled down to her shoulders, a plain red t-shirt with a provocative penis-shaped L on the front, a black mini skirt which revealed pale thighs and legs and crimson Nikes. Her colouring fitted what my daughter Regina had recently described as 'the caramel generation'. When her mother had asked for an explanation, Regina had said 'They are the colour of caramel: a mix of brown Polynesian and white Pākehā.'

'And you're not of that generation?' her mother had asked.

Regina had replied, 'Do we have a hidden Pālagi in either of you or both?' Andrea had smiled and looked at me.

'Don't look at me,' I'd laughed.

'Caramel is such a sweet and beautiful colour,' Andrea had added, 'but I'm afraid we're both plain brown.'

'But of course Amataga *is* caramel, eh!' I'd acknowledged. Regina and Andrea had laughed.

I went over and, avoiding the eyes of the woman behind the counter, ordered a latte (double-shot) and my usual brunch: creamy mushrooms, bacon and toast.

'Where's Andrea?' she asked, as she wrote down my order.

I glanced up and recognised her – the owner, and smiled. 'With family at the Dawn Parade,' I replied.

Ancestry

'My husband and three of our kids are there too,' she said. 'His grandfather and my grand-uncle died in Gallipoli.' And she waited for me to list my Gallipoli dead.

It came quickly. 'My grandson's great grandfather and, I think, a cousin were killed in Gallipoli,' I said. My grandson was the only family member who, through his Pālagi father, Ralph, would have had ancestors at Gallipoli. On my way back to my table, I realised that was the reason why Regina and Andrea and Amataga were at the Dawn Parade. It didn't matter that Amataga's father, a wastrel and womaniser, had left him and Regina last year; Andrea wanted our grandson to learn about his Papālagi ancestors and honour them.

'… Another bloody protest to do with the Treaty,' I heard the young man saying, as I passed their table. He was holding the previous day's paper in front of his partner's face and pointing at the headlines on the page.

'I don't want to go down that groove, Jet!' She stopped him dead in his tracks. 'I don't want to!'

'Why not?' he objected, his red face redder still.

'Cos ya've always refused to listen to my views!' She paused and, gazing straight into his face, emphasised slowly, 'And in case ya're blind, Ah'm Māori!'

Their argument about the Treaty seemed incongruous in the context of Anzac Day. I took my seat quickly and turned my back to them and tried to concentrate on looking at Williamson Avenue. Obviously, some of the vehicles were heading back from the Dawn Parade: in some of the cars, I glimpsed men in suits and chested with their service medals, and with them were their younger descendants. Every year the media talked about how the younger generations were returning to the Dawn Parades to honour their dead relatives; hundreds were now even visiting Turkey and Gallipoli for the memorial service there. The previous year I'd watched Helen Clark on TV speaking at that service to a huge audience of solemn and weeping Kiwis; mainly young ones.

'… And don't forget, if ya don't recognise the Treaty then you and ya fuckin' ilk are in Aotearoa illegally!' the woman in the café was saying. Throughout my life, every time the Treaty and the debates that raged around it erupted in my purview I *curled* away from them. That was the term I'd coined to describe accurately how I felt. I was *fascinated* by the debates, but whenever I wanted to involve myself in them – even with Andrea and Regina – I *curled* away from them, like a foetus; half-opened my eyes and ears and merely observed.

'… We're now beyond viewing our history and future through the Treaty,' the man was insisting. 'It's too narrow a frame to see ourselves and our history through. Plus, we can't continue viewing our history through the grievance mode!'

'Pull me other tit, bro!' She deliberately stereotyped herself.

'… Besides, most people now know about the Treaty and have it in their hearts!'

'Fuck, Jet, ya're so fuckin' dishonest hiding behind that liberal colonial bullshit. Most non-Māori don't have the Treaty in their hearts!'

She reminded me of Regina and Dad and how they argued about the Treaty: passionate, direct and courageous. But even here I was curled, merely observing and trying not to take sides. I must admit though, I was getting – if not angry – *impatient* with Jet. I looked around: the place was filling up with family groups who looked as if they'd been to the Dawn Parade.

A chair screeched behind me as someone got up angrily. I glanced back: it was the young woman, and she was stuffing her things into her large handbag, and the man was half on his feet, crimson face frozen in a look of offence and embarrassment. 'Stuff you, dickhead!' she said. She gathered up her handbag and started stumbling out, with the man in front of the fire smiling and everyone else trying not to look at them. 'Stuff ya all!' she declared. I liked that; yes, I did, I realised, and was surprised and pleased with myself that I felt that way.

I paced my eating until I saw people opening the doors of Foodtown across the road. I hurried over and, because it was still largely empty, didn't take long buying the things Andrea and I had listed yesterday evening. Because our grandson now spent a lot of time with us, much of the shopping was for him. Andrea and Regina banned soft drinks and sweets and other junk food from our home. However, whenever I shopped I sneaked in some of Amataga's favourites – Coke, jelly beans and chocolate fish – and hid them in the laundry, and when he and I were alone we feasted on them. My dad used to do the same with me. As I was loading the shopping into the boot, I missed having Andrea there. Over the years, like most marriages, ours had settled into well-established routines, such as doing the supermarket shopping together. She hadn't come the last few times, though. That added to my aggravation.

There was more traffic on Williamson Avenue as I drove home. As I turned along Ponsonby Road and into heavier noisier traffic, I remembered, with immediate apprehension and worsening aggravation, that Andrea hadn't narrated her dreams to me over the past six weeks. And yet her dreams and our detailed interrogation of them had become an essential part of our life.

I was finishing mixing the salad dressing when I heard footsteps hurrying up the front steps and recognised them as Amataga's. Immediately I headed for the front door, my heart quickening with love and anticipation. I grasped and turned the door knob and, pulling back the door, knelt down to Amataga's three-year-old height, and he squealed and burst into my wide embrace. 'Grundad, Grundad!' He cried into my neck, his face feeling chilly against my skin.

'You're cold,' I said, lifting him up. To stop himself from sliding down, he wound his legs tightly around my stomach.

'Samoan, Dad,' Regina said into my left ear, as she unwound her long red woollen scarf from her neck.

"I, fa'a-Samoa i le tama!' Andrea reminded me too.

'Sorry,' I mumbled and, hugging my grandson, carried him into the sitting room. We'd installed central heating years before at my insistence, so our house was cosily warm. "Ese lou mālūlū,' I said to him.

'I'm not cold!' He insisted, as I kneaded warmth into his hands.

'Fa'a-Samoa; speak Samoan,' Regina reminded him.

'I wanna speak Pālagi today,' he said, and looked at me for support. I unzipped his thick waterproof jacket, took off his scarf and All Black beanie and handed them to Andrea, who hung them up in the corridor.

"Ese lou laki, Amataga,' Andrea said. 'E lē to'atele tamaiti e iloa Fa'a-Samoa.'

'And speak with the "t"!' Regina insisted. Poor kid: not only did he have to speak Samoan, despite not having many friends who spoke it, but he had to speak with the t, which most speakers didn't use in conversation.

Since Amataga's birth, this debate had become a major theme of our life together: Regina wanted her son to be to be fluent in Samoan, and she had us trapped in the guilt of not having taught her Samoan. Like my parents had, we'd insisted to her that learning Samoan wasn't *useful* in New Zealand: mastery of English was her way to a 'good future'. So, like most of her generation, she knew little Samoan – and we were to blame for that! Although I didn't admit it to Regina, every time I was with our grandson and we used Samoan, our relationship *felt* deeper, more intimate; more so than my relationship to Regina had been at his age. Like it was a 'secret' language, reserved specially for us and our alofa for each other.

Because I'd migrated to New Zealand when I was only five, and my parents had discouraged me from learning Samoan, my Samoan was nowhere near as fluent as Andrea's; she'd shifted to New Zealand only after she'd graduated from high school in Samoa. Our grandson was enrolled at the Richmond Road School Āʻoga Samoa and, because Andrea was far more knowledgeable than me about things Samoan and the language, she quickly became one of the āʻoga's main advisers, and we, two of its most generous donors.

A short while later we were seated round the lunch of beef burgers and green salad that I'd prepared. "Ai lau salaki, darling,' Andrea urged Amataga, who again glanced up at me for help. I looked away and left him to his grandmother's and mother's mercy.

'Yes, darling, ʻai lau salad,' Regina emphasised. We knew what he was going to do next: he got me to cut his burger into quarters, then he ate each quarter quickly, observing all our rules about eating cleanly and silently, and then, closing his eyes and withdrawing into himself, he started spearing each bit of lettuce and tomato and cucumber and avocado firmly, pushing each bit into his mouth and trying to swallow them without chewing.

We applauded when he swallowed the last bit and, his eyes choking with tears, dropped his fork onto the plate. I handed him a tissue to dry his eyes with. 'There, it wasn't so bad, eh?' Andrea consoled him.

'So tell Grundad what happened at the Parade,' Regina urged him.

He wrapped his arms round his chest and, avoiding my scrutiny and squirming as if he was being tortured, whispered, 'Jus' lots of soldiers ...'

'Faʻa-Samoa!' his mother ordered.

'Okay, koʻakele fikafika ...'

I had to save him from being told to speak with a t by saying, 'E māgaia ʻofu o fikafika ma lakou folegi?'

Ancestry

"I, ese le magaia.' He brightened, sitting up at attention and swinging his arms in marching style. 'Ga masi fikafika pei se ami!'

'Ia, fa'aali iā Grundad le masi a fitafita!' Andrea encouraged him. Regina nodded enthusiastically. And he was on his feet, at attention, facing me.

'Squad!' I ordered, 'Forward march!' He stepped left foot forward, fists clenched tightly, head held with eyes fixed straight ahead, and started marching round the kitchen.

"Ese lou poko e savali fa'a-fitafita!' Andrea congratulated him.

'Ga fa'aali mai e Grundad!' he said, proudly, and my heart continued to swell and encompass all of him and the joy he was in my life.

Except for his unusual morning blue eyes, Amataga *was* caramel, from his skin to his hair. We were relieved that his eyes were the only feature he'd inherited from his father. The rest of him, according to Andrea, was from his 'Samoan side': from her father and mine. (Andrea's father had died in an accident at sea in Samoa, so I'd never seen him.) Yes, Amataga uncannily reminded me of my father, in physical appearance, in the way he moved, in the way he talked and smiled. My father had died from pancreatic cancer six years before: it had been a slow and excruciatingly painful death, and, in his usual stubborn and courageous way, he'd fought against it. I'd wished – but told no one – for him to give into death early and be free of the profound pain, but he'd fought on. So when Amataga was born and Ralph and Regina had agreed to our request he be given my father's name, I had wept uncontrollably, stopping only after Regina had placed Amataga in my arms and whispered, 'He's with us still, Dad.'

Ancestry

'So why didn't you bring it up while Regina was here?' Andrea asked after Regina and Amataga had gone and she was stacking the dirty dishes and cutlery into the dishwasher. I glanced at her. 'About why we went to the Dawn Parade?' she reminded me.

'When you got ready this morning and left, I didn't even think to ask,' I lied.

'Didn't you think it important – mysterious and out of character?'

'I worked it out while I was having brunch at the Café Oceania,' I replied, knowing she wouldn't like my avoiding her question. 'Worked it out when I went to order my meal and the owner gave me a full list of her war dead at Gallipoli, and then expected me to list *my* Gallipoli dead …'

'Which you did …'

Nodding quickly, I said, 'I figured out rapidly that you could only be at the Dawn Parade because of Amataga's Pālagi connections and Regina's insistence. Correct?' She smiled and nodded. 'Told her Amataga's great grandfather and cousin had died in Gallipoli.' She smiled more widely. 'What is the correct list?' I asked.

'His maternal grandfather and one of his brothers on his father's side,' she said. 'You know how thorough your daughter is when she researches something she considers important.'

She shut the dishwasher and turned it on. As the machine started churning and swishing, we picked up the coffee I'd made and, with a plate of afghans – her favourite biscuits – went into the sitting room.

'I also had a dream which may be related to that,' she said after she had lain back on the La-Z-Boy and I was seated on the sofa opposite her.

Then she anticipated me by saying, 'I know we haven't been interrogating my dreams over the past few weeks, and I'm sorry about that, but this one, we need to interrogate.' That didn't soothe my aggravation, but I hid that from her.

'Everything was in red, in all the nuances of red, and for a while as I waded through it, I felt there was nothing unusual about it. Immediately I recognised it was our street and it was deserted but I *knew* that behind each front door people were celebrating Waitangi Day – yes, Waitangi Day – and I was puzzled by that, but, strangely, I considered it aptly appropriate they should be doing that. What kind of celebrations? You ask. I thought it usual that each family group – which numbered seven persons each – should be in a circle holding hands, heads bowed, and the elders – all women of my age but with brilliant red hair – chanted the same karakia in a mix of Māori and Samoan and Kiwi English, which I didn't understand but didn't mind not understanding. I didn't recognise any of the people, but again I felt completely safe with them because soon, very soon, they would come forward and embrace me as a long lost relative. Out of the stained glass front door of our house I saw the number sixty-three growing like a large ear. Again I felt there was nothing unusual about that. So I moved up the twelve steps – why twelve? – turned and placed my right ear to the door's ear, which felt like live flesh, and waited. "Did you bring your grandson?" I heard, and immediately recognised my grandmother Faivai's voice. "Yes, he's inside," I replied. "What does he think of Waitangi Day?" she asked, and I thought her question normal and said, "He supports it!" "How can you be so sure?" she asked, and for the first time I experienced uncertainty. "Don't worry," she comforted me. "As you well know, our lives are governed by the principle of uncertainty." "True, but Amataga is 110 percent sure about his support of Waitangi Day!" I insisted. The next moment the door and the ear weren't there and I was tip-toeing into our house, wondering where Faivai had gone and why she'd used English to talk to me, especially when she didn't know any English.'

'Strange coincidence,' I said, 'but at the Café Oceania this morning, a young Māori woman and her Pālagi boyfriend had a very heated argument about the Treaty – and she ended up walking out on him.'

'Good on her!' Andrea said, and then asked, 'Why the colour red? Why a blood-red world?'

'My parents' favourite colour, remember?' She didn't react to that. 'The colour of birth, good fortune and blessing?' I suggested. She nodded repeatedly. 'And why celebrating Waitangi Day with seven people in each group holding hands?' I now got into it. 'And the karakia in Samoan, Māori and English?'

'Despite what may now seem strange and eerie, nearly everything in the dream was *normal* when I was in it.'

'Except what?'

'Except Faivai, who didn't know any English, speaking to me in it.' With her long forefinger nail, she cut open the packet of afghans and extended it to me. I took one and she took one and, in her usual way, bit off a quarter of it and started chewing that slowly, thoroughly, her face scrunched up in deep contemplation. 'You're right, I think; it's about

Amataga's birth into a world that is now fortunately integrated in one karakia. And don't forget, seven is our lucky number …'

'… And our grandson was born on the seventh of October!' I reminded her. I poured and sugared our mugs of coffee. She took hers and, after blowing on it, sipped carefully, her long fingers curled around her mug. As I gazed at her fingers I *felt* as if they were wrapped warmly around me.

Smiling, she said, 'Amataga is so lucky to be a 110-percent supporter of Waitangi Day. As you know, there are lots of Kiwis who aren't.'

'Including his father,' I intruded, *feeling* the heat of her fingers radiating into my body.

'He tried to hide it from us. But let's not go there, darling. I'm just glad he's not around any more.' She'd supported our daughter's decision to marry Ralph and, because I'd opposed it openly, I now didn't want to say 'see, I told you so!' 'Besides, my dream of our house having a super-ear shows we're acutely aware of whatever is happening around us, especially to do with our family.' I reached over and, with both hands, held her right foot. I started massaging her toes. 'That's nice,' she said, squirming deliciously and shutting her eyes. 'The dream also allowed Faivai to visit me again. It's been a long time since her last visit.' She lifted her right leg and I started massaging the sole of her foot in long lingering strokes.

Regina and Amataga lived in Newton, in our old family home, which my parents had bequeathed to Regina. Amataga was ready when I knocked on their front door. 'Got to go shopping,' Regina excused herself. 'You look after Granddad, darling,' Regina said, hugging and kissing him. He gripped my right hand and started tugging me down the front steps into the sparkling bright morning. "Fā, Amataga!' she called, but he didn't acknowledge her. 'Don't forget to speak Samoan,' she reminded me.

Amataga grinned and said, 'So we don't have to speak Hamo today?' as I strapped him into his car seat.

'If ya don't want to,' I replied.

I got into the driver's seat, strapped myself in and, turning on the ignition and hearing the car purr into life, said, 'Ready? Let's go and see Papa and Mama.'

As the car moved forward, he clapped once and said, 'Grundad, don't forget the flowers.'

'I haven't,' I replied, showing him the large bunches of flowers that were lying on the passenger's seat beside me. I'd bought them at St Luke's, earlier.

'So, let's go, Grundad,' he urged.

It was the last Sunday of the month, the day I usually visited my parents' graves at Waikumete Cemetery. Ever since he was a baby, I had taken Amataga with me. Sometimes Regina came. For a few months after my dad's funeral, Andrea came, then she began to miss visits, and about two years later stopped altogether. While Andrea and I were still at university, I think she and my father came to an unwritten understanding they would politely tolerate each other and, in my presence and that of my mother, never show their basic distrust of each other. Many times I sensed Andrea was on the frantic verge of expressing her true feelings about my father but she never did – and I didn't encourage her

Ancestry

because I knew – and so did she – I would defend my father fiercely, and that would result in ugly rows between us. On the other hand, my mother and Andrea got on like a house on fire. They were so different: physically Andrea was half my mother's abundant size, fastidious and tidy in her ways, while my mother kept everything clean and healthy but infuriatingly untidy. Andrea was frugal and always careful about money, while my mother spent or gave it away generously, especially to our 'āiga. Andrea was guarded and reserved with new people, while my mother immediately offered her alofa to anyone who came into her perimeter. When my diabetic mother died unexpectedly of a stroke three years before my dad, Andrea had gone into what I could only call a period of deep mourning, about three months of refusing to let us mention my mother, and late night sobbing in the toilet, until Regina told her: 'Stop being so bloody selfish, Mum, we are grieving for her too!'

My parents' graves were near the back boundary, so we had to drive through the large cemetery of undulating flats, gullies and rises covered with graves. Everything shone with the brightness of sun, so I put on my sunglasses. The light turned a dark red, mellow on my eyes. Along the way, we saw many people weeding and cleaning the graves of their loved ones. I turned into the lane of high trees that led to our graves. 'Look!' Amataga said, pointing out. To our right, a large group of mainly Polynesian mourners surrounded an open grave, singing. I rolled down my window and immediately recognised the hymn as Samoan. 'Grundad, we sing that song at Ā'oga,' Amataga said.

Ancestry

He knew our routine so well now. We parked under the shady kahikatea beside the graves. Quickly he unbuckled, opened his door and dropped to the ground. He hurried to the back and was opening the boot when I got to him. He pressed open the lock on my large toolkit and got out his small rubber gloves and I helped pull them on, the rubber snapping as I did so. I pulled on mine. He picked up the trowel and a roll of supermarket plastic bags and went to the graves. I got out the secateurs, hand broom and pail and followed him, again marveling at the similarity of his walk to his great-grandfather's.

He went up and, stopping in the narrow gap between the two graves, said, 'Yuk, they're dead.' The flowers we'd brought four weeks before were now black withered stalks in the vases, which were filled with smelly mud-thick liquid. I picked up the vases and poured their contents in to the trough below the tap under the kahikatea.

When I got back after washing the vases in the tap, Amataga was carefully brushing the dirt off Dad's gravestone. 'I know what that says,' he said, pointing at the writing on the gravestone under Dad's black and white photograph. He couldn't read; he'd memorised the texts on both graves, so I played along. Looking at the bilingual texts as if he was reading them, he didn't stumble as he 'read' Dad's and then Mum's gravestones.

Poko kele, Amakaga,' I congratulate him.

'I can read in Pālagi and Hamo, eh!' he boasted, examining my face to see if I really believed him.

'So you can, so you can,' I said, 'Ese lou poko!'

He whooped and then said, 'I fooled ya, Grundad!'

'So you did!' I laughed, ruffling his large frizzy hair, which, Andrea and I agreed, he'd inherited from my mother.

I got him to talk about his school, friends, sports and anything else that caught his fancy while we weeded round the graves, cleaned and scrubbed the gravestones, arranged the flowers in the vases and cut up the rubbish and put it in the bins. For me the time passed in profound happiness, working with my beloved heir, repeating and reaffirming that line of descent that I'd learned and inherited from my parents and they from theirs. When we finished, we washed our hands and rested under the kahikatea.

'Papa was seventy-one when he died, eh?' Amataga asked. I nodded. 'That's very old, eh?' I nodded again. 'And Mama was how much?'

'Sixty-eight,' I replied. 'That's old too.'

Then, scrutinising me intensely from under serious eyebrows – just like my father before he asked a serious question – he asked, slowly, 'And how old are you, Grundad?'

'Fifty-five years and four weeks and two days,' I replied.

He withdrew into himself quickly, figuring; then, with that shining look of having discovered a marvellous revelation, he declared, 'You got a long time to go, eh, Grundad?'

I didn't hesitate. 'Yes, a long time before you and your mum will have to come and take care of my grave,' I said.

'That's good, Grundad,' he whispered. And my future with him stretched and stretched out in unlimited happiness and distance.

Ancestry

On the way home, we stopped at Reina's Treats, our favourite ice cream place on Ponsonby Road. He had his usual hokey pokey ice cream topped with maple sauce and sprinkled with macadamia nuts and I had my usual single soft serve of strawberry yogurt.

That night, in bed, I told Andrea about Amataga's revelation. 'I love you too,' she whispered, embracing me. 'We have so much time left together and so many dreams to interrogate, darling.'

FIRST CLASS

If it wasn't raining heavily, he walked to and from work. Because of his high cholesterol and blood pressure his doctor had recommended that he exercise regularly – a brisk thirty-minute walk or jog each day would be ideal. He also enjoyed the route down Woodlawn Drive, then across the sports field of Noelani Elementary School, and round the back streets and through St Francis High School and the Newman Centre and into the campus. The route was lushly rich in fruit and flowering trees and plants – mangos, avocados, bananas, vī, papaya, ginger and frangipani – and the ever-changing aroma of flowers and the stream. Most fascinating for him was the inescapable presence of the Koʻolau Range.

If he was walking away from the Koʻolau, he would sometimes play games with it, unexpectedly looking back over his shoulder and catching it observing him – yah, gotcha! – and smiling to himself, knowing it was always going to be there. Most inviting though was his return, his walking up towards the range, and watching the light and clouds and shadows changing constantly on the mountains. When the range was still blazing with light, he felt it was disappearing into the heavens, and he had to look at his arms and reaffirm he wasn't disappearing with it. When swift winds were driving large clouds across it, outracing their immense shadows, which swam in and out of the ravines and valleys on its slopes, he raced with them, letting his heart and belly sing with the speed.

Once, and the memory of it still awed and frightened him, he'd stopped in the middle of the Noelani school field as evening was happening, his feet deep in the dry grass, and had gazed up at the Koʻolau. With mounting fear, he had watched the last rays of the setting sun contracting into one quickly reducing sliver of brilliant light, which, as it slid and slipped across the massive contours of the mountains, as if someone was pulling it towards the west, looked as if it was never returning. That night, he'd tried recording the experience in a poem, and had managed only one worthwhile line: *The light is pulling out.*

The back of his aloha shirt and armpits were soaking wet from the brisk walk from his apartment to his office through the mid-morning sun, and he didn't have the time to let his office air conditioning cool him and dry off the sweat. His first session with his 313 Writing of Poetry class was five minutes away, and he was never late for any class, and, as usual, he was stressed – that tight dry starting-to-churn-up feeling in the dead center of his stomach – anticipating his first session with new students he knew little about. Though he'd taught American students in his first semester and had found most of them – especially the Asians and Hawaiians – welcoming, considerate and respectful, he still considered himself ignorant of their ways, finding even the ways they spoke difficult to understand. Also, in his eighteen years of teaching he had always dreaded first lectures; sometimes the fear was so demanding he suffered nausea and vomited.

As he hurried down the corridor to his lecture room, he recalled that when, during his first year as a lecturer at Auckland University, he'd first told his mother about his dread, she'd laughed and had repeated her core philosophy: 'Daniel, you in the lion's den; get out of it. Just act; be an actor like Marlon Brando. That's what they want, a performance like *On the Waterfront*! All through my schooling, I wanted for to see acting, but my bloody ignorant Hamo teachers were not John Wayne or Bogart.' Another time, when she caught him spewing in the toilet before his lecture, she'd said 'Hey, Daniel in the lion's den, why you sick with worry? They only bloody Pālagi. You, beloved, you the brown Brando. Yes, you be like me: act through your life: act, act, act, that's the only way you going to get somewhere.'

Just before he turned the handle of the door into the lecture room, the tight ball of stress in his stomach began easing away. His mother had certainly been the most accomplished, unrelenting and devious actor he'd ever known. It wasn't lying, she'd insisted, when his father discovered in the pay slip from her first job at the hospital laundry that her name was now Emerald Malaetau; and she had repeated that denial when he'd later accused her of conning her way into a secretarial job in the Social Welfare Department under the name Janine Elizabeth Wiley; and then later when he was at university studying Shakespeare and she'd persisted in walking round him, while he was trying to analyse *Macbeth*, reciting Lady Macbeth's lines and claiming that she'd first read Bill's – as she always referred to Shakespeare – work in Samoan in her village, and, ashamed and exasperated, he'd accused her of lying about that; and she'd continued repeating her denial whenever he or his father or anyone else, including the police, had accused her of lying. Even if you're caught red-handed, never admit that you're guilty. Why? Because the so-called 'truth' came in many forms and guises. Isn't that what Albert Einstein meant in his theory of relativity? After Albert, her favourite philosopher, everything was relative, depending on your individual perspective and viewpoint. 'What about agasala, sin? You know, doing wrong?' his father had insisted. After Albert, there was no such vicious creature, she'd argued, only illness, and lack of certain chemicals in the brain. 'Where you learn all that lāpisi from?' he'd countered. Look around you, she'd pointed out; look at all your extremely poko and brainy son's books! Go into his computer and up into the space, into the internet! Listen to his very clever talking, to him and his godless and intellect-whatever-that-word-is friends! And go to the movies, Lemu, then you no longer be slow but become fast in your brain and learn as fast as the computer in 2001 Space Something-or-Other.

Since he'd first looked up his fifteen students' names on the computer registry, two weeks previously, he'd wondered what they looked like – and, in Hawai'i, how many were going to be Hawaiians/Kanaka Maoli, Pacific Islanders and Asians, but he now couldn't look at them as he walked self-consciously across the room in front of the blackboard,

First Class

feeling their heavy curiosity enveloping him, placed his folio of lecture notes and a copy of their only class text on the desk, stood with head bowed, hands gripping the front corners of the moveable lectern for a deeply silent moment, and then, letting his shoulders sag as if he was now ready to relax and get into it, gazed up and into the expanse that was filled with their curiosity and expectations of who and what he was like, this Samoan/Polynesian professor from New Zealand, a country they knew little about and cared even less about. With his mother's absolutely winning Joan Crawford smile, he extended his arms in the manner of Miss Baystall when she'd first welcomed them to school, and, in Brando's voice as Mark Anthony in *Julius Caesar*, said, 'First of all I'd like to welcome myself to our class, 313 Writing of Poetry!' He felt them lift instantly: a short high but quickly suppressed exclamation of surprise. Some of them laughed, and he now had the attention of even the professionally bored-looking ones, so he declared, 'For me it is wonderful for a change to be in a class in which most of the people look like me!' Nearly all of them laughed, the professionals trying to disguise their pleasure at such a totally unexpected and witty observation. 'You are also one of the handsomest classes I've ever taught.' Instantly, many squirmed in delight and elated embarrassment and oh Jesus, we're not that good looking but thank you for saying it!

'Yeah, bro!' exclaimed a handsome Samoan with a Dwayne 'The Rock' Johnson haircut and a taulima tattoo around his thick biceps. He was ensconced in the middle of the back row between a hefty Samoan woman trying to appear disassociated from the rude and foolish dude who'd just broken the Samoan taboo against being too forward with your elders and teachers and a beanpole thin and angular haole whose grin was telling him he was now expecting an even more unexpected repartee.

So he gave it to them. 'Apart from the fact we're all handsome, most of us have one other thing in common.' He waited, and they were dying for it. 'We are all permanently suntanned!' The Samoan with the Rock haircut raised his fists and pumped them into the handsome air, the beanpole thin haole inflated to twice his size with laughter, the hefty stern Samoan woman slapped at her massive thighs, which were threatening to burst through her jeans, and crooned, 'Right on, uso!' and the rest of the class laughed, knowing they were never ever going to forget this charismatic guy and his unique remarks and humour. No, dis professor from Noo-Zeeland/Arrruuteeayroar was cool, man! You are the bomb, bro! he imagined all the Polynesians in his class saying to themselves.

His dread had vanished; gone without him observing it, worrying about it. He had them, in the cool of his acting. Like his mother had always said, it's all acting; give them your best Brando performance. But he'd learned early in his teaching career that he also had to know his subject, in depth, and, in his individual way, show he had a passion for it and infect his students forever with that passion and the desire to learn more. His mother was a massively talented actor who could mesmerise most audiences into believing any role she played, but sometimes she was lazy, overconfident and arrogant and didn't research the roles intimately, and suffered the consequences of an indifferent, uninformed performance.

First Class

In triumph, he swept his euphoric, possessive gaze lingeringly over his enraptured audience. Good, wonderful, wonderful. Once more, another sweep, enjoy, enjoy. The left-hand corner of his left eye threatened to snag on someone at the back left-hand corner of the room, but kept sweeping. His students were all satisfied – no, elated – no, absolutely taken with him. It was going to be right on, brother, for the rest of the semester! Then he glanced over at the back left-hand corner. He detested snags, students who weren't convinced of his mana, but there she was, scribbling intently on a yellow pad, the light caught in long wavy hair that hid most of her face from his view; scribbling, scribbling and paying him no attention whatsoever.

'Please answer when I call your name,' he instructed. She continued scribbling. He read out their names carefully and ticked them on his roll. The most difficult names for him were the Hawaiian ones – twice he had to ask the individual students to pronounce their names so he could learn them.

'Are there people here whose names are not on our list?' he asked. This time the snag raised her right hand in a slow calculated upward movement that seemed to establish her permanently and fully in the centre of his view, and also made him aware she was older than the other students; at least ten years older, he reckoned when he examined her face. 'Please come and see me at the end of this session,' he told her. She nodded once and, for the first time, dropped her pencil onto her yellow pad, and focused on him.

Ancestry

Quickly he distributed blank index cards, instructing them to write their names, addresses and phone numbers on them. 'Despite the fact that the confidentiality laws of your very litigious nation don't allow me to compel you to do even that, I want you to also put in some brief information about your private selves.' Some laughed, but he was inexplicably uncomfortable 'feeling' the snag observing him, though he sensed she was trying not to.

'Whad sorta information, professor?' the angular haole asked.

'Such things as: if you've survived any writing classes before, especially poetry classes; what you read; do you like films and plays and the other arts we of the bourgeoisie are supposed to love; do you play the uke; you know, anything that'll help me help you improve your writing, or amaze me with your boundless talent and your ability to hide, from me, the real truths about your lives, because that's what we and all other autobiographers do.' He stopped and glanced at her and caught her smiling for the first time. That he interpreted as her congratulating him on his performance, but he didn't want that; he wasn't a child.

The rest of the session was him taking them through the course prescription, schedule and reading list, explaining what he was hoping they were going to study and write during the semester. He ended by giving them a potted history of Hawai'i and the other Pacific countries out of which the literature and writers they were studying had emerged. Throughout it they were quite respectful and open about questioning him on aspects of the course they didn't understand.

First Class

Most of the class thanked him as they started leaving. As she strolled up to him, he was surprised; she was much taller than he'd thought, even taller than him by a few inches, with extremely wide shoulders, a long powerful torso, long arms and large hands – no nail polish – small breasts and narrow hips, tightly muscled flanks. Her deeply tanned body literally glowed with health. She was obviously into body-building, sports and exercising regularly at the gym. 'My name's Lanimua Niuhi,' she introduced herself, still avoiding looking into his face as she reached out and he had to shake her hand. 'I'm Kanaka Maoli and from Hawai'i, the Big Island.' He paused, and he wasn't going to ease her discomfort by talking in turn, so she added, 'I rang you about two weeks ago, and then again last week, and left messages about wanting to enroll in this class, professor.'

'I'm sorry, but I haven't opened my voicemail in weeks.' He tried to turn his neglect into a joke.

'I hope my messages are on it, because I really want to be in your class.'

'Have you done much writing?'

'Not much poetry or fiction, but lots of memos and reports and letters.' She smiled. 'Had to earn a living.'

Before he could stop himself, he suggested, 'Perhaps you should try and get into a first-year writing class; all the students in this class have done at least two years of creative writing.' When he sensed her disappointment, he quickly added, 'This class is also limited to fifteen students only.'

Ancestry

'I wanted to be in your class because you're one of only three Polynesian instructors in creative writing in this department.' She looked into his face for the first time, right through his performance, and then added, with a touch of admiring shyness, 'And I've read all your books – and love them!' Praise always sent him into a painful adolescent squirming and embarrassment, which completely disabled him from replying coherently to it.

'It's all right, Miss – Miss …'

'Lanimua Niuhi, Professor Malaetau,' she saved him.

'I'm – I'm glad you liked the books,' he mumbled.

'Everyone calls me Mua,' she helped him again.

He couldn't look into her face, realising he was now cauled firmly in the aura of her imposing height and physical presence. 'I think I can allow one more into our class,' he heard himself admitting defeat, but he was relieved; in fact, very pleased about it.

'Thank you, professor,' she said.

They were all waiting for him when he entered the room for their second session. They'd rearranged the seating into a semi-circle with his desk and chair at the open end. He liked that. He paused and looked at them: the Samoan athlete sat first to his left, then the angular haole, then the Samoan woman. Lanimua occupied the seat just where the circle curved towards his right, so she was side on to him.

'Is it possible to turn the air conditioning down, professor?' Lanimua asked. 'It's chilly in here.'

First Class

'I don't think you can,' he replied. 'Any others finding it chilly?' A few nodded.

'I think if we leave the doors open, that'll lessen the cold,' she suggested. He nodded and she hurried to the back door, opened it and wedged a chair against it to stop it from re-closing. The angular haole did the same to the front door.

'Now that we've made our little contribution to our consciences for not pandering to the expensive and eternal chill that enriches the electricity corporates, we shall begin,' he pandered to his inner moral discomfort. But the irony was lost on most of them. And Lanimua looked puzzled; slightly skeptical.

Quickly he told them to look at their copies of the course prescription he'd distributed the day before. He knew it. It happened every time, everywhere, with university students. Two of them boldly raised their hands and asked for copies. 'Let's get this clear; we are writers, we are professionals, and professionals do not forget the stuff they need for class, at home!' They squirmed as he handed them copies. 'We must not reinforce the public's stereotype of us writers as being disorganised, irresponsible, impractical, always-late dreamers, who rarely meet their obligations and deadlines.' They all drew silent and couldn't look at him. Good. No irony now, no subtle joking. He then re-explained the prescription, and re-emphasised what he expected of them in terms of how much poetry they had to have in their final folios by the end of semester and on which they would be graded. 'Now, please hand in the index cards I wanted you to fill in.' For an annoyed instant he thought he saw in the body language of a few of them that they'd forgotten the cards. But all the cards came in.

He'd prepared the first poetry exercise he was going to give them, the week before, but another inspiration came unexpectedly, and he couldn't deny it. He said, 'I'm now going to explain the exercise I want you to do.' He paused. He went on to explain that, before Hawai'i, he'd not liked air conditioning, having grown up in the temperate climate of New Zealand in which you didn't need it. In Samoa and Fiji, where it was just as hot as Hawai'i, and where he'd worked at the universities, his offices had been well ventilated and hadn't needed air conditioning. You switched on the fans if it got too hot. It was also a matter of principle: in a poor country air conditioning was absolutely wasteful. Did they know that capitalist America wasted at least three-fifths of the world's energy resources? And he was now in tropical America, in which, whenever you went indoors, you were in the air-conditioned nightmare. But, lo and behold, within a matter of weeks – suffering the relentless heat outside and in his apartment – he'd grown accustomed to his workplace being in perpetual cold and artificial light. 'As you well know, our lecture rooms get chilly, really chilly, because you can't control the temperature and there are no windows we can open out to the outside world of natural heat and light. And I'm behaving like most people and putting my physical comfort ahead of my so-called principles. I need air conditioning. My conscience, as usual, has learned to live with that.' When he looked at them, the professionals tried to look as if they understood what he'd said;

the angular haole looked pleased with himself; the two Samoans looked lost; and the rest of them, except for Lanimua and a few of the locals, looked offended; yes, offended.

'Some of you obviously disagree with some or all of what I've just said,' he offered.

'Yes, professor,' said the short, muscular blonde with the extremely short Levi's skirt that revealed her solid legs, who was sitting opposite him. Mainland America, he identified her; not a trace of Hawai'i in her accent. 'We *need* air conditioning in the heat of Hawai'i; in this room, too, otherwise we won't be able to think and write.' Paused, ran her tongue over her lips. 'And your – your attack on America was unfair, professor.'

'What attack?'

'Your claim that capitalist America is wasting all that energy,' the untidy, flimsily dressed haole next to her replied.

'Well, isn't it?' the Samoan woman asked.

'We only have the professor's word for it!' the short blonde scoffed.

'So you're saying Professor Malaetau is lying!' The interjection was issued without any trace of anger in the voice but with utter clarity. Everyone looked at Lanimua.

'No, I'm not saying that,' the blonde tried regaining the high ground.

'So what are you saying?' Lanimua asked. The blonde and her friend from the mainland retreated.

'She's saying that some of us are fed up with the misinformation and unwarranted attacks on *our* country!' This time it was a haole man with a chunky physique, square shoulders, thick overtrained biceps and a number two haircut. Another mainlander, one with military training. 'Our boys are dying in Iraq to protect freedom …'

'That's it!' Professor Malaetau cut it off. 'Let's not go there.' He was surprised, and somewhat shocked, that it took only a quite harmless discussion about air conditioning to bring out the battle formations in his class. Even more upsetting were the arrogance and ignorance of some of the students from the Mainland. He'd seen a little of it the year before in his other classes. He glanced over at Lanimua. She refused to look at him. 'Now, for your first exercise. I want you to write a poem, no more than six lines in length, on the topic of cold. I want you to use the present tense and set the poem here in Hawai'i. Any questions?'

'Six lines, in the present tense, in Hawai'i, about the cold, professor?' the angular haole summed it up.

'Yes, and do not use the I perspective,' he said. When he noted the puzzled looks on the faces of the two women from the Mainland, he said, writing on the blackboard at the same time, 'Not in the I perspective, meaning not in the first person. Okay?' Most of them nodded.

'And can we use it to spread *misinformation* about the great ole' US-of-A?' He was surprised it was the Micronesian woman, who'd been silent up until then, and not Lanimua. With bold mischief in her eyes, the woman was gazing directly at the mainlander with the number two haircut.

Supressed laughter among some of the Hawaiians and locals. 'Yeah, ya can' wride ah po-eeem about da killing cold in Hawai'i, man!' One of the men exaggerated his Hawaiian accent.

'Yeah, bro', an' in seex lines', a friend continued to parody.

'... An' in da presen' tense', another one added.

'... An' widoud da eye, man!' another one ended it.

'Yeah, does that mean you write it blind, professor?' Lanimua finished it. The whole class, including the chunky number two haircut, erupted with laughter.

That night, with the trades shuffling through the louvres and cooling his apartment, and dressed only in an 'ie lavalava, he studied their index cards, jotting down on the cards the observations he'd made about them in class, and filing them in individual folders. He always found it difficult to remember peoples' names, so, at the start of each course, he tried to memorise his students' names by visualising them and attaching to them easily remembered features, mannerisms and history.

For instance, the haole with the number two haircut was Malcolm Lowry Unders, twenty-one years old; he had shifted, most of his life, from military base to military base with his family, his father being an officer in the Marine Corps; this was his first year at UH; he loved jazz and marching bands, and played the trumpet; he had read a wide range of poetry, especially American poetry; his favourite poets were the ones shaped and published by the *New Yorker*; his favourite writer and philosopher was Ayn Rand.

The striking Micronesian woman, who'd challenged Malcolm, was Maria Gomez, from Guam. A brief four lines scribbled at the centre of her card read: 'I am Chammoran. Third year at UH on scholarship.

Ancestry

Have not done much writing but joined your class because I admire your writing, especially *The Final Return Home*. Want to learn from you. I love Māori writing too.'

The angular haole was Nigel 'The Hammer' Blathmire. He had spent since the late 1990s traveling around Asia and the Pacific, attending some of the universities there. He *loved* Hawai'i and Hawaiian music and culture, and was learning to play the slack guitar. Had published a few poems in various magazines. Considered Robert Lowell the 'awfullest' poet in American poetry. 'Fuck the American academy for inflating Lowell's importance. The King of Poetry is Bukowski!'

The Samoan athlete was Nathaniel Matagi: 'everyone calls me Nat. Born in Tennessee but am Samoan at heart and muscle and soul.' The Rock was his hero because 'The Rock can rock any honky out of the ring and is Samoan and proud of it. Want to be a novelist like Albert Wendt whose novel *Sons for the Return Home* changed my life.' Hadn't written any poetry at all but he wanted to learn from Daniel Malaetau, 'the greatest poet on the planet and Samoan.'

Folole Misamalosi, the Samoan woman, was from Pago Pago, American Samoa, and didn't want to live anywhere else 'cos Pago is the Paradise of the Pacific.' She claimed she was living in exile in Honolulu because she wanted the best education so she could help her people. Wanted to be a lawyer. That way she could kick arse, especially those of the 'ignorant, arrogant Palagis who dominate my beloved country.' Wanted to be a poet so she could be more eloquent when she argued her court cases. Praise God!

First Class

Shirley Anne Beems was the name of the short obstreperous blonde. She was originally from Iowa City but had lived and studied in numerous other places on the Mainland. This was her first time overseas. She was attracted to Hawai'i by the 'surf, sun, and the movies about Hawai'i.' 'Haven't read or written much fiction but written lots of poetry. Guess it's what you call "confessional stuff".' Hated Sylvia Plath though. 'I want to write a novel in verse about surfing, sun, the movies about Hawai'i and getting away from your hopeless parents who are drowning in their expensive middle-class shit.'

Her friend was 'Just call me "Michel" with the surname Nargler'. Who loved 'any kind of poetry written by any kind of woman anywhere.' Most male poets were full of macho shit and blather, and Bukowski is the 'blatherest'. Will spend her semester trying 'to fish love poems out of 'the female universe that is still becoming.'

Last but now the most compelling presence – and he was in self-denial that she was attracting the usual fire in his body – was Lanimua, call me Mua. Again he reminded himself that in his whole career as a teacher he had never had an affair with any of his students or colleagues. No. Definitely. Too right he'd suffered huge temptations, which sometimes he had almost given way to, yes. Most difficult were those students who came onto you openly, without shame or false modesty. Almost irresistible moral and jail bait. And now, when some of those lurid episodes threatened to swamp him, he jotted down these notes about Lanimua: in her late thirties, she had not finished her degree when she'd first attended UH fresh out of high school. 'Too many irresistible distractions.' (He wondered what those had been.) Then worked. (Nothing about what that had been.) Was now back to finish her BA in English. 'Love the writing by Kanaka Maoli and Pacific writers, especially John Dominis Holt, Haunani-Kay Trask, Joe Balaz, Victoria Kneubuhl and Imaikalani Kalahele.' At the bottom of her card she'd scrawled, as an afterthought, 'My aumakua is the niuhi, the white shark.' Yet he concluded – but didn't know why – that that was the most important thing she'd said about herself. The other thing that struck him was that she'd said little about what she'd done since her first stint at UH.

He finished compiling the information on the students by about ten o'clock, then turned on the TV and watched *Law and Order*. Lanimua continued infiltrating his attention and diverting it from the dedicated team of detectives as they hunted another devious serial killer.

The following Wednesday when he arrived for their session, they were all in their seats, trying to appear relaxed and unconcerned about having to read out and discuss the individual poems, on cold, they'd written during the week; their first exercise and leap into the evaluation and critical judgment of people and a professor they didn't yet know. Strangers to the slaughter. You were putting your head and heart and imagination and everything on the block, in the form of this six-line poem. It was the same every year, and he needed to reassure them, so he did what he did every year. He held up the sheaf of copies of the poems they'd emailed him (and one another), which he'd read and studied carefully, writing careful and encouraging remarks on them, and said, with his most genuine smile: 'These are good, people. I like them very much.' He could see their bodies relax, whaarr, releasing the tension and apprehension. (Lanimua looked the most relieved and, without make-up and in a simple yellow t-shirt and jeans and jandals, the most attractive.) 'Of course, being your first poem for me, there may be things you need to revise.' Malcolm looked startled. Nigel, Nat, Maria and Folole nodded in agreement. 'Right now, I have to remind you that you won't be a good writer if you don't revise and revise and revise your work.' Shirley looked superior, above that advice, and Michel copied her.

Not long after that, he invited them to read their poems aloud, and again anticipated that no one would offer to go first. They all avoided his scrutiny. His anticipation was dead right. So he asked again, 'Isn't there a courageous poet in this class?'

'I'll read,' Lanimua offered, almost inaudibly. Most of the others looked as if they'd been saved from drowning. Her face was now turning pale, as she struggled to swallow back her fear. 'Okay, this isn't a good poem – it's the first poem I've ever written.' Paused, swallowed again.

'Our aumakua lives in Te Moananui-a-Kiwa

It swims, moves, weaves in the cold depths

It mustn't stop – if it does it will drown

Our niuhi lives in perpetual motion

beyond the cold and the edge of stillness.'

'Are you sure, Mua, it's the first poem you've ever written?' he asked deliberately, smiling.

She started chortling. 'Well, if you call the couple of poems I tried to write in elementary school poems, professor!'

Ancestry

Now he invited them to comment on Lanimua's poem. Most of the others looked away from him. He turned to the hand as it rose. 'Name's Jake Nakasone,' the slender, black-haired young man with the fine bone fish hook pendant said. 'Ah'm jus' puzzled, professor; I thought the poem was to be about the cold.' A few others nodded.

'You want to read your poem again, Mua, and talk about it a little bit?' he asked.

Reluctantly she reread it, and then said, 'Some sharks, especially the niuhi, the great white, are built not to feel the cold, so I think the cold is in the poem but the niuhi can't feel it. It lives beyond it. It also can't be stationary; it can't just lie down on the ocean bed and have a sleep.' Some laughed. 'It has to keep moving.'

'Yeah, in perpetual motion,' Folole remarked. 'That's a very apt way of puttin' it. Imagine, you can't sleep, you havta keep movin' and movin' and movin' until you die …'

'… Beyond the edge of stillness and the cold,' Maria added.

'Yeah, I get it now,' Jake nodded. 'It's a beaudiful way of puttin' it, Mua.'

'Frank's my name,' another Hawaiian student said. 'The poor sharks have had a very bad press since Hollywood turned them into ferocious, man-eating monsters …'

'But that's true, man,' Malcolm interjected. 'I saw a documentary about sharks off the tip of South Africa. They even attacked the scientists who were in steel cages filming them.'

'Hollywood made millions from turnin' Mua's aumakua into Jaws, a frightening monster,' Frank countered.

'Yeah, like haole and the tourist industry continue to make millions by selling everything Hawaiian,' Lanimua continued.

'So you don't believe in the sayings about sharks?' Malcolm said.

'What?' Lanimua demanded, final and deadly.

'Loan sharks, business sharks etc?' Malcolm was oblivious to the corner he was painting himself into.

'Those metaphors are in the cultures of people who know fuck-all about sharks!' Lanimua attacked. And he didn't want to stop the argument. 'People who don't even read the scientific studies done by their own scientists about sharks.'

'Ah thought we were writing and talking about poetry.' Jake tried rescuing the situation.

'I thought the discussion so far is about that,' he said. 'Mua's poem is about sharks; a particular shark: the niuhi and its role as aumakua.'

'Let her tell us what Hawaiians believe sharks are really like,' Maria insisted. 'So much bullshit has been fed us about sharks by haole films and TV!'

Lanimua glanced over at him and he nodded. 'Okay, if we believe the films, most sharks are large and ferocious. In fact, most sharks are quite small, ranging from a few inches to a few feet in length. Those movies portray sharks as feeding in packs and doing so in day-long feeding frenzies. In fact most sharks eat less than 10 percent of their body weight each day. That is less than most animals. And they feed individually, not in packs. And they certainly don't attack out of some innate sense of ferocity and violence. They're not crazy feeding and attacking machines. I'll stop there – I'm boring you.' Some asked that she continue, but she refused.

'And now that I know all that,' Jake said, 'I can see some of the complexity in Mua's poem.'

'And when we know more about Hawaiian culture and the history out of which the poem has come, obviously, that complexity will increase,' he added.

'For instance, Mua,' Michel said, 'what is an aumakua?'

Lanimua was trying to be patient. 'It is a family akua or god. Other families had other creatures as their aumakua. Our niuhi protected us, fed us, provided us with a role model for courage and patience, etc. Even today there is a shark heiau in Kaneohe Bay. And sharks still come there to spawn and grow.'

'In Fiji, the great white shark is one of the important gods,' he added. When he glanced at the class, he noted most of them wanted to move onto the next poem, the next victim. 'So, who's going next?' Paused. 'Mua, thank you for being the first in our class.' She smiled, glad she was no longer the centre of attention.

'Professor, the name's Shannon; may I read my poem?' It was one of the Hawaiians who'd joked about the cold at their last session. Dark, black wavy hair, a trace of oriental features. 'Okay, here we go.'

'Before the haole came we had no words for snow, ice, sleet,
   and all those elements produced by the cold

First Class

Those were not in our lives.
So what did the first bit of ice feel like
in the amazed hand of a Hawaiian who didn't have the vocabulary of the cold?
That touch would have fired his search for that language.'

Paused, eyes lowered. 'Ah'm not happy about it; not happy about the las' line especially. And I need to condense it further, eh?'

From past experience, he anticipated that a few – maybe three – would try and cruise their way, with the minimum effort, through the course using smooth articulate talk and bluff, and he was again correct. Jocelyn Kim, a slim young woman who was deliberately trying to be inconspicuous, and whose name he asked for when he sensed she was not going to offer her poem, read her poem with enormous verve and confidence, but that didn't fool him into believing she'd spent much time on it. After the others had discussed it, saying it was a quality poem, he said, curtly, 'You need to revise that numerous times and show it to me again next session, okay?' And as he anticipated, she smiled beautifully and said, 'Certainly, Professor Malaetau!' That would have conned other men, but he was used to working with such confidence tricksters! The challenge was to turn her confidence into a talent for using her writing to con readers into believing anything she wanted them to believe. That's what art was all about.

He was disappointed that Nathaniel, a fellow Samoan and a straightforward, uncomplicated soul, though not a confidence trickster, was expecting to get through the course with first drafts as final ones. Nathaniel read his poem in the voice and manner of The Rock:

'In winter, bro, it's cold in Tennessee,

so cold your ears and other valuables can freeze and break off.' (A wave of suppressed laughter from the class.)

'Playing football in winter is a shit

You can't feel anything in your hands …'

He lost interest in Nathaniel Matagi's poem right there. He didn't even wait for the others to comment. 'You need to revise that many times, Nathaniel. It's like practicing a move in football until you get it perfect. How do you do that?'

'Over and over again until it looks and feels easy,' Nathaniel admitted.

'Yeah, bro, in football you get killed by the opposition if you don't rehearse and practice, right?'

'Right!' Nathaniel replied.

He was also disappointed in Shirley Beems' effort – or lack of it. He smiled but was blunt. 'How many times did you rewrite that?' he asked, immediately after she read it. He refused to set her free from his gaze.

She squirmed, and then admitted, 'Twice.'

'So, class, I expect you all to revise and revise your work, otherwise drop out of this course now and do something you can con your way through!' He laughed; the others didn't because they knew he wasn't bluffing.

Apart from those three, by the time they'd all read and discussed their poems, he was enveloped in the usual feeling of relief and self-satisfaction and euphoric keenness to write their next poems that was emanating from the rest of the class. It was like that in each course, at the end of the first readings and critiquing. He was especially pleased that no one had been insensitive, arrogant and destructive in their analyses.

'Next week's exercise is this: Write a poem no more than eight lines, again without the I, but in any tense, and using in the poem the words *she, fire, lava* and *blue light*.' He wrote it up on the board. 'You will also continue to revise the poems you wrote for today and keep them in your folios for me to look at again later on.'

'Before we finish, professor, may I ask Mua another question about sharks?' Nigel 'the Hammer' Blathmire, who'd said little during the class, asked.

'Go right ahead, Mano Kihikihi,' Lanimua replied, with an ironical smile.

'I mean, if sharks were ancestral gods, why did Hawaiians eat them?' the Hammer asked.

'We, Kanaka Maoli, are a spiritual but very practical people,' she explained, eyes twinkling mischievously. 'Not all mano, or sharks, were aumakua. We ate those who were not our aumakua. And we only caught what we needed, and it wasn't just for the fins to make shark fin soup or to mix some concoction to try and get our limp hopes erect again!' Most of the class, including the Hammer, laughed with her, and for the first time he sensed they were becoming a class, a group held together by mutual respect and trust.

That evening at home, he got out his Hawaiian dictionary and looked up 'mano kihikihi', and laughed to himself when he saw the meaning: hammerhead shark.

HAWAI'I

The automatic doors slid open and as he pushed his suitcase-laden trolley out of the restricted area she waved and smiled and again wondered why David always looked *defenceless* whenever he came off a long plane trip. He wore a crumpled crimson aloha shirt with yellow frangipani motifs on it, the dark blue linen trousers that she'd gifted him for Christmas, and his favourite sandals. A week in the sun had deepened his tan to a shiny ebony. Defenceless, yes, but strikingly handsome, and she sensed many of the women looking at him.

It was just after midday, and the arrival area was crowded, so he had to stop and search the crowd for Taimane. She pushed forward between two Polynesian men, raised her arm and waved. He saw her and hurried over, smiling widely. After nine hours crammed into an economy class seat, he felt dirty and smelly, and wanted a hot shower.

'Good conference?' she asked as they embraced. David kissed her on the cheek. He smelled of sun and sunblock lotion.

'Yeah,' he replied, 'and I missed you.' But when she nuzzled closer into David's arms he held her off; it was too public, too many people around. Not long after they'd met, she'd realised he didn't like showing affection for her in public and she been hurt, believing he was ashamed of being seen with her. But it had been three years now – she knew it was just how he was. He wound his right arm round her shoulders and, holding the trolley with his left hand, steered her towards the exit. 'It's good to be home.'

'Great tan – how was Hawai'i?' she asked, taking the trolley and steering it. 'Still paradise?' David had taken her to Honolulu the year before for another conference, which had been held at the Mānoa Campus of the University of Hawai'i. They'd stayed at the Rainbow Hotel in Waikīkī, right on the beach. And then explored Hawai'i and enjoyed the most wonderful holiday she'd ever had.

'Yeah, still has the best climate on the planet.' As they wove their way through the parking area, Taimane gave him the car keys. 'My paper went well,' he added.

'I'm sure it did; I'm sure they loved it.' She paused. 'Fantastic title: "The Netherends in Epeli Hau'ofa's Fiction".'

'Had a packed audience. I've sent a copy of it to Epeli.'

'That's brave! What if he doesn't like it?'

'He's liked my earlier stuff about him.' David had introduced Taimane to Epeli Hau'ofa at the closing dinner of a conference David and his English department had organised and held at the impressive Fale Pasefika a few months before. Epeli was a tall Tongan with a bushy beard and sparkling, mischievous eyes. Later, Taimane laughed her way through Epeli's collection of satirical stories, *Tales of the Tikongs*.

After accompanying David to the opening of that Hawai'i conference in a large, nondescript lecture theatre with about two hundred other participants, where she really *tried* to focus on the keynote address by a stumpy, bald-headed professor from New York as well as three other so-called 'papers' (which their presenters crammed into their prescribed fifteen minutes by reading them at a rapid, jargon-filled pace), she'd told him that such academic brilliance about literature and the Pacific diaspora wasn't for her illiterate mind, and that she would only come to David's session the following day, before enjoying the 'sea, sun, and volcanoes of Paradise' for the rest of their stay.

'Don't you want to meet some of the writers in the conference?' David had asked, affronted that she wasn't prepared to give the conference a chance and worried that his friends would conclude that she wasn't well educated or literary. 'I'll meet them at the social functions,' she'd replied.

He'd stopped himself from reminding her she'd promised with boundless enthusiasm that she *really, really* wanted to attend her first ever literary conference and would *really, really* love it.

'I'm an illiterate lawyer who needs to learn about the literature of Oceania, your specialty, darling,' Taimane had declared. 'And I want to hear *your* paper.' One morning of the conference – admittedly the keynote speaker and the other three papers had been, even for him, pretentious and boring – and she'd had enough. A feeling deeper than annoyance had surged up from his belly, but, as was now usual in their relationship, he'd blocked it in his chest and swallowed it. She'd sensed his rising anger but knew he wasn't going to confront her. Besides, she *had* been genuine about wanting to participate in a literary conference and learn more about his work and the scholars and writers he worked with across the world.

After putting his suitcase and satchel in the boot, they got into the car. She immediately leaned across and held him and kissed him passionately. 'I missed you,' she whispered, and then bit his left lobe, her hot breath surging into his ear. 'Wow, now you've got me all randy!'

'Calm down,' he said. 'We don't want an accident on the way home!' They headed out of the airport through the busy traffic. It was another hot summer day. It felt good after being in Hawai'i's clean, tropical heat.

That first day, straight after the last conference session, Taimane had taken him back to their hotel, where she'd put on her black bikini, white bathrobe and jandals, all the time hurrying him out of his clothes. They'd elevatored down into the crowded lobby area and walked out, through the other tourists weaving through the corridors and onto the hotel's spacious back lanai and swimming pool. He'd felt *exposed*, his skin unused to being naked in that heat after being cooped up all winter.

There'd been few swimmers round the pool – most people were down on the beach under brightly coloured beach umbrellas, or sunbathing on the sand, or out in the waves surfing and swimming. A cool breeze wove round them, and he'd hoped she'd stay on the lanai so he wouldn't have to suffer the scrutiny of the beach crowd, but, face flushed with joy, arms outstretched, Taimane had jumped down onto the white sand. And he'd followed her. The sand had felt pulpy and wet and warm around his feet, as he'd stood surveying the stretch of mythical Waikīkī.

'Did you get the chance to have a holiday?' Taimane asked, snuggling into his side and slipping her hand between his legs. He tried to pull away, but she said, 'No, you don't, keep your sexy eyes on the road, darling, or you'll crash us.'

'I took some friends to Waimānalo and swam and picnicked there for the day. They loved it …'

'Like we did, eh?' He was hardening. 'Wow, darling!'

After their first swim at Waikīkī, during which she'd felt as if her whole body and breath had been cleansed of its physical and emotional impurities, they'd returned to their luxurious room, where she'd quickly sketched out a schedule on hotel stationery for what she'd called their 'holiday in paradise'. She'd known David would protest like he always did, but with a little persuasion (and *allowing* him to believe the final schedule was really his), she knew he'd come round.

As she'd predicted, David *had* protested: 'What about my missing out on most of the conference?'

'But darling, how many papers are there that you *really* can't afford to miss?'

He'd scrambled and could only come up with two.

'See, and those are on tomorrow in the afternoon. Yours is in the morning.' She knew she'd won. 'So, darling, we'll spend tomorrow at the conference and then have a two-week holiday.'

'Two weeks?'

'Why not? I'll ring my office and tell them. And you're on mid-semester break.'

Within minutes, she'd left their hotel room and booked their schedule with the tour company in the lobby.

'How's work?' He tried distracting himself from Taimane's marvellous grip. The thick traffic ahead on the motorway, the summer light flashing off the vehicles, threatening to blind him.

'Fine, fine, busy! A difficult divorce case starting on Monday …' She sucked in her breath. Her throat and eyes were parched dry and her voice trembled as she gazed admiringly down at her hand. 'Wow, wow!' she whispered. She knew this was one of his favourite ways of getting aroused, and when he was aroused, her desire fired, too. 'Eyes on the road, darling. Eyes on the road!' When she started unzipping him he reached down and grasped her hand.

'No, not here; wait till we get home!'

His first impression of Taimane – when they'd shared the same table at his cousin's wedding reception – was that she was demure, reserved, almost shy, stand-offish. He'd seen her once before at a Laughing Samoans' performance at the Aotea Centre; he remembered that she'd been in the lobby before the show, drinking wine and laughing softly with a man and three other women. She was tall, wide-shouldered with slim hips and long, silky black hair and absolutely striking in her dark blue woollen overcoat, tight-fitting black puletasi and black pearl earrings that hung down almost to her neck. He'd heard she was a lawyer in a firm of three Samoan female lawyers. At the wedding, when he realised that she was avoiding him, he'd decided right then not to talk to her either.

Like most of the Samoan community, she knew who David was; there weren't many Samoan university lecturers, and even fewer who were also writers. She'd read one of his novels and had found it compulsively engrossing but frightening and upsetting in its portrayal of the paradisiacal Samoa her mother had nourished her on. Did he need to be so anti-faife'au and anti-church, and so gratuitously graphic with the violence and sex? She wasn't going to read any more of David's books! Now she had to sit opposite him, that person who *obviously* knew little about Samoa and was giving people everywhere a grossly false, unfair, malicious picture of *her* people and culture! She'd had enough of up-themselves Samoan men like him (*and* that high school teacher she'd just dropped, after tolerating almost six months of his egotistical behaviour)!

During the wedding breakfast, while the others at their table were busy eating and talking, the urge to penetrate Taimane's aloofness gripped David, and he reached over and grasped her left hand.

Startled, she pulled her hand away, which startled him in turn. 'Sorry – I'm sorry.'

'Don't worry – don't!' she automatically responded, making eye contact with him for the first time.

'I'm David, David Tulafono.'

'I know,' she'd said. 'My name's Tai – Taimane Falemalu.'

A week later they went out to dinner at his favourite Thai restaurant in Ponsonby, near the two-bedroom apartment where he lived alone after he and his wife had separated. Within half an hour, she was surprised, breathlessly elated, to find herself talking more freely about her life than she'd ever done with any other man. David seemed wholly focused and interested in what she was saying; *such* a good listener, a total contrast to the arrogant, anti-Samoan writer she'd believed he was. She heard herself saying, 'Once I thought, after reading one of your books, that you were a really arrogant person. Now, now …' She flung her hands up, admitting how wrong she'd been. He smiled, eyes concentrated only on her, and didn't say anything. 'Really arrogant,' she repeated.

She continued telling him her story. An only child, she'd been raised in Grey Lynn by her mother and grandparents, who were poorly educated but hard-working, loving, God-fearing people, who'd put her education and upbringing before anything else. Sunday school and church twice on Sunday *and* youth group on Wednesday nights, an A-student all the way through Auckland Girls' Grammar and then university, and – 'Would you believe it in this day and age?' – she was chaperoned everywhere. She wasn't allowed to play sport or have boyfriends, because those were distractions from her education, being successful and becoming 'a true

Samoan woman'. Whenever she stopped talking, worried that she was boring him, he would nod and ask her a question that would set the next direction to her story.

'And would you believe it, even when all my friends and other young people around me were doing what they wanted, not once did I ever rebel against my strict upbringing! How could I? My mother and grandmother worked in a factory during the day and as cleaners at night, and Granddad drove a bus and was a security guard in the weekends. All for me.'

He found everything about Taimane captivating: her unawareness that she was physically beautiful, the iridescent glow that emanated from her whole being when she was discussing things she believed in and her voice, throaty, deep and rising from the depths of her belly, firing long shivers down his back.

It was only when they had finished their desert of fresh mangos and vanilla ice cream that she realised he'd not given much information about himself. 'Bloody hell, I'm so sorry. I've been telling you tons about myself!'

It was at that pause, that moment of formulating his reply, that the sharp finger of doubt first jabbed into the credibility of the life Taimane had storied to him, but he dispelled it immediately.

'There isn't much to tell.' He looked away from her. 'I was married for eight years, have an eight-year-old daughter, Gaualofa, and have been teaching at Auckland University for eight years.' He laughed. 'My life works in eight-year cycles!' They laughed some more and he noticed that her eyes glistened like diamonds.

Ancestry

He couldn't sleep for a long time that night, trying to deny his doubts about her life story. Of one thing he was irrefutably sure: Taimane was the first woman since his separation that he had felt more than lust towards. He wanted to know more about her; even perhaps be with her beyond an affair.

When the automatic garage door closed behind them, they didn't even bother to take out his luggage as they rushed into the house and onto the sitting room sofa. As they fucked wildly, her crying out, 'Hawai'i, Hawai'i!', vivid memories of their holiday in Hawai'i and their lurid lovemaking – on the beach, in the car, in their hotel rooms and once, almost in public view, on the cliff at the highest point on Waimea Canyon – as they'd travelled round O'ahu, to Hilo and around the lava fields of Kilauea Volcano and the Big Island, and on to Kaua'i fuelled the intensity and variation and duration of their love-making.

'Now do you agree that ditching that *literary* conference and *doing* Hawai'i and those sexy volcanic fields was worth it, darling?' she laughed, as they showered afterwards.

'Too right, too bloody right!' He rubbed body gel over her back.

'And for your sake, I hope you didn't have a holiday like that this time!' She turned and rubbed her lathered face into his chest. 'Did you?' she asked, pretending she was still joking.

'Of course not,' he replied, knowing Taimane was serious and suspicious – but he wasn't going to reveal it. 'There were some awesome papers and some of my close friends were there.'

He hadn't slept much on the plane, so David retreated to bed after their shower while she went into her study and tried to work on the divorce case. Instead, she found herself recalling in hypnotising detail their car trip into the National Park and up through those amazing lava fields ablaze with light and heat waves, to the edge of the Kilauea crater. It was like she was watching a silent black and white movie being projected from her eyes.

'See the fissure down there where the molten lava and fire are coming out?' he'd asked as they had stood at the edge. 'That's Halemaʻumaʻu, home of Pele, the akua of volcanoes.' As the acrid smell of sulphur had grown stronger, she'd cupped a couple of tissues to her mouth and nose.

Following their Thai dinner, the compulsion to be with each other was undeniable. So they usually met after work for drinks or dinner, or spent long periods talking on the phone. Not once did either invite the other to their apartments.

Once, David asked her where her grandparents were now. He caught the hesitation in her eyes, in her hands, and then Taimane said, 'Oh, once I was settled into my law job, they decided to go back to Samoa and live. My mother and I built them a modest house there, and they're very happy living on their New Zealand super in the community they grew up in. Mum and I also send them money every month.' The need to know more was urgent, but he tried to sound nonchalant as he asked after her mother.

Oblivious to his suspicions, she answered, 'She's living with her sister, my aunt Fausia, and other ʻāiga in our home, which I had totally renovated two years ago.'

Trying again to quiet his doubts, David offered information about himself; that both his parents had died in a car accident when he was ten and that he'd been raised by his uncle and aunt in Ponsonby.

Taimane reached over and grasped his hand. Before she could ask, he added that his uncle and aunt, who had a grown-up son and daughter, had been marvellous parents – better even than his biological ones. She caressed the back of his hand. 'Had been?' she asked softly. He nodded once, and told her his aunt had died of breast cancer four years before and his uncle of a broken heart a few months later. With both hands she gripped his, tightly, and gazed at him, tears in her eyes. 'Of a broken heart? What a wonderful, wonderful story, David!'

And she meant it. He reached over to her and she thrust her head forward, cupping the side of his head with her hand, and they kissed for the first time. Long, searching, urgent.

The next afternoon in the middle of a lecture he was giving to his graduate class on Sia Figiel and her views on how Samoans defined I, the self and the individual, bewildering doubts about her life story again clogged his attention. For a moment – during which his students looked up at him, puzzled — he lost the thread of his discussion, retrieving it only when he decided he had to satisfy those doubts immediately.

That afternoon, he started gathering information about her, and felt highly relieved he wasn't experiencing any guilt doing it. To his relief, the first informants he rang reinforced much of the story she'd given him. He remembered her mother's name and rang her, pretending he was a *New Zealand Herald* journalist doing a feature story on Taimane and two other Pasefika lawyers as outstanding examples of the new generation of Pacific lawyers in Auckland.

As the woman answered his questions, he didn't want to believe the obvious discrepancies between her story and Taimane's. Taimane had claimed that her mother and aunt and grandparents were poorly educated, yet her mother was speaking fluent, lucid English. How had her daughter done at Auckland Girls' Grammar? he asked. Auckland Grammar? No, the woman said, her daughter had attended Massey College, where she was still the head of maths.

His breath snagged in his throat. The father, who had been absent from Taimane's stories (he'd assumed it was because she was ashamed of him), turned out to be a highly respected paediatrician who was still practicing. And instead of being an only child, she was the youngest of four. As for doting grandparents, they had died before Taimane was born.

There was nothing in her family and history to be ashamed of, so why the lies? A lacerating mixture of betrayal, anger and bewilderment threatened to choke him. David went to the long windows of his office that overlooked the harbour and took long slow breaths. He persuaded himself that Taimane would soon tell him why she'd lied about her family. Right now, all that he was, even his lust, needed Tai. Yes, absolutely. So he decided to discontinue his investigation, and he knew he'd never reveal his findings to her.

It was almost seven, and David had been sleeping since he got back from his trip. As Taimane watched him from the doorway, the light from the corridor fell across the bottom of their bed and up over him. He was on his stomach with the sheets tangled round his legs.

So much of her and her life had changed over the three years she'd been with him – and for the better. He wasn't going to wake for dinner; she'd let him sleep through the night, so she turned and went into the kitchen, where she made an avocado, tomato and ham sandwich and lemon tea and sat down at the dining table – he insisted that they always do that.

As she ate, she remembered the first time she and his wife Ariel had met. She was now sure Ariel had *deliberately* planned it. In the Foodtown supermarket on Williamson Avenue of all places! She was selecting a bag of seedless grapes when someone wearing the strong scent of Poison came and stood beside her. Taimane almost stepped away when she recognised Ariel from photos she'd seen of her. 'Oh, hello,' Ariel said, smiling. 'What a surprise.' Taimane would never understand David's attraction to blonde Pālagi women – it was strange, considering his staunch, outspoken views about racism, colonialism and the rights of indigenous people.

She didn't know what to do, and heard herself mumbling, 'Good to meet you. Gaualofa is a very well-behaved child.' Ridiculous thing to say; why talk about Ariel's daughter?

'Thank you,' Ariel said. 'You don't mind looking after her in the weekends?'

'No, no!' She replied. 'She's a good girl and David loves having her with us.' The separation agreement between David and Ariel gave him the right to have Gaualofa the last two weekends of every month and some of the school holidays. Since shifting in with David two years before, Taimane had established, if not an intimate, fully trusting relationship with Gaualofa, one that was *workable*. At first Taimane had found it painfully difficult sharing David with a child he doted on. She didn't know much about children or care very much for them; especially prepubescent girls who couldn't stop talking and whining and demanding things. Once, when Gaualofa refused repeatedly to clean her room, Taimane had grabbed her shoulders and ordered, 'Do it now!' David slid into the room and, embracing his sobbing daughter, carried her out, shouting over his shoulder, 'Don't you bloody well treat *my* daughter like that again!' Since then – and after a few more confrontations with Gaualofa, which only ever resulted in nasty arguments between her and David, and the bitter realisation she could never compete with Gaualofa for his affections – she left the parental control and responsibility to David.

Now, Gaualofa's mother was in front of her, another competitor for David's attention, if not his love. As long as Taimane was with David, Gaualofa and Ariel would be there too. She cursed that, dreaded it, but had to accept it.

'Would you like to have coffee?' Ariel invited her. Taimane hesitated. 'Don't worry,' Ariel chortled, 'David is no longer on my radar. And he tells everyone he's totally smitten with you.'

Near midnight, her eyes heavy with tiredness after working on the divorce case, she brushed her teeth and undressed. Getting into bed, Taimane snuggled up against David's back, buttocks and legs. Yes, she fitted so comfortably into him, and, yes, he into her, and, yes, she was so glad he was home.

On Monday morning she was ready for work and having her usual black coffee and single piece of wholemeal toast with marmite when David came into the kitchen. 'You were dead to the planet last night! My case starts at ten – I have a few more things to prepare for it.'

David kissed her on the cheek and told her he had a lecture at 10.30. 'Talking about three Hawaiian poets,' he added.

'Who? Do I know any of them?' she heard herself asking.

He poured coffee into his favourite mug, and said, 'I think two of them. I introduced them to you at that conference.' He poured in some milk.

She remembered. 'What was her name? The very beautiful one feared by all Haole and colonisers?'

He used a teaspoon to scoop up a large dollop of honey, and stirred it into his coffee. 'Haunani-Kay Trask.' He pushed two slices of bread into the toaster and came to the table.

'Should I read her work? You told me she was so angry about what America had done to her country.' She didn't quite understand why she was pursuing this.

He started chuckling. 'She scares the shit out of Americans – and the other groups who colonised her country and are still wrecking it!'

She remembered that while they'd been in Hawai'i he'd tried to get her interested in its history and what was happening there, but she'd been too preoccupied with enjoying herself. 'And the second one I met?' she asked, now regretting not knowing more about Hawai'i's anti-colonial struggle.

'Mahealani Kamau'u, that's her name,' he replied. 'She's a lawyer.'

'She's a beauty too,' she said. She waited for David to continue, but he went and got his toast.

'And the third poet – or should I say, poetess, is?' She didn't care any more what she was revealing with her questions. The crackling sound of his buttering his toast scraped across her hearing. As he cut his toast in half, the crunching cut open her annoyance.

'Rachel Wong,' he said nonchalantly, and took a large sip of his coffee.

'What sort of Hawaiian name is that?' He could be *so* deliberately hurtful in his treatment of her when he didn't like what she was inquiring about. So fucking cruel! She stood up and started gathering her used dishes and cutlery.

'That's why I wanted you to learn more about Hawai'i,' he said, continuing to eat as if he wasn't aware of her true feelings.

There it was again: his cruel streak of deliberately playing on her weaknesses. 'So now I'm ignorant, now I don't care about Hawaiians –'

'I didn't say that, darling.' Noisily, he sipped his coffee. 'Most of Hawai'i's population is part-Asian, and most indigenous Hawaiians, like Rachel Wong, are that –'

'How could she be indigenous then?' As soon as she spoke she regretted it, but it was too late to withdraw her words.

David spread a thick layer of marmalade over his second piece of toast, taking his time and then, gazing up at her, said, 'Being indigenous has little to do with blood quantum and everything to do with *gafa*, genealogy, darling. You know that.'

She tried to lay her dishes into the sink quietly. 'I might be home late from work,' she said, and headed out of the kitchen. 'And enjoy your *indigenous* Hawaiian poetesses!' she called over her shoulder. 'Especially Miss Wong!'

He got home at six, after a day plagued by his mounting frustration about Taimane's unreasonable suspicions, which had worsened over their time together. To distract himself, he started cooking their dinner. Taimane was a hopeless cook, a hopeless housekeeper, a hopeless shopper for food and a hopeless budgeter. And she was supposed to be Samoan, the ideal Samoan woman! Admittedly, since they got together, she'd been willing to learn how to cook and he was enjoying teaching her. However, she refused to learn how to clean the house or budget properly – her supermarket shopping consisted of buying anything she fancied, irrespective of the prices.

'I can bloody well afford it,' she insisted. 'I can also pay for people to come and do the cleaning. If I had to pay myself or you to clean at the rates we earn, we wouldn't be able to afford it!' He had to agree with that. 'Besides you're a gifted cook, darling, and you love doing it.' He had to agree with that, too. He found himself cooking three of her favourite dishes: pork sapasui, faʻalifu talo and green bananas and a salad of mixed lettuce, avocado, tomato, capsicums and feta, sprinkled with roasted pine seeds and a light French dressing.

As he was setting the table, he heard Taimane's car enter the garage, her car door slamming and her high heels clicking up the front steps. Her key slid into the keyhole, the door swung open and then slammed, and she was there in the kitchen, dumping her heavy satchel onto the side table. His heart quickened and his body tensed. 'Hi,' he said without looking at her.

'Had a fucking awful day,' Taimane sighed dramatically as she slid into the dining chair facing him. He opened the fridge and got out a cold Heineken, opening it and placing it in front of her. 'Thanks.' She picked it up and in one long swig drained half of it, her eyes watering immediately as the cold hit the back of her head. 'Needed that.' As he started putting the food into serving bowls and dishes, Taimane finished her beer and got another out of the fridge. 'Smells delicious! Haven't eaten all day.' She drank the second bottle quickly too, and sighed as if her life was in a hopeless mess. He refused to take the bait.

After he laid out the food, he brought a chilled bottle of chardonnay and two wine glasses to the table. He opened the bottle and filled their glasses, while she watched and thanked him for cooking some of her favourite food. 'Sorry about your tough day,' he said, and then, raising his glass, added, 'Cheers, darling!' They clinked glasses and, for the first time, Taimane smiled. Her eyes were bloodshot with tiredness.

At first, he'd been surprised by the way Taimane ate whenever they were alone. Then he was annoyed, and finally, resigned to her eating habits. Tonight though, he didn't really care; he was more concerned about her being tired and stressed.

Ancestry

While she continued to tell him about her court case and how badly the husband and his lawyers were behaving, Taimane scooped large helpings of food onto her plate until it was almost overflowing. Using her hands and fingers and the serving spoon, she devoured her meal, cheeks bulging, mouth moving in a huge chewing movement, pausing only to emphasise a point. Not that the food stuffed in her mouth interfered with the clarity of her speech; he understood everything Taimane said. 'Guess what the bastard and his lawyers are trying to hide, David?' She waited, eyes swallowing him, her face round with food. 'Go on, darling, guess.'

'Most of his assets and sources of income, especially those overseas,' he played her game.

'Right on, darling.' She licked her coconut-covered lips clean. 'Wow, if I keep eating this marvellous fa'alifu, I'll have an incredible multiple orgasm like yesterday!' Taimane chuckled deep in her throat, rolling her eyes at him, and he had to laugh. 'Yeah, the bastards have revealed only four companies and a piddling number of his investments and shares and fixed deposits overseas. At first I couldn't prove otherwise and, believing the stereotype that fulltime housewives don't understand their husbands' dealings, didn't bother to ask my client – his wife, Martha – about it. I mean, what do domesticated women who spend their days baby-talking to their kids and entertaining their husbands' clients know about business?' Another large spoonful of sapasui into her mouth. Another contented sigh. 'Martha was so quiet while I was preparing our case that I thought she *was* a dumb housewife! I didn't realise it was because she was in deep shock and grief, caused by the break-up of her twenty-six-year marriage to a man she'd loved and served faithfully before he betrayed her. Martha told me she wanted to die and I thought she was *such* a cliché!'

Though he and Ariel had been married for only eight years, David understood some of Martha's pain. Ariel was the one who'd wanted out of the marriage. She told him she was in love with someone else. He'd suspected nothing, so it had come as a numbing, almost unbearable shock. Shock turned to dismay, self-recrimination; he even grovelled to try and get her back. Then that turned to grief, during which he felt empty and wanted to die. When that turned to anger, he started healing. He'd not told Taimane any of this.

'… Today, after getting *nowhere* with trying to get those wankers to admit they were hiding the rest of their client's wealth, I stormed back to my office, where I found Martha and her eldest daughter. I could feel it when I looked at her: Martha was angry, really angry, steaming, ready to go to war! Martha handed me a thick file of papers and said, "That should fix the selfish, unfaithful prick!" So I now have some *interesting* reading for tonight.'

He cleared the table and washed and put away the dishes while Taimane showered. When he went into their bedroom, Taimane was already in bed, laughing smugly as she read Martha's file. He showered and, naked, snuggled up against her side and kissed her shoulder repeatedly. 'That's nice, nice,' she murmured, but her attention never left the file. 'Good on ya, Martha! We've got the pricks!'

Ancestry

On Saturday, he woke and found a note telling him she had gone to get Gaualofa for the weekend. Suspicion and worry radiated through him. This was the first time she'd done that. She'd not offered before, which suited him because of the potentially inflammatory results of a meeting between Taimane and Ariel; plus he didn't want Taimane to learn more about his failed marriage. Gaualofa and Taimane weren't yet trusting buddies, either.

He prepared Gaualofa's favourite breakfast of strawberry yogurt and muesli and a well-boiled egg. For Taimane, two strips of lean bacon, a tomato cut in half and steamed, and two pieces of wholemeal toast and marmite. And just as he finished laying out breakfast, Gaualofa burst through the front door, scuttled down the corridor and, jumping into his arms, screeched, 'Daddy, Daddy!' He hugged her tightly, kissed her on the forehead and eased her into her chair.

'She was dressed and ready when I got there,' Taimane said as she took her seat. He wanted to ask if she'd talked with Ariel but didn't. 'Gaualofa has already told me what she wants to do today,' Taimane said. She waited for Gaualofa to say what that was, but the girl was engrossed in her yogurt and muesli, so Taimane told him. 'She wants to go to Western Springs Park and feed the birds and eels. Is that right, darling?'

'Yeah, Mummy takes me there sometimes and I love feeding the ducks and swans and pūkeko and creepy eels and I want to take you there, Daddy!' she replied, carefully spooning up the last remnants of her muesli.

'I'd love to come,' David said to his daughter. She noticed that David was using the voice that he reserved specially for Gaualofa, and which signalled she was now excluded from their intimate circle. At first she'd been intensely jealous, but, over the years, she'd had to accept it. She didn't want to jeopardise her relationship with David.

'We'll go later this morning,' David said.

'By the way, Ariel said to give you her love.' Taimane couldn't believe she'd said it. She caught the tension in David's stance. 'She's looking well. Still *very* attractive.'

'Is Mummy working yet?' David asked his daughter, his attention focused on Taimane.

Gaualofa shook her head. 'She only works sometimes in the library.' Taimane noticed with satisfaction the momentary flicker of exasperation on his face. He was still paying Ariel generous child support, and resented it. Taimane resented it too; after all, that money was partly hers.

'Gotta go to the toilet,' Gaualofa said, and left the dining room.

'So she's still attractive, eh?' David fumed. 'The – the bloody lazy –' He couldn't say it. 'She should be out working fulltime!' Taimane was surprised and wickedly pleased – this was the first time he'd ever derided his former wife to her. 'Did you know she was the one who wanted to end it?' He stopped abruptly.

'I'm so sorry, darling!' She grabbed onto this new knowledge. 'I didn't know.'

He couldn't stop now that the wounds were open and bleeding again. 'While I was busy slogging my guts out to support her and our kid, she was, she was …' Again he couldn't say it. And he didn't care if he was on the verge of tears.

'I'm so sorry,' she repeated as she hugged him closely, burying her face in his warm hair. She'd always meant to tell David about her first meeting with Ariel at the supermarket, and then having coffee with her, and the two later lunches they'd had in Newmarket. About how, though she was wary of Ariel's sincerity, she'd ended up believing her. According to Ariel, David had been unfaithful, having an affair with one of his graduate students, and when Ariel had found out, he'd simply admitted it and had declared their marriage over. Ariel told Taimane how she'd pleaded with David, but he'd just walked out. She said she still loved him, but she was happy he'd found someone as beautiful, caring and loving as Taimane. How could Ariel have lied to her so blatantly?

When they heard Gaualofa returning, he broke from her, dried his eyes and started clearing the table.

By high noon, the sun had sucked up all the shadows. Because of the heat, most people remained under the trees or beach umbrellas. A few hardy joggers and walkers went by on the birdshit-stained main walkway and paths. Taimane sat at the massive wooden table by the lake, under the large, rainbow-coloured beach umbrella that she'd bought in Honolulu, watching David and Gaualofa, who were a few paces away, feeding the mix of pūkeko, ducks, seagulls and geese milling round them.

Gaualofa was heavy for her age, with blue-green eyes and a shock of golden hair; a miniature version of Ariel without visible signs of David or being Samoan – partly Samoan, Taimane corrected herself. Now that she knew the truth about his marriage break-up and how terribly he'd been affected by it, every time she looked at David she experienced a melting sadness and concern and love – yes, love – and the desire to help heal him. But she knew that if she intruded into the father-daughter circle that was bound even more tightly by the joy David was deriving from watching Gaualofa playing so happily with those birds, she would be rejected. She could see, anyway, how being in that circle was helping to heal David.

So she opened their large chilly bin and carefully took out their lunch and drinks and laid them out on the picnic table. She knew this was going to attract the birds so she quickly called to David, who put an arm round Gaualofa and brought her to the table, followed by most of the birds they'd been feeding. Here's trouble, she thought. David picked up Gaualofa and placed her on the bench, above the birds. The birds, especially the geese, were already more aggressive, their demanding heads and beaks thrusting forward repeatedly, even at Gaualofa's feet and legs, and honking louder. Gaualofa was squealing with delight. Sparrows and other smaller birds were scrambling across the table. Gaualofa moved to break some crusts for them.

'No,' David said. 'They'll only get worse. Put the food away.' Taimane quickly packed the food away, while David took down the umbrella.

As they fled from the table, Gaualofa protested, 'I don't wanna go; don't wanta!', but David hurried her away. The birds streamed after them for a short distance until, realising their feeders were no longer tossing them food, stopped and started looking for other sources.

'Those geese can be really vicious, eh?' David sighed.

Ancestry

Taimane agreed. 'They're supposed to be good guards for your property, better than dogs. My grandparents in Samoa keep a small flock of them for that purpose.' Was that another lie? He immediately regretted his thought. His deep distrust of Ariel and the pain she was still inflicting on him was making him suspicious of Taimane again.

A short while later, they found another table at the edge of the children's playground. It wasn't too crowded. Gaualofa rushed over and, getting into a swing, pushed herself back expertly with her feet and then forward; she was soon away, her flight getting higher and higher and more daring. And very risky, he concluded, so he hurried over to her and stood at the side as she laughed and whooped, her eyes wild and bulging with joy.

Taimane didn't put up their umbrella again. She wanted suddenly to be in the full force of the heat and sun. Dressed in jean shorts, a bright red t-shirt with ALOHA HAWAI'I emblazoned along the front of it and yellow jandals – or slippers, as Hawaiians called them – she wanted to *feel* Hawai'i again, revel in it, in the boundless amazement she'd experienced moving through the landscape; the healing wrap of the balmy sea unthawing her of all stress and worry and inhibitions, the exhilarating cool of the trade winds that fingered and flowed through her pores and cleaned out all her regrets and grudges, and the magnificent lava fields that spread around her for miles and miles and miles – not a place of desolation and fear and sadness, but of gods and hope and promise and David.

'Tai, Tai, may I have a drink?' Gaualofa's voice broke the spell.

She blinked and smiled. 'Of course, darling,' she said, pulling out a cold can of Coke.

'I'm not allowed fizzy drinks,' Gaualofa said, regretfully. 'Mum says they're unhealthy.'

Of course she and David knew that, but she glanced conspiratorially at David. 'One won't do you any harm,' she offered. Gaualofa nodded eagerly and looked at her father, who nodded back. Gaualofa grabbed the can, pulled open the tab and started sucking up the Coke.

'I'll have one too,' said David. It was bloody time they weaned Gaualofa away from her manipulative, heartless, unfaithful mother.

The can hissed sharply as she opened it and extended it to David. She opened a can for herself and clinked it against David's and Gaualofa's Cokes. 'Here's to us and to all the birds!' They drank together.

FAST

...And it is blinding morning, laced with the unpleasant odour of winter mud, bursting through the gap under your bedroom curtains and flowing over your duvet and up over your chest and into your nostrils and eyes. You remember, you push your legs out of bed, your feet find the floor and you re-hitch your 'ie lavalava round your waist and start rushing for the bathroom. Shit, shit, shit, you're going to be late for your 9.30 am lecture, again! No time to shave or have breakfast. Final week of lectures and then finals, and hopefully the completion of your MA and your graduation and getting a teaching job. You have to be at Professor Thalmer's last class of the year because he is going to tell the class what is in your final exams on The New Zealand and Pacific Novel.

All your family have left already: your father to his chef's job at the Battersea on Ponsonby Road, your mother to the Williamson Street Foodtown and your sister and brother to Auckland University of Technology, where she is completing a BA in film studies and he is studying for a diploma in nursing. You fling your haversack into the back seat of your 1996 Honda Civic, which your parents bought for you two years before as a reward for completing your BA – you are the first in your 'āiga to graduate from university. You slide into the driver's seat, start the car and head for university, which, if the traffic is light, is only ten minutes away.

Once you're into Grafton Road and turning into the Owen G Glenn Building and parking, you know you'll only be fifteen minutes late.

Through the narrow glass partition in the back door, you look into the small brilliantly lit lecture theatre. Professor Thalmer is down in the front behind the desk, his purple-rimmed glasses glinting, and behind him on the screen is a PowerPoint slide of a list of items. You count the students quickly. You're the only one absent out of the fourteen. And Graeme, your ally, is there.

You pull back the door quietly; your heart is thumping like thunder and you hope beyond hope no one, especially Professor Thalmer, is noticing your entry. You start towards the empty seat beside Graeme. 'So, my handsome Samoan Viking, I'm so glad you're able to be with us today.' Professor Thalmer catches you on your third slow step. Excruciating embarrassment: your ears hot, your heart thumping, your throat parched dry.

'Hi, Jonas,' Graeme whispers. On his retirement as a highly successful architect, Graeme decided to pursue the love of his life: poetry and the literature of his country. Balding, with long straggly wisps of white hair and a few days' growth of white stubble, paunchy, always dressed in black polo necks, navy blue corduroys and thick-soled suede boots – he claims he'd been a beatnik. He is by far the oldest in your class and the one Professor Thalmer is most *careful* of.

Using his prepared PowerPoint presentation, Professor Thalmer takes you quickly through a summary of all the topics and the novelists you've covered this semester. You've spent four years with him, from Stage One New Zealand Literature through his second-year course on the New Zealand/Pacific Short Story to his third-year paper, 'Post-colonialism and Pacific Literature', and now The New Zealand and Pacific Novel. Because New Zealand and Pacific literature is your passion, you've studied hard, doing far more than the required reading and research and writing and handing in your assignments on time, and he's given you an A-minus average for each course, your best grade in all your studies. Yet you've never felt he respects your intelligence and ability; you've suspected that he's unconsciously assumed that being a Pacific Islander, a Samoan – at least he knew that! – English is your second language, and because of that you're struggling to cope with the literature of that language. So you can never break that A-minus barrier. (It is a joke among PI university students that all PI students start with C.) So it's strange, bloody strange, that you continue to hold some admiration and respect for him. Or is it out of the fear that if you don't pander to your lecturers' tight-arsed egos they won't give you good grades?

'… So, I'm now going to go through the exam questions – oops! Sorry!' Professor Thalmer's eyes shine with fake horror. There's a scatter of student laughter. Graeme doesn't laugh. Professor Thalmer sniggers and corrects himself. 'Sorry, I'm going to talk about the topic areas I'll be giving you exam questions on. If you're shrewd, you can just get the last three years' exam papers and all the questions will be there.' You and Graeme don't join the laughter of your class mates.

'God, he loves himself,' you hear Graeme whisper. 'We're going to need a strong cuppa coffee after this corny shit.'

Looking straight at Professor Thalmer, you reply to Graeme, 'Shit, yeah.' Over the last three years, Graeme has been the only student who has been in all your Professor Thalmer classes, and you usually have coffee or lunch together at least once a week. As a superannuitant, Graeme can simply audit his courses and does not have to do the assignments or sit the exams, but he always does, and insists his lecturers award him grades for them. When he doesn't like the grades or disagrees with his lecturers' remarks on his essays he challenges them. Graeme doesn't take notes at lectures but recalls everything almost verbatim, and when he makes a presentation, he doesn't refer to notes or a prepared text, yet he is always absolutely fluent and delivers without faltering. Name any poet he admires and he can quote verse after verse from their work. Photographic memory? You've wondered but have never asked him.

All your sessions in this class are student seminars, each presenter talking about the topic for at least twenty minutes and then leading a class discussion for the rest of the session. At the start of the course, Professor Thalmer got you to choose your seminar topics, and then set a date for each seminar. Graeme chose to give the third seminar, on the intriguing topic 'Courage and Architecture in James George's

Fast

Novels'. As usual, it was flawless in delivery and innovative and original in analysing the novels, complex and sophisticated in the way he wove in the latest theoretical readings while simultaneously undermining them with a mesmerising sense of irony and fun, which, you sensed, Professor Thalmer didn't appreciate because it was aimed at *his* style of lecturing and reading. And as usual Graeme conducted the class discussion with verve and tolerance and insight, getting every student to participate fully and with enjoyment. He also used it to murder the theoretical jargon that Profesor Thalmer and his pet students are fond of using.

'Well, Jonas,' Graeme says as you leave the lecture theatre, 'we've survived another semester of the great Professor Thalmer.'

'He's not *that* bad,' you try to say.

'Contrary to the Kiwi stereotype of you being violent and mean, you Samoans are too generous, Jonas,' Graeme says, chortling.

'Thank you for *your* generosity,' you say. Graeme guffaws and punches you lightly on the arm.

Graeme needs a left knee replacement, and he refuses to use a walking stick or crutches, so you have to walk at his hobbling pace to the Student Union building. Once you jokingly suggested he should get one of those fancy motorised wheelchairs that go faster than Superman, and he'd laughed and said those were for 'the lazy Kiwi middle class, who are too cowardly to face the cleansing pain of worn out joints and souls'! That comment still puzzles you.

Ancestry

Since your first coffee together, Graeme has insisted that he pay. 'You're a bloody poor student, Jonas,' he'd reasoned. 'And I know you Samoans are big on reciprocity, so I'm reciprocating you, Jonas, for your generosity towards egotistical pricks like Thalmer and your kindness towards old bastards like me. Is that fair enough?'

You take the lift up to the restaurant.

The café is fairly full but there is an empty table near the front windows. Graeme joins the short line at the counter while you hurry over and take the table that looks down at the courtyard four stories beneath you. Your legs grow goose pimples and nausea nibbles at the tip of your tongue. Heights have always frightened you. You look away from the drop, and sit down with your back to it. 'What's the matter? You look as pale as a Pālagi,' Graeme says when he sits down opposite you.

'So you know what the Samoan is for Pākehā?' You try distracting him.

'Too right, mate, I have a good teacher of Samoan!'

'Your teacher is shit-scared of heights,' you admit.

'Just like Melissa,' Graeme says. Melissa is his wife, his third one, and at least fifteen years younger than him. 'I designed and built at least six of Auckland's highest buildings and she's absolutely refused, even at their official openings, to go above the third floor. And would you believe it? She's the most nerveless person I know, afraid of nothing, except heights of course.'

You first met Melissa at their home, in Freeman's Bay right at the water's edge and looking across the harbour and up at the Bridge, at their oldest grandson's twenty-first birthday. (You'd not wanted to go, but Graeme had insisted over three lunches that his 'bloody wasteful mokopuna need to meet someone who's focused and bloody hard-working. Besides I need an intelligent drinking mate'.)

You don't know much about art, but you recognised a Hotere and a Pule as Graeme took you into the spacious sitting room. You'd expected a large, palatial home with a swimming pool, and it *is* large, three split levels large, with lots of rooms and equipped, furnished and carpeted lavishly, and there is a swimming pool, but as Graeme said it was 'a very messy, shambolic reflection of me and my beautiful Melissa.'

You'd expected it to be a lavish, expensive party with lots of wild students and their wild friends and raucous music and dancing fuelled by unlimited alcohol and food such as caviar and champagne and whatever else rich people's parties are supposed to have, but you counted only about fifty guests, including Graeme's two daughters from his first two marriages and their husbands, his son with Melissa and his wife, his four grandchildren, other relatives and Ralph's, the birthday boy's, friends. You've grown up with Pālagi but you've never felt fully comfortable at their functions, but after Graeme introduced you to Melissa and some of his family, and he put a glass of champagne in your hand and said 'Ia Manuia! and you drank with him, and his grandchildren immediately drew you into their celebrating circle, you slid right into their family and into the party. You'd expected Graeme, like your father would have been, to be in control of that gathering, but you soon observed he wasn't. Melissa, a tall, stately woman with short-cropped silver hair and wearing what appeared to be a Pacific-blue puletasi with light frangipani motifs on the front and black pearl earrings, was in charge, in a quiet, almost unnoticeable way. You recalled Graeme telling you that Melissa had been a VSA volunteer in Samoa, years before.

Over dinner – after Melissa introduced Ralph and you all toasted him and he spoke and thanked his parents and grandparents and then blew out the twenty-one candles – Melissa brought her food and sat down beside you at a table beside the swimming pool. 'I expected someone older,' she told you. 'Graeme finds all young people, including his mokopuna, *difficult*, so when he came home and told me he'd found a good classmate, I assumed it would be someone older than "young people".' She laughed softly. 'You must also be exceptionally bright and able, because he can't tolerate "unbright" people who believe they're brighter than they are! And best of all, he's so chuffed you're the first Samoan friend he's made, without my help.' She went on to talk about her VSA year in Samoa and 'her Samoan 'āiga', which now had a branch in Auckland and which she maintained close ties with. Since that party, you've lunched with her and Graeme many times.

The waiter brings Graeme's double-strength latte and piece of carrot cake with a dollop of cream, and your flat white, mince pie and mixed salad. Two Samoan students you know wave at you; you wave back and hope they don't come over – they don't. Three of your MA class smile and head towards you, but when they see Graeme they veer off to another table. 'Do I have a bad smell?' Graeme asks. You pretend you don't know what he's referring to. 'Are they scared that my making *their*

Professor Thalmer look like an amateur will jeopardise their grades?' You don't understand that. 'That because I'm belittling Thalmer's ego he'll take it out on the whole class?' he explains.

'I guess so,' you reply.

'Then how come you don't mind being seen with me?'

'Cos, no matter what, I'll get another A-minus, as always.' You both laugh.

He spears his carrot cake, digs out a hunk of it and shoves it into his mouth. 'You know what we should revive?' he asks through his bulging mouth.

'Yeah, cannibalism!'

His eyes bulge with mirth and he can't swallow his large mouthful of cake. You hope he doesn't choke as he laughs, bits of food flying out of his mouth. 'That's good, yeah, fucking cannibalism so we can gobble up second-raters like our Professor Thalmer!' You're no longer self-conscious about laughing with abandonment in that public place.

A short while later, after Graeme dries his tears of mirth and wipes his face and clothes clean of food, he asks, unexpectedly, 'What are you going to do with your MA?'

You shrug your shoulders. 'Teach at high school,' you reply. High school: that's what your careers advisers and your teachers told you best suited your abilities, strengths, interests and grades. Because of that, your parents have supported that too. So you've never seen yourself doing anything else.

'Are you interested in doing a PhD?' he asks.

'You must be joking! With only an A-minus average, the department won't let me do a PHD.'

'Have you actually talked to the head of department about it? Even Thalmer?'

You shake your head, and say, 'You know Thalmer gave me the A-minuses.'

'Okay, so just tell him how you feel about that; just let him have it.'

'That would shut the door completely,' you say, but you feel encouraged.

'Are you bloody sick of hearing the self-righteous confessions of old fogeys?' he asks, from under his closely cropped white eyebrows. You can almost hear him chuckling.

'Not as long as it is a captivating, inspired, meaningful unpacking of that old bugger's story.' You imitate Professor Thalmer's tone.

He guffaws. 'Throughout my childhood and early life you know what my teachers and parents and everyone else, including my classmates, came to believe? That I was a mental retard: mentally handicapped was the uncool vocab of that time. In a literate culture if you can't read or write properly, you're fucked. They knew nothing about dyslexia in those terrible days. I couldn't read, and they equated that with retard intelligence. So they "promoted" me from class to class to get rid of me. And as I suffered my bloody parents' abusive treatment, I believed I deserved it. At the age of sixteen they took me out of school – I wanted out too – and apprenticed me to a butcher, a friend of my father's.' Graeme went on to explain that he was so ashamed of himself he even believed that his obsession with drawing — he drew on everything and all the time — was another feature of his retardation. At the butcher's, because he didn't have to know how to read and write properly, he learned by doing whatever the butcher showed him, and found his body, his eye, his memory absorbing everything with faultless accuracy, but again he was too unsure to reveal that to anyone. And he continued to draw with an obsessive compulsion, finding he was drawing everything he was doing at the butcher's, right down to the minute details of the various parts of the slaughtered beasts, and learning the names of all those parts. 'Is your dad a kind and generous man towards you?' Graeme suddenly asks. He waits for you to decide.

'My father is tired and stressed most of the time: the result of working too hard to pay for us to get a good education and never have to do what he and our mother do,' you confess. 'It is also not the Samoan thing for a man to show affection for his loved ones, publicly.'

'And your mother?' He pursues you, and you don't understand why.

You nod repeatedly, annoyed. 'She's a bit overboard with the public display of parental love.'

'Well, mine simply saw me as a burden, a lifelong burden, and a public stigma, evidence that their genes might not be *normal*. So when I got my first pay packet they arranged for me to board at a male boarding house mainly for sickness beneficiaries,' he continues. You can feel the bitterness in his voice. 'At first I felt utterly abandoned, but …' – his eyes light up with a piercing brilliance – 'a few weeks later, alone in my spacious room away from every element of my dreadful serfdom, I suddenly felt *released*.

I had a sanctuary in which I could do what I liked and not be judged useless, a nong, a halfwit, a moron, an idiot, a dummy, a mental retard, and now "an intellectually challenged person".' He pauses, breathing deeply, elated. 'And at work, that kind and generous butcher Fred Calhoun found my stack of drawings behind the freezer and, instead of berating me for wasting my time and his, simply went through them, studying each one slowly. Yeah, Jonas, he didn't need to tell me how he was feeling, no. I could feel it, observe it in his manner, hear it in his silence. And for a moment I couldn't believe it. He was, so he told me a few minutes later, amazed. And what was I doing there instead of developing my talent?' Graeme lowers his head and gazes into his coffee. He goes on to say that Fred gave him time off work to attend the art classes one of his friends was teaching at a nearby polytech. In those days it didn't matter how talented you were; you had to write essays and sit written exams. Failing those meant the end of your studies. So he started printing the words he wanted to learn into his drawings and memorising them visually. He would take his textbooks and course hand-outs home and pay one of the beneficiaries to read them aloud to him. He would memorise those, or at least those sections he had to know to pass. And as he did that he was composing his essays in his mind and then, after he was satisfied with them, laboriously writing them down. 'Melissa reminded me years later that I was doing what you Samoans did before the introduction of written language: memorise everything, catch reality in your memory, translate it into oral language – poetry, oratory, song, music; carve it out of your environment, out of the spirits in the wood, the clay … Fuck, I'm sounding like all our over-literate academics, tied to the technology and limitations of writing and written language, eh?' He gazes across at you, unsure of your reaction.

'What happened to Fred Calhoun?' you hear yourself asking, and wonder why.

He hesitates, surprised. 'I worked for him for another five years, until I'd completed my diploma in art and my confidence in myself was strong and I knew that I wanted to study architecture.' He stops and looks as if he's forgotten what he's been talking about. 'Bloody Alzheimer's!'

'Fred Calhoun?' you remind him.

He smiles, relieved, and says, 'He and his doting wife Jill and their two kids became my 'āiga – right word?' You nod. 'Yeah, they saved me, Jonas. I never lived with them, but their home was always open to me, and when I established mine, it was open to them. Whatever success I made was theirs. They were my special guests at all my graduations, parties, openings, birthdays, everything, Jonas. I made sure they needed for nothing. In their retirement, I designed and built them their dream home at their favourite summer beach, Whangamata, and filled it with a selection of those drawings I'd done when I'd been his apprentice. And when Fred died of prostate cancer twenty or so years ago, Jill and I carried out his last wishes: that he be cremated and his ashes scattered at our favourite fishing spot in Whangamata Bay.' He pauses again, looking inwards, and then ends his narration. 'Jill died two years later and we buried her beside her parents in Taihape – her last wish.'

The café is now crowded, and many people are looking for seats. You and Graeme ignore them as you sit in that special healing quiet that eventuates when a confessor has been relieved of his burden, his story, by the listener, who, in this case, will continue to try and unpack the full implications of his wise confessor's tale, at least until their next lunch together.

'For many years I regretted that they didn't know anything about dyslexia then; maybe they wouldn't have treated me so unkindly. But, Jonas, don't you think that's what turned me to whatever I am today?'

'Shit, yes!' You hear yourself celebrating his triumph over circumstances and ignorance.

'I like that, Jonas, I like that you agree with me!'

That afternoon, just before you go into your class, Shakespeare in Film, your cell phone rings. 'Hi, Jonas!' It's Donna (Samoan name Matagi, which she doesn't like), and you're immediately wary because she's been pressurising you, mainly over the phone and through common friends, to restart a three-month relationship you'd had the previous year. After four years of revelling in a rollicking social life, she is still trying to finish a BA in journalism. 'How was your Poly lit class this morning?' she asks. You've never liked the way she exaggerates the way she talks, like a stereotypical Poly student, and you resent the way she always seems to know what you're doing.

'Fine, great.' You replicate her jovial tone. 'Gotta go into my Bill Shakespeare class now.'

'Awesome. I *love* Shakespeare films, man, I really do! By the way, who was that old Pālagi dude you were lunching with today? Your prof or something?'

'Naw, he's just a classmate.'

Staccato laughter, and then she says, 'Where's he bin all these years instead of getting a degree?'

Now you have to work hard at suppressing your rising contempt. 'Donna, the old guy's a retired architect who's keeping his mind alive studying literature.'

'Our other Poly friends tell me he's bloody rich and famous …'

'Fā, Matagi, gotta go to class!' you interrupt her, and switch off your phone.

It's your turn to cook at home, so after your Shakespeare class you stop at the supermarket where your mother works, and she helps you get the supplies you need. 'Who's that wealthy Pālagi businessman in your class? Ben told us last night that you spend a lot of time with him,' she says in Samoan. Again you have to stop yourself from being angry openly. The whole fucking Samoan community must know about it! 'Ben says he looks as ancient as Moses!' She laughs.

You try to smile. 'Yes, e makuā pei o Moses but e kelē aku aga kupe,' you say in the usual mixture of Samoan and English that is your language at home. 'Plus he's lāuiloa i Giu Sila!' You exaggerate.

'We're having Dad's fifty-fifth birthday next Friday, don't forget. Why don't you invite Moses and his wife to come?' You can't escape her scrutiny. 'That's if you think we're good enough for them!'

You're trapped. You have to nod and say, 'I'll ask them.'

You're intensely worried about how you're going to ask Graeme, and how your asking is going to put Graeme in an awkward position, and if he and Melissa come, how they are going to react to your family and vice versa. And you're not going to feel good if you lie to your mother that you asked Graeme but he already had another commitment to go to. You've lied before about other things, but this is too important to lie about. So you keep putting it off and suffer the dreaded signs – unrelenting stress and lacerating stomach pains – of your recurring duodenal ulcer.

Four days before your father's birthday, while you're in your usual computer booth on the fourth floor of the new all-glass Student Study Centre, trying to finish your last assignment of the semester, your cell phone rings. You hurry out to the corridor to answer it.

'Still being a diligent student, Jonas?' Graeme greets you. You say hello, and try not to sound guarded. 'I'm also trying to finish my last essay, but have given it up and am now having a cuppa coffee, would you like to join me?'

Shit, accepting his invitation means you *can't* postpone inviting them!

A few minutes later, there's a flat white waiting for you as you join Graeme at one of the tables by the windows. And some Melissa-baked shortbread, Graeme's favourite. 'She told me to bring those for you.' He looks more fragile and vulnerable; a sickly paleness is pushing up through his skin, the wrinkles on his face are more numerous and deeper, and his coffee hand is shaking visibly whenever he lifts his cup to his mouth.

'Melissa was a VSA in a village in Samoa, eh?' You keep postponing the invitation.

He sits up, obviously excited about the topic.' Yeah, in the village of Pou-tassy. Is that correct?' You nod. 'On the north-eastern coast of Upolu.

Fast

She was only seventeen, just finished high school. She lived with a family there while she taught at the school. Learned a lot of Samoan, loved it; loved the whole place and people. After she returned and graduated as a teacher she kept going back to visit her Samoan 'āiga during her holidays. She helped many of her 'āiga migrate here. When she left teaching and became an architect and ran her own practice, her visits to Samoa dropped off. But she still participates in her 'āiga's affairs here in Auckland.' You recall her telling you some of that the first time you were at their home.

You have to do it now, while he's least expecting it; while he's wowed about Samoa and Samoans. 'Graeme, mydad'shavinghisfifty-fifthbirthday ...'

'Hey, Jonas, slow down, man!' He laughs and, gazing at you, waits for you to calm down, then he says, 'Now, let's hear it.'

You swallow once, twice, look unflinchingly across at him, and say, 'My 'āiga would like you and Melissa to come to my dad's fifty-fifth birthday on Friday night next week.' You've said it, and it's like ridding your throat of a sharp fishbone.

'Thank you, Jonas, Melissa and I accept your 'āiga's generous invitation and will come on Friday, at what time, sir?' His eyes twinkle – are those tears?

'About 7.30 pm, my silver-haired lord!' You parody him. You start to write down the address for him, but he reminds you he has an 'infallible memory' like all pre-literate Samoans.

As you enjoy your coffee and shortbread, you find yourself telling him about your 'āiga – did he steer you to that? – and enjoying it. You

Ancestry

tell him your mother had only a village education, your father graduated from Samoa College; they met here while going to the same church, in Mangere, 'fell in love, so the story goes', married and had three heirs: Jonas (named after his father's father), Ben (after Charlton Heston as Ben Hur) and Diana (after Diana Ross, his mother's favourite singer.) You laugh with Graeme at that last bit. You father, while labouring on a building site, attended cooking classes at night, then got a job as a waiter in a flash restaurant; worked his way into assistant chef, then chef. Your mother cleaned, and when you were born and she had to stay home, she cleaned at night. Finally a cousin got her a job at Foodtown as a shop assistant. 'By the way, in that whole saga of migrant success, my parents deliberately kept away from what they called "the wasteful, expensive fa'a-Samoa", so they could afford to get a good home and get us educated. They've not gone back to Samoa since they got here, even.'

'What do you think of that?' Graeme asks.

'In the last few years, I've felt deprived of the fa'a-Samoa and my roots. So have Ben and Diana.'

'Have you told your parents that?'

You shake your head and drink the reminder of your coffee – it tastes bitter and cold. 'We don't want to hurt them. They've sacrificed so much for us.'

'Jonas, I wish my spoilt mokopuna were like you and your sister and brother and didn't want to *hurt* their elders!' he declares. 'They don't even recognise there are such creatures as elders.'

Fast

You look at him with shrewdness and irony, and ask, 'And whose fault is that?'

His eyes light up with mock surprise. 'Jonas, you've got me there; right there where the blame should be.'

'But you didn't raise them: their parents did.'

'Yeah, I suppose, but to protect myself and Melissa from their rapacious free-loading and keep them at bay, I keep giving them anything they want.'

You recognise Donna's scent before Donna and a friend, Cushla (Samoan name, Teuaute), are upon you, right at your table, casting their shadows over you. Graeme looks up and smiles. You push back your seat and, without looking up at them, say, 'Graeme, these are Matagi and Teuaute!'

Graeme extends his right hand to Donna. 'How are ya?' They shake hands.

'Pleased to meet you, sir!' she greets him. Graeme moves to shake Cushla's hand, but she hunches up and shies away. 'And how are you, Jonas?'

You make no move to invite them to sit down. 'Good, good,' you mumble. 'Graeme and I were just leaving to go to a class.' You're relieved Graeme hasn't asked them to join you.

'Shit, I almost forgot!' Graeme improves on your lie. 'You, beautiful young ladies, want this table?'

'Yes, thank you.' Cushla speaks for the first time.

Graeme gathers his satchel, straightens his clothes and shoves on his Hurricanes sports cap while you all watch him. When he tries to get up, he grabs at his bad knee in pain, so you reach forward and help him up. 'I bloody well need that knee replacement Melissa and you keep urging me to have.'

'And when are you having that done?' you ask, trying to avoid Donna's intense scrutiny.

'Straight after our finals, and this time Melissa is going to kick the shit out of me if I chicken out again!'

'Good luck with your operation, sir,' Donna says, and you know she means it and recognise, from your past relationship with her, that she does have many appealing and decent qualities. 'And good luck with your finals,' she says to you.

'Thanks, Donna,' you say and mean it. 'And good luck with yours.'

'Lovely meeting you,' Graeme says to Donna and Cushla.

'I'll ring you,' you hear yourself saying to Donna, and gaze fully at her for the first time. Yes, she is beautiful. And as you and Graeme walk away from the table, the exciting, wild imagery of your sexual life with her starts capturing you.

'What was that all about, Jonas?' Graeme asks, softly.

'Donna and I used to have a relationship …'

'Used to, and it's now called a relationship, eh?' Graeme slaps your shoulder.

'Yeah, used to.'

'She's a very beautiful young woman!'

Fast

'Yeah, straight out of Prof Thalmer's lecture and presentation on "Dusky Maidens and Gauguin in the South Seas", eh?' You start laughing at your own comment.

'Too right,' laughs Graeme. 'Too bloody right!' He holds himself up by leaning onto your shoulder as you laugh and weave your way down the corridor through the stream of students and staff now coming in for lunch.

Like most families that you know, you, Ben and Diana and your parents have *evolved* – or is it developed? – ways that enable you to live together fairly harmoniously. Some of that harmony you achieve through avoidance of areas of possible friction. For instance, if you watch the television news or eat together, you and your parents never discuss politics or current affairs or the behaviour and lifestyles of young people. On your political scale, but you've never accused him of it, your father is even right of Ayn Rand. You gave him *Atlas Shrugged* and it became his second bible, which he quotes from to justify his unshakable belief and faith in capitalism and his being a totally self-made man who has arrived where he is through the honest sweat of his brow and the strength of his own hands; Samoans who remain poor are that way because they're lazy and want to live off the sweat of hard-working taxpayers like himself and your mother. Mention things like socialism, the Labour Party, the welfare state, the rights of unions to collective bargaining and welfare benefits for single parents (especially unwed ones) and he (and your mother) become Emperor Nero at the gladiator games, callously turning down

Ancestry

their thumbs for the final kill. You recognised early that that was why for them it was thumbs down on the fa'a-Samoa out of which they had come. It was socialistic: 'āiga before the individual, communal sharing, compulsory contributing to family and community affairs and projects, and what your father condemns as 'a bloody system of sweat-eating, with too many sweat-eaters and too few sweaters'. So over the past few years you've preferred to get your news coverage off the internet through your computer in your room. But tonight, you can't avoid being in the sitting room with them, in front of your Mum's new humongous flat screen television. It is Ben's and Diana's turn to cook dinner, so they're in the kitchen and dining room doing that. You'll watch the news – Dad prides himself on being 'well informed' – and then over dinner discuss and finalise the arrangements for his fifty-fifth birthday party, which he insists is your mother's wish.

You get stubbies for Dad and yourself and a Bacardi and Coke for your mother, as the signature tune for the TV One six o'clock news starts. You sit down in the armchair on your mum's right, away from your father. You take a deep drink on your ice-cold beer as the news headlines begin: Prime Minister in Beijing for free trade talks; two teenagers die in car accident in Mangere, alcohol and speed suspected; Minister of Justice accused of conflict of interest …' You don't pay too much attention to the headlines as you continue drinking and waiting for the news details.

You get a second stubby out of the fridge and start returning to your seat when the face of someone you feel you should recognise comes on to the screen, and the announcer is saying, 'This morning at his home in

Fast

Freeman's bay …' It is old black and white television footage of a youthful long-haired Graeme; he is being interviewed without sound while the announcer is talking. 'Graeme Hudson, one of New Zealand's most distinguished architects, collapsed and died of a massive heart attack …' You sit down quietly. You feel nothing. Not shock nor sorrow nor pain. '… Mr Hudson designed some of our country's landmark – and what some have called controversial – buildings and complexes …' On to the screen come some of those, and snippets of Graeme and his staff designing and directing their construction. 'Graeme Hudson achieved all this despite suffering from a severe form of dyslexia. He went on to become the most generous patron of the Dyslexia Society …' You watch the bespectacled head of the Dyslexia Society being interviewed about that. Now you refuse to believe the news: you had lunch with Graeme only two days ago!

'Isn't that your friend, Jonas?' you hear Ben asking. He is standing just behind you.

'Is it?' your mother asks, turning down the sound. 'Is it?'

Everything immediately sounds loud and demanding and focused on you. You now have to face it. 'Yes,' you whisper. 'Yes, it is.'

'The one who is supposed to be coming to my birthday?' your father asks.

'Yes.'

It is a calm morning full of sun and squawking seagulls and mollyhawks and the gullet-deep growling of the sea as it surges in from under the Harbour Bridge. You walk between your father and Ben, wearing formal 'ie lavalava and 'ulafala. Your mother and Diana walk a few paces ahead of you, holding the 'ietōga between them, displaying its ancient and silky beauty as it shimmers in the light breeze. Your mother told you it was the mat they were saving for your graduation; it has been in her 'āiga for years. The night Graeme's death was on television, you'd insisted with your parents that even if they didn't believe in the fa'a-Samoa, you wanted them to do it for Graeme's funeral. 'But your friend and his family know nothing about the fa'a-Samoa!' your father had objected. 'His wife knows a lot about it; she lived in Samoa for a long time and has Samoan 'āiga,' you had countered, unafraid of him for the first time, you will recall later.

You start up the long massive front steps that lead into the house. You can't see anyone about. The wide sliding doors in the front are open, and you can smell fresh greenery and flowers. At the threshold, you all take off your sandals and line them alongside the footwear that is already there.

You notice that the pillars immediately inside the door and holding up the high ceilings of the house now have long garlands of flowers and nīkau palm leaves woven round them. Everything, including the art, has been removed from the massive room and the whole floor is covered with Samoan mats and siapo. You realise that the house has been transformed into a fale-tele. In the centre of the space, on top of a thick layer of siapo and 'ietōga, lies the white casket. Beside it, at its head, sits Melissa in a plain white puletasi. Behind her sitting in a group are some of their children and grandchildren and a few of Melissa's Samoan 'āiga. To her left facing you are two grey-haired matai, bare-chested, wearing only plain siapo, their tatau glistening. It is obvious that Melissa has consulted and assembled the 'āiga. You are in awe. You look at your father and see that he is awed too, but there is also fear there: he'd not expected such knowledge and correct observance of Samoan protocol and customary funereal practice.

You have Graeme's cell phone number and, after you'd seen the news on television, you'd debated all night if you should ring it. Early in the morning, you'd done so, hesitantly. You'd jumped in fearful surprise, expecting Graeme to answer, when the voice said, 'This is Melissa Hudson speaking.' Clear, unemotional. 'You must one of the thirty people Graeme allowed to have his cell phone number.' Is she amused by that?

'This is Jonas,' you reply softly.

'Tālofa, Jonas, I've been expecting your call,' she said. 'Why? Because being Samoan, you know what to do when a loved one dies and an 'āiga needs comforting and consoling.' That's not true for you, but you decide not to contradict her.

You'd rehearsed what you were going to say but lose all of that and blurt out, 'Mrs Hudson, I'm very sorry about Graeme …' and go blank and try to control the sadness surging up in your throat.

'Jonas, he died the way he wanted: quick, unexpected, and reading *The Crocodile*, which you gave him …' She stops, catching the first signs of sobbing in her gullet and holding them there.

'Is there anything I can do to help with his maliu?'

'Thank you for thinking about that, Jonas, but Graeme's Pālagi 'āiga and my Samoan one are arranging everything.' Her voice is clear again. She itemises those arrangements. 'By the way, there will be no Christian service. As you know, apart from being a loudly loquacious atheist, your friend Graeme considered all religions as "the causes of the worst massacres and wars on our planet". I've had to work bloody hard persuading my Samoan 'āiga about not having a Christian funeral. And we're bringing Graeme home for the day and night before his cremation.' She pauses. 'You bloody Samoans are so difficult; I had to persuade my 'āiga that cremating Graeme isn't inconsiderate and insulting!' She pauses and, breathing in deeply, says, 'If you want to come and see your friend, come here when he's home.'

Melissa nods and smiles at you as your party enter and sit down cross-legged on the floor. The two matai start welcoming you in high oratory, which you don't understand because the language is ancient, allusive and metaphorical. You glance at your father, whose head is bowed, beads of sweat starting to drip down his face, and you hope he can cope with the level at which the ceremony is being conducted.

When your father starts to reply, almost inaudibly, his head rises slowly, and when his gaze is directly on Melissa, his speech grows more confident and louder. He replies in the ornate language used by the matai, who nod often and congratulate him on his oratory. Then your father, unexpectedly, cracks what is obviously a joke in Samoan, and the matai and Melissa laugh. That immediately dispels the solemnity and seriousness. 'Because most of the people here today do not understand our language, I would like to speak in English,' he says, and doesn't wait for a reaction. 'I acknowledge and greet all the sacred 'āiga of Graeme Hudson. I greet the chiefs and orators of those 'āiga and, in particular, Mrs Melissa Hudson, the grieving wife and mother …' As he speaks, you scepticism turns to surprise that, though he has denied you the fa'a-Samoa and you were convinced he didn't know much about it, he is now showing he does. 'We are here because of the friendship between our son and Mr Hudson. This mat is to acknowledge that friendship and alofa.' Your mother and Diana rise and, again displaying the 'ietōga, take it towards the matai.

'Mālō, fa'asāō!' The women in Melissa's 'āiga praise the beauty of the mat. Two of them come forward. Taking the 'ietōga, they fold it and place it beside the matai.

'The mat is called "Matagi Mālū", "Cool Wind", which is an apt name in the cool vocabulary of the uncool young people today,' your father continues. 'We kept it over the years to present to our son on his MA graduation, but he wants it presented to Mr Hudson on his graduation to Le Lagituaiva.' Melissa clasps her hands together and laughs. The matai and some of the elders laugh with her. You don't understand the reference to the Lagituaiva. 'For the benefit of uninformed people, like our children, the Lagituaiva is the Ninth Heaven in the Samoan cosmology of ten heavens.' He laughs softly with Melissa. 'Even this "never-been-to-university Samoan" knows about cosmologies.' You survey Melissa's Pālagi 'āiga: they too are enjoying your father's performance. 'In our ancient religion, when you die and you've lived a virtuous and generous life, your agāga, soul, goes to le Lagituaiva, the highest heaven for humans. The Tenth Heaven is reserved specially for Tagaloaalagi, our Supreme Atua. This humble person is sure that Mr Hudson is on his way to Le Lagituaiva. To help pay for his fare, here is an envelope with a humble sum in it.' All the elders are now laughing openly. To Diana, he hands the envelope with the money you'd put together the previous night, and with bowed head she takes it to the matai. Your father ends by speaking directly to the casket: 'Lau susuga, Mr Hudson, go with our alofa, go safely and go well. The Atua will protect you all the way. Soifua!' Many of Melissa's Pālagi 'āiga applaud.

As your parents approach the casket, Melissa rises to her feet and embraces your father, then your mother. 'Thank you, thank you, for your alofa!' she tells them. They kneel down beside the open casket, and your mother, without hesitation, caresses Graeme's hair and then kisses his forehead. Your father does the same, then they turn and embrace the matai. 'Come, Jonas,' Melissa beckons you. The restrictive, terrible self-consciousness that usually infects you on public occasions like this is gone, completely. You slip into her embrace, she gazes up into your eyes and you kiss her on the cheek, and hold her and hold her.

The start of finals is only a week away. You wait outside Professor Thalmer's office for your 10.30 am appointment. Only a few minutes to go. You'd expected to be gripped by apprehension, fear and trepidation, but you're not experiencing any of that. Since Graeme's cremation, which was restricted to only his immediate family, the two matai elders and you, you've prepared yourself for this meeting with meticulous care: the kind of care Graeme would have taken. You've selected all the possible scenarios, worked out all the arguments and their supporting data, and then memorised all of it. You've been in Professor Thalmer's office a few times before, mainly to discuss the seminars you were giving. Those times, he did most of the talking.

You knock with confidence. 'Come in!' you hear him calling.

You open the door and meet the pleasant smell of books and papers – and is that strawberry yogurt in the mix? You see the opened yogurt container, with a plastic spoon in it, on his desk. Professor Thalmer is one of the few lecturers who hasn't adopted the more egalitarian, less threatening arrangement of not having your desk between you and your visitor. Behind his desk, he is writing furiously in a pad, and looking neat in his purple-framed glasses, his long brown hair freshly washed and combed. Without looking up he waves you into the chair directly in front of his desk. You deliberately focus on his shiny forehead. That does it. He drops his pen and glances up. His eyes brighten in recognition. 'Ahh, Jonas!' Then he remembers, and his beaming smile changes to an expression denoting sadness. 'I'm so sorry about Graeme Hudson. I know he was a good friend of yours. So sudden, so quick.'

'Yes, Graeme helped me a lot with my work – and other things.' You look appropriately sad. Graeme is there beside you.

'He was a – a marvellous student who contributed a lot to our class.' He pauses and looks away from you. 'I understand he was also a good architect who contributed much to the development of that field.'

'Yes, all the media praised him for that.' You stop deliberately; you don't mind the awkward silence that is going to happen. You wait and gaze intensely at him.

Ancestry

He looks at you and away, fidgets and eventually has to ask, 'Now, Jonas, what can I do for you?'

You take your time. You hear Graeme's ironical chuckling. 'Yes, I have decided that I would like to do a PhD in New Zealand and Pacific literature.' Thalmer looks as if he hasn't heard you. So you repeat, 'I've thought about it very carefully, and have decided that I would like to do a PHD in this department.' You know he is going to give you the stock reply to such a request.

'For that, you need to make a formal application to the head of department, who will then refer it to our graduate committee, who will make the final decision.' He gives that stock answer.

You again wait and watch him. 'To succeed, what do I need to have?' you ask slowly.

'You need to have a research topic and a staff member in the department who can and is willing to supervise your research and thesis,' is his automatic reply. And then, trying to deemphasise its importance, adds, 'You need good grades as well.'

'I have a topic, Professor. I want to do a thesis on the topic "Politics and the Pacific novel: with special reference to the novels of Sia Figiel and James George".' You and Graeme wait and watch.

'Good, good,' he says. He stretches back in his chair, gazes up at the ceiling and asks, 'And do you have someone in mind as your supervisor?' You and Graeme continue to wait and watch. Thalmer names two possible supervisors on the staff.

You then attack. 'Professor Thalmer, I know you are the international authority on those authors.' You pause and watch his eyes, his ego, bloating. 'In all the four years I've been in your marvellous classes I have never doubted that. I have read almost everything you've published on New Zealand and Pacific literature, Professor.'

'Thank you, Jonas, it's very flattering that you believe that, but there are many others in the field who are admired and respected more.'

You and Graeme allow him time to enjoy his self-importance and then ask, 'What sort of grade average do I need to have for the department to consider my application seriously, Professor?'

'Usually, you have to be in the top 2 percent of your MA class, Jonas, but – but the department has made exceptions in the past. What sort of grades have you had for your MA courses?'

You pretend you're trying to remember. And then say, 'Nothing above an A-minus, I'm afraid. You've given me four of those. Two of my other lecturers have also given me A-minuses.'

You and Graeme sense Thalmer is now worried about those grades but that he is quickly finding a way out of that dilemma. 'A-minus is a very good grade, Jonas. When I give an A-minus it is a *very* very good grade. I will not hesitate in telling the graduate committee that!' You know that he is chairman of that committee. 'I will also remind our department that it has always been university policy to encourage and support students from underrepresented groups, such as women, Māori and Pacific Islanders. I will also remind the department that over

Ancestry

the last twenty years only two Polynesians have ever finished a PhD with us: Meilin Hansen and Selina Marsh.' He is breathing heavily, triumphantly, as he declares, 'You should be the third one, Jonas. I – and I'm sure all the other right-thinking members of staff – will support your application.'

'I'd hate to be anyone who tries to stop that!' Graeme laughs.

RANFOR

Summer was cleaning out every cold and dark corner of Ponsonby, and it was ten days before Christmas, a season Professor Harold Thalmer wished didn't exist because it meant he had to again cope with the undiminished anger of his former wife, Lucille, and his sons, Matt and Otis, who were failing at university while he had to pay for it. Outside Harold's study, up in the neighbour's high Phoenix palm, a couple of nesting thrushes were crying with a loud, consistent TWEET-tweet-TWEET, obviously objecting to a stalking cat underneath them. He tried not to be distracted by it, though he knew the culprit was their cat, Ranfor.

Attraction had little to do with love – whatever that is – and almost everything to do with your genitals and lust, was the theme he was now pursuing as he continued writing his paper on what he was tentatively calling 'Love and Lust in the New Zealand Novel'. His graduate class in New Zealand literature had recently inspired it, when he'd arrived at their lecture a few minutes late to find the class in high hilarity debating the topic. They didn't notice him standing at the back of the room.

Ancestry

'... When a new couple meet and they're *attracted* to each other, it's all got to do with lust and sexual desire,' claimed Dalphine Mavrock, the oldest in the class and a twice-divorced lawyer who, disillusioned with law, was finishing a master's thesis on Patricia Grace's novels. Some were sniggering, but most were nodding in agreement.

'So what about all that bourgeois fiction – since the invention of the novel – about romantic love, virginity, innocence, chastity belts, loyalty, fidelity and women swooning at the loved one's touch?' Lance Westright, who was a James Joyce addict, asked, his voice rich with irony.

'Yeah, what about that?' others chorused.

'All dainty bullshit that denies us existing below the navel!' Dalphine pursued.

'So over the long years of English departments researching and teaching fiction, our professors have forced us, gullible students, to study that above-the-navel-bourgeois bullshit?' someone at the back continued teasing. Most burst into laughter.

'Yes, because all the writers were conditioned and forced to write above their navels!' Dalphine persisted.

Lance raised his hand and declared, 'So if free and unashamed guiltless sex – Freud's cure for everything – had been the order of the day and our writers, like the delicate Jane Eyre, had written from the basic truth that lust and sex and sex and sex are at the core of how we view reality, Henry Miller's and Joyce's ancestry would have stretched right back to the beginnings of the novel?'

'Too bloody right!' Jonathan Smittle, a red-haired fan of Miller, replied. His supporters grunted in support.

Thelma Horne, stately, usually unflappable and a staunch member of the Students' Christian Movement, blushed a strawberry red, and accused, 'Are you saying that right now, you and your supporters are *looking* at us and seeing us only as sex objects?'

'Are you saying that?' a few other women echoed her.

'You're flattering yourselves!' Dalphine betrayed them. 'So during the two hours we spend with Professor Thalmer and with one another, you don't experience a Joycean stream of consciousness that is rich and raunchy and deliciously turns some of us into what you call "sexual objects"?'

'Not even one Rabelaisian image?' someone added. The Christian Thelma and her cohorts looked offended – and cornered.

'Not even one smidgen of lust?' Another pressed the attack home. 'Not even to do with the handsome, sexy Professor Thalmer?'

'Yes,' stuttered Thelma, 'but that doesn't dominate my whole time in our class or elsewhere!'

'Be honest: lust, delicious lust, is the name of the game!' someone else called out. The majority of the class agreed.

'That's not true,' someone mimicked Thelma. 'When I meet a hot guy I just want to hold hands and say beautiful clean things to him and vow to be faithful forever and ever.'

Thelma and her cohorts looked extremely upset, so Professor Harold Thalmer knew he had to intervene.

Ancestry

There was a hushed, awkward pause when he walked down the aisle, chortling and shaking his head. 'May I ask you to tell me what your generation thinks about how boy-girl or boy-boy or boy-whatever relationships begin?' he asked.

For a rich moment no one responded, unsure if he was being serious or not. Then Mark Brethland, who was prematurely grey and usually reticent about expressing his views, said, 'A mix of a lot of factors, Professor. For instance, you may be attracted by the person's intelligence and personality …' This time, even the Christians laughed.

'So for nearly all of you, it's all lust and sex and more sex?' he concluded.

Evelyn Ragg, daughter of a wealthy architect, who'd already published a much-heralded essay entitled 'Gender Politics in the Poetry of James K Baxter', gazed directly at him, and said, 'Of course, and it's lust and sex and more sex until it all becomes humdrum and boring, then the next raunchy guy comes along and lust raises its undeniable head again!' He was surprised she was capable of such frankness.

'So all these couples who supposedly marry for love and vow to be together forever are just …' he challenged her.

'… just adhering to society's expectations,' Evelyn said. 'Or *having* to.'

'Look at the divorce rates, Professor,' Dalphine argued. 'One out of every four marriages now ends in divorce. The average length of marriage is eight years and getting shorter.'

'And she's the handsome example of it,' Thelma tried to get her own back.

'With the pill and vasectomy and the legalisation of abortion, you can pursue your genitals' desires until boredom's end,' Jonathan said.

'What happens when your genitals break down or age prematurely and you can't fulfil lust's demands?' he asked, trying to keep a straight face. Surely you're not that ignorant and naive? He saw that in the way they were scrutinising him.

'Your machinery may break down, but that doesn't mean your lust breaks down with it,' Evelyn declared.

'Besides, enjoying the handsome salary of a professor, Professor, you should be able to afford the magic pill that'll put the mana back into your machinery.' Jonathan dared cross the line between professor and student. Suppressed tittering and sniggering round the class.

He tried to keep a straight face as he said, 'Perhaps you, Mr Brilliant Jonathan Smittle, should write a dissertation on the topic of "Colonialism and the Capitalist Hegemony of Cialis".' A river of laughter swept through the room, Dalphine laughing the loudest.

A whole chorus of sparrows and blackbirds were now accompanying the alarmed thrushes as they objected to Ranfor's dangerous presence, when Harold got up to go and make a cup of tea.

The door to Marilyn's study was open and she was working on her computer, the sun streaming in through the front windows and encasing her with a skin of golden light. So beautiful, he thought. In the first few months of their relationship, when he was still married to Lucille, if he'd seen Marilyn on fire like that lust and desire would have immediately driven him to her and they would have fucked as if nothing else mattered.

Ancestry

Sometimes they'd spent all day in bed. Finally, he couldn't do without that unbelievable sexual connection, and had walked out on Lucille and their two sons. His relationship with Marilyn was now five years old, so, according to Dalphine's statistics, they had one or two years left before breaking up. Lust had cooled down to perhaps twice a week, and it was now more out of habit than blood-thumping, absolutely mind-blowing experimentation and exploration of each other's sexual possibilities. They kept agreeing they were *best* friends, and that was more important than anything else, but what they both secretly wanted was to discuss what they should do about their now staid, routine lovemaking. 'Want a cup of tea?' he called.

Without turning from the computer, she said, 'Yes, please, darling.' He turned to go into the kitchen, when she added, 'And please get Ranfor to come in; she's scaring those poor bloody birds to death.' She'd procured Ranfor from the SPCA near the Airport, when Ranfor was the size of her hand, and they'd agreed to call her Ranfor because she was the only kitten who had broken from the litter and run to her when she'd looked into their cage. Now Ranfor was two years old and they were both besotted with her. Since she was a teenager, Marilyn had always had a cat: always tabbies, always female. Before Ranfor, there'd been Humor, who'd been hit by a car; before her, Manono, named after the island in Samoa where she'd carried out her six-month research on the Samoan concept of mana; before her, Mānoa, the name of the fabulous valley in Hawai'i where she'd spent what she'd expected to be an incredible few days of sexual exploration with the darkly handsome Professor Nicholas

Beet, who was in his silver-haired sixties and the world authority on Rapanui, but her expectations had proven too demanding, and the distinguished professor had almost suffered a heart attack – she could laugh about it now. Before Mānoa, there'd been Vericose, and so on. She knew more about cats, tabbies, than even Ranfor's vet, she reminded Harold when the vet tried to sell them an expensive life insurance policy for Ranfor. She'd told the vet she wasn't a bloody fool about to spend hundreds of dollars on an animal; even one she loved more than people!

The previous year, after publishing her latest book, a tome on the concept of mana in Polynesia, which had taken her a decade to research and write, she'd been promoted to professor in her anthropology department and invited to give the highly prestigious annual Michael Neill Lectures. This morning she was completing the PowerPoint presentation that would accompany those four lectures, which she was giving the ironic title: 'Paradise: Michener, Brando and Raymond Burr in the South Seas'. Her throat and eyes were parched and her lower back ached painfully from sitting at the computer since breakfast, so she rose to her feet, stretched her arms and back and hurried to the kitchen, eager to see Ranfor.

When Harold had left Lucille, he'd shifted into Marilyn's Mission Bay home, which she'd inherited from her father, who'd been a professor of archaeology and an avid collector of classical Polynesian art and artefacts, which now cluttered the house. After a week of living there, they decided it didn't fit them as a couple, so, after Harold's meticulous house-hunting in central Auckland, where they agreed they wanted to be, they bought an old but expensive villa in Lincoln Street, Ponsonby, hired an architect who specialised in restoring and renovating villas, and, preserving the villa's basic structure, had it raised for a two-car garage underneath, and the rest of it renovated extensively. For instance, the two bedrooms were enlarged, studies and sky-lighted bathrooms were added, modern insulation was put under the floors and into the walls and ceiling, the ancient gas heaters were replaced with an electronically controlled central heating system and all the floors were stripped and carpeted. Harold (with the architect) supervised all this – Marilyn claiming she was useless at such things. She even refused to see any of the renovations until they were completed. 'This is splendid, darling, marvellous!' she exclaimed repeatedly as she inspected their new home. And as soon as they shifted in, she insisted that they should, like cats – her favourite creatures – mark and claim their territory by 'spraying and rubbing our scent' all over it. So, with incredible intensity, passion and daring, they made love all over their new home.

He plugged in the electric kettle, opened the French doors and stepped out onto the back deck. Standing at the railing and looking down across their back lawn and overgrown garden, he called, 'Ranfor, Ranfor, c'mon, girl, c'mon!' No sign of her, but he knew she was hidden somewhere down there, for the birds were still objecting. One thrush in particular was now standing as a sentinel on the centre of their circular clothesline, crying TWEET-TWEET-TWEET-TWEET! and thrusting her head and beak forward in stabbing motions. He started returning to the kitchen when he felt Ranfor weaving like a warm wavelet round his ankles. He scooped her up.

Marilyn stopped in the kitchen doorway and watched Harold, who had Ranfor cradled in his arms while he stroked her and crooned, 'Hey, girl, you've got to stop scaring the birds; you've got to!' She didn't mean it to, but the observation intruded that he looked tired and older, more wrinkled and sallow in the face, his hair greyer and so thin now she could see right through to his scalp, yet he was only fifty and a year younger than her. Where was the zip, the unquenchable vitality, the ihi?

When he turned and focused on her, she smiled and rushed forward, and he released Ranfor into her arms. 'Darling, my little darling, you should leave those poor birds alone!' Ranfor purred loudly as she stroked her.

'What kind of tea, darling?' Harold asked.

'Green tea, please,' she said, releasing Ranfor in front of her food dish on the floor. While Ranfor dug into her food, her teeth crunching sharply as she chewed, Marilyn refilled her dish of water and put it beside the food. She squatted down and, while Ranfor ate, she ran her long fingers from Ranfor's neck down her back, saying to Harold, 'She's beautiful, eh? In good form; a fit and mighty hunter!'

He put two food mats and a small plate of gingernuts and Krispies on the white table under the large beach umbrella on the back deck. He brought sugar and honey too, and then poured their cups of tea and took them to the table, and sat down in the red canvas chair. 'Darling, your tea's out!' He glanced back and caught her rubbing the side of her face into Ranfor's back, her eyes glazed with happiness.

'Isn't she beautiful?' Marilyn sighed.

So *were* you, so were you, he thought, and, for the first time, didn't feel any guilt at thinking that. He started sipping his tea. When he'd first seen her around the university at various meetings and gatherings, his lust antenna hadn't registered any interest. He saw her as a nondescript, slightly untidy woman without make-up and usually dressed in black trousers with a heavy leather belt inlaid with white pearl shell, navy blue sweater – too hot for summer – black pearl earrings and thick-soled boots, who was always forthright in her views and expressed them with authority, lucidity and persuasive charm.

Māori Studies, Pacific Studies and Anthropology organised a conference titled 'Post-colonialism and the Indigenous Body', and invited him to give one of the keynote addresses. At that time, he was enthralled with Albert Wendt's novels, which a famous French professor at the University of Bourgoyne had recommended to him, so he wrote a paper called 'The Anthropology of Guilt and Redemption in Wendt's *Pouliuli*', and delivered it to begin the second day of the conference, to a packed and what he felt was a hugely appreciative audience, in the magnificent Fale Pasefika.

That afternoon, in the same venue, he was preparing to leave after trying to stay awake during three trying, boring papers, when Marilyn walked up to the lectern again, th... ther. 'Cheers, Beloved!' He saluted her.

For a while, he didn't recognise her. The transformation was amazing. The glowing, perfectly groomed woman with the slow beguiling smile in front of him was certainly registering on his lust meter, especially when the richly ringed, crimson-red manicured fingers of her slender right hand started adjusting the height and position of the microphone and looked as if they were stroking him. And when she spoke in a deeper voice, which seemed to be coming from the core of her belly, his lust really kicked in – or was it out? And his weakening resolve to remain faithful to Lucille dissolved instantly.

He hurried up to Marilyn after her paper. 'Impressive paper; really inspiring and innovative analysis of mana and how it operates in Samoan society,' he congratulated her. 'Best paper I've heard on the subject.' Though she squirmed with embarrassment at being praised with such enthusiasm, her whole face and eyes lit up with gratitude, pride and self-satisfaction. For the remainder of the conference he made sure he was near her everywhere, and he sensed she wanted to be near him too.

Back at work, they rang each other often, both welcoming the almost uncontrollable lust that was enveloping them. On the third day, she invited him for coffee in her office. No preliminaries: she locked her office, he swept everything off her desk and she slid onto it, lay back and raised and opened her shaking legs – she wasn't wearing any panties, and he buried his burning face and mouth and hungry tongue in her. And the rest is history, he now told himself as he watched her playing with Ranfor. Only this time, he experienced lust not for her but for a new woman, any woman. Like the Marilyn he'd first met at that conference on the 'indigenous body'.

She sat down in the canvas chair opposite him, with Ranfor in her lap. He pushed her cup of tea over to her. As usual she wasn't wearing make-up. Her face was drawn with fatigue, and her wrinkles, blotches and brown age spots were more pronounced. Her old and faded Nike sweat suit, which she wore round the house almost every day, emphasised the fact that the flesh on her arms and neck was loosening and starting to sag and droop.

'Anything wrong?' she asked him unexpectedly. He shook his head and reached over and caressed Ranfor's head. For months now she'd felt belittled by his close scrutiny whenever he believed she wasn't aware of it. Belittled and deeply resentful at being belittled! 'You don't look well; you shouldn't work so hard, darling,' she returned his belittling. Ranfor slid off her lap and, before she could stop her, was leaping down the deck steps onto the lawn, again setting alight the loud chorus of frightened, offended birds in the Phoenix palm, shrubs and neighbouring trees.

Like he did at every morning tea they enjoyed together, he half dunked a gingernut into his tea, soaked it for a moment and then bit off the soft half and ate it. After the second gingernut, he took a large mouthful of tea and swallowed that to clear his gullet. Suddenly he was aware she was observing him closely, from the corners of her green-grey eyes, with disdain, and, at first, he couldn't believe she was doing that, but then when he gulped down the rest of his tea and rose to his feet to leave and he sensed that her scrutiny was now even more disdainful, he felt *exposed*, naked, stripped of his integrity. 'Got to finish my paper,' he mumbled.

'Good on you, darling,' she said, and he believed there was a cruel, jeering tone in her voice. 'I'll enjoy the sexy sun for a while longer and then return to *my* lectures.' She watched him going back into the house, and concluded he was definitely looking *empty*; definitely aging quickly, prematurely.

She put on her sunglasses, lay back in her chair and closed her eyes. Yes, she was again definitely *interested* in other men, and had tried to deny that to herself over the past year. Before she'd started the affair with Harold, she'd been celibate for a year, devoting herself wholly to finishing her tome. Because she considered sex a need like food, which you ate whenever you were hungry, she'd lost count of the males (there had been three women) she'd dined with before Harold had come along. (She liked that metaphor.) For about four years she and Harold had enjoyed the wildest, tastiest, most satisfying, most eclectic, most extrovert and no-holds-barred sexual feast she'd ever helped to concoct, cook and serve. And it was so, so disappointing – but inevitable – that the feast was now a morning tea with dunked gingernuts. She almost laughed making that observation.

When she heard Ranfor's purring and felt her paws kneading her belly and then her warm, warm weight settling down on her, she whispered, 'Hi, my darling, my beautiful darling!'

He *knew* who it was when the phone on his office desk rang, and he let it ring for a while. He'd just finished a lunchtime lecture on the poetry of Hone Tuwhare to his stage one New Zealand literature class, of almost two hundred and fifty students. He hated lecturing to first-year students, many of whom were only taking the course as a prerequisite for other non-literary degrees such as law, and didn't really care about the literature of their country; most were content with handing in shoddy, mediocre work. But it was a long established policy in his department for professors to take a stage one class. He felt down, stressed, cynically disappointed by his students' indifferent reaction to Tuwhare's poetry. What do you expect when you have such a large class and you can't get to know students individually? He picked up the phone without thinking, and muttered, 'Hello, who is this?'

'You don't have to speak like that to me!' Lucille's annoyance jabbed into his head.

'Sorry, I'm sorry,' was his automatic reaction, and he immediately regretted regressing to his manner of reacting to her anger when they were married. 'What the hell do you want?' He compensated for it.

A shocked gasp, then she snapped, 'You may speak to your bloody girlfriend like that but …!'

'I *can* speak to you like that: I didn't ring you; you bloody well rang me!' A needle of pleasure pierced his tongue when he heard her snivelling, swallowing back tears. 'You rang me, Lucille, so tell me what you want.'

'Remember your sons? They're still alive – as if you care one fucking bit!' she attacked. He let her rave, telling him Matt and Otis had rung her complaining about him not fulfilling his promise of paying their fares to the Makaha Surfing Championships in Hawai'i. 'Promises are promises, Harold, despite the fucking fact you broke your promise to me and your kids and took off with that – that whore of an anthropologist!'

'I did not make such a promise,' he cut her off. 'And I am not going to pay for their surfing when I am bloody well paying thirty percent of their annual university expenses and they continue to fail and fail. Goodbye!' He slammed down the phone. And felt splendidly elated and free for having at last denied Lucille and his sons something.

When he got home to Marilyn and a light evening meal of scrambled eggs, cheese and French bread, plain low-fat yoghurt and a glass of red wine, and told her about Lucille's call and his 'fucking lazy, spendthrift sons', she tried to look interested in and offended by what Lucille had said and done, and said, 'She actually called me a whore? Who the hell does she think she is? Does she think the whole university doesn't know she puts it out even for her first-year students? Bugger her!' She was surprised that she was *really* feeling offended.

As they washed the dishes, Ranfor purred loudly, weaving round their legs, and a disturbing question, prompted by Marilyn's comments about Lucille, grew more and more demanding in Harold's mouth, though he tried to swallow it. She dried her hands, picked up Ranfor and, cuddling her, started to go to the sitting room. 'Darling,' he stopped her, 'is it really true that everyone at the university believes – believes she's a …?'

Marilyn didn't hesitate. 'A whore?' He nodded. 'What you really want to know, darling, is: did your beloved wife play around with other guys when she was married to you? Isn't it?' Typical male paranoia and hypocrisy: you can fuck around but your wife can't!'

Ancestry

'No, and I don't care if she did!' Harold tried to sound unconcerned.

Marilyn held Ranfor up against her cheek, and Harold had to gaze into both their faces. 'So you don't really want me to give you a truthful answer, darling?' She focused right in.

'I don't care,' he murmured, smiling to try and hide his fearful apprehension.

'So, my darling Ranfor, shall we give your other darling the truth and nothing but the truth?' She could feel her whole being glowing with joyous triumph. 'Don't worry, Harold, what I said is not true,' she lied. 'I made it up because of her hurtful remarks about me.' She could see relief, profound relief, rising from the depths of his eyes and in his almost inaudible sigh. 'Besides, is it *that* important? I mean, we started our marvellous affair while you were still married to her.' Ranfor squirmed deliciously in her arms and she pushed her into Harold's arms. 'Here, at least Ranfor'll never lie to us. A cat is always a cat.'

ONE RULE

'Don't forget Marcus is coming tomorrow morning at ten,' Mauga reminded her. The strong smell of coffee and cooking toast was spilling out of the kitchen onto the deck and up into the bright morning sky. From through the trees at the back of their yard and over the neighbouring houses came the rising noise of the city traffic.

Emelia poured his coffee and he got the toast. 'Are you sure he said Tuesday?' she asked. He slid two pieces of toasted crumpet onto her side plate.

'Yeah, I'm sure,' he replied, 'and isn't it Tuesday tomorrow?' The toast was burning his fingers, so he dropped it onto his side plate. After five years of not having to go to work and attend functions and other commitments to do with their work, counting the days or remembering which day of the week it was wasn't important to them any more. When they needed to know, they asked each other or consulted the small calendar she had magnetised to the fridge door.

Ancestry

'Is he in trouble again?' She tried to sound unconcerned about it so as not to stress him some more. They were on the back deck round the oval teak table and in the red canvas chairs and under the sturdy beach umbrella their daughter Lagi, Marcus's mother, had bought them for his seventieth birthday the year before. He sugared his coffee and didn't reply. 'Is he working?' She couldn't leave it alone.

'How should I know?' he said, curtly. She handed him the Olivani.

'He tells you everything.' She tried to sound gentle. Whenever it came to their discussing their four grandchildren she had to be careful, walk that territory with perceptive gentleness, so as not to upset him or fire his anger; especially anything to do with Marcus, who had always been his favourite, despite his trying to hide that from their family.

'He doesn't, darling, he doesn't,' he said, the coffee turning bitter in his mouth. 'None of them do. They tell us what they think we want to hear!'

'So what *did* he tell you when he rang last week?' She agreed with him about their grandchildren but especially about Marcus, the oldest of the four.

'That he *really* wanted to come and see us because he hadn't seen us for *such* a long time.' He imitated the intonation his grandson used whenever he wanted something from them. 'What's happened to our mokopuna?' he declared, needing her sympathy and agreement. Their daughter Lagi and their Pālagi son-in-law Timothy had Marcus and Betty; Errol, their son, and his wife Margaret had Moe and Safata.

'Not all of them are like Marcus,' she insisted. 'We've not had any serious trouble with the two girls.'

'But they all behave as if everyone owes them a living!' Even when he said that, he knew it wasn't altogether true – he was just exasperated and desperately disappointed with Marcus's behaviour, but was refusing to admit that to himself. 'Lagi and Errol were never like that,' he added.

'No, but don't you think they and their spouses should accept some of the responsibility for how …?'

'Of course, but I wasn't talking about that …'

She had never liked the way he interrupted her whenever he was annoyed or angry, so she continued, '… As I was saying, their parents should not have been so indulgent in giving them whatever they wanted, and letting them behave so – so inconsiderately and selfishly.'

'Are you inferring I did that too?' he demanded.

'No, I'm not saying that.' She had to control her rising anger and avoid another taxing argument about their grandchildren, and about Marcus in particular. Ever since Marcus had dropped out of high school without completing his Year Twelve, absolutely convincing his grandfather to pay for him to learn how to fly, and promising he would then go to university and get that civil engineering degree his grandfather's heart was set on, things had started going awry in their relationship. 'I have to accept some of the blame too,' she said. 'I indulged them too.' She paused, debating whether she should say it. 'For a long time I believed – yes, believed Marcus's stories and excuses,' she admitted.

'I've believed all his – his bullshit all these bloody years, and I'm still hoping …'

'We both did – and still hope he turns out good – because we love him, and you love him more deeply.'

'Yes,' he admitted for the first time in a long while. 'Why him out of all our mokopuna?' He was talking more to himself. Marcus started his expensive flying apprenticeship and kept telling them how well he was doing, until they found out through his mother (who'd found out from the flying school) that he wasn't attending classes any more and was hanging out with friends from high school in the nightclubs, bars and cafés, drinking and smoking dope. 'He was such a happy, intelligent, obedient, loving boy, at primary school, wasn't he?' As usual she didn't reply, knowing this was his way of talking the pain and regret and remorse out of his heart. 'Such a beautiful boy!'

'Who reminded you of our Errol, his uncle – and who you still hope becomes a brilliant achiever like Errol,' she helped him. Errol had sailed triumphantly through high school with straight As; was head boy and captain of the first fifteen and debating team; had acquired his medical degree with distinction, had married another doctor; had done postgraduate diplomas in surgery; and was now a highly respected orthopaedic surgeon in Remuera.

'That's probably why I've never given up on Marcus,' he said, then, gazing at her, added, 'And he's still *only* twenty-two.'

She didn't want to go there, remembering that after the fiasco at the flying school, Marcus had persuaded his grandfather to pay for his

One Rule

training as an IT technician, had gone to only a few sessions and, without telling his grandfather, had then told his enraged parents that computer programming wasn't for him. For once when his grandfather forced himself to chastise his grandson about all the money he was wasting on him, Marcus had broken into loud tears and apologised, 'Granddad, I'm hopeless; I can't find what I really want to do! Forgive me!' And his grandfather forgave him again. Three weeks after that Marcus took a friend's car without permission, partied with friends, crashed it and landed in court for the first time. She'd had to rush Mauga to their doctor for medication to calm his raging anxiety. Lagi had refused to help Marcus, so they'd hired a good lawyer, who got Marcus discharged without conviction, only having to pay for the value of the car. Without her knowing, Mauga had paid that. That was only the beginning of Marcus's brushes with the law.

'Whatever happens, darling,' she tried consoling him, 'no one can say we didn't do our best by him. We've stuck by him, even when his stuck-up mother and pretentious father kicked him out.'

He took a large gulp of coffee. 'This is bloody cold, and so is the rest of our breakfast – see what their awful behaviour does to us?'

'You haven't taken your pills,' she reminded him, trying to distract him. She handed him his glass of water. She watched him take his four pills: one for cholesterol, one for his prostate and two paracetamols for his lower back pain.

'Don't they know we now have to live on pills?' he exclaimed. 'And have to survive on the pittance of a superannuation?' A bout of self-pity always felt good, so why not continue this one? 'Doesn't Marcus and our other spoilt mokopuna know that if we keep spending at the rate we're doing – and especially on them – we'll die in poverty? And do they care?' As he continued this tirade – careful not to be loud enough for the neighbours to hear – his heart and lungs and breath felt free and strong and everlasting. He ignored the contradiction at the core of his monologue that, despite their small government pensions, they had over the years amassed a healthy portfolio of shares and bonds, fat savings accounts, innumerable fixed deposits in three banks and a very valuable collection of New Zealand and Pacific art, and were part-owners of six apartments and houses their children and their spouses had bought as investment properties. 'I'm not going to give them any more money,' he vowed at the end of it, flushed with conviction and finality.

'Good on you, darling,' she said, looking forward to seeing if he'd do that with Marcus on Tuesday. He brought her a glass of cold water and she took her daily baby aspirin and her anti-high blood pressure pill.

When she woke as usual at six he was already dressed and getting things ready, and she knew he'd had a bad night. By ten o'clock, with temperatures again in the high twenties, which they both liked, everything on the back deck was ready: the sun umbrella, the teak table and canvas chairs – he'd added a third one – the dishes and cutlery, two of the Brickle coffee mugs that he usually reserved for his closest friends and a cup and saucer for her, a ripe papaya and a dozen French croissants, strawberry jam and other goodies that Marcus liked, which he'd driven to Nosh up the road

One Rule

to get. As she'd helped him prepare, she'd grown more breathless and agitated from the anxiety she was experiencing trying not to think of Marcus arriving late, as he'd done for most of their other meetings, and dreading what he would look like, and hoping, with all her strength, he wouldn't be under the influence of alcohol or, worse still, marijuana. She didn't want Mauga to be devastated again.

It was five minutes past the arranged time, and he was again preparing for the frantic, painful disappointment and anger that would envelop him if Marcus was late, when the front doorbell BBRRIINNGGED once, twice. He started hurrying for the door. She clutched his hand and stopped him. Have to go slow; let him wait. So he waited. One more ring – this time longer. He glanced at her; she shook her head. Another ring, this time laced with impatience. She turned and headed for the back deck.

'Coming!' he called. 'Coming!' He caught the rising agitation in his voice. This time he had to dictate and control and be prepared to deny Marcus whatever he was after. He'd decided that during the sleepless hours of last night when he hadn't been able to stop himself from reviewing – in extremely painful and accusing and remorseful detail – his life with his grandson. Most excruciatingly painful was the fact – and he had to accept it whether he liked it or not – that Marcus had *used* them, without conscience; exploited their love and trust and forgiveness. His hands shook as he opened the door and pulled it back.

For an incredible moment, he held his breath, believing he was gazing into his reflection or, more accurately, into a life-size photograph of who he'd been in his twenties: Marcus was over six feet tall, on the thin side, with rich curly black hair, hollow cheeks and that charming smile, that stance of taking the weight on the left leg, shoulders pulled back, right hand in the back pocket, left hand with thumb hooked into the silver-studded leather belt. Cool, his mokopuna would describe it. That photograph disintegrated when his image said, 'Hi, Granddad!' Smiling brightly, Marcus moved forward to embrace and kiss him, as their mokopuna been raised to do, but Mauga thrust his right hand forward and Marcus had to shake it. 'How are ya and Mama?' Marcus asked.

In one quick survey Mauga noted that Marcus now looked older than his years: pale pockmarked face, thinning hair, a few days' growth of beard, shoulders in a permanent stoop, tiredness round the bloodshot eyes – but he was relieved he couldn't see drugs there. 'Good,' he mumbled, and turned.

'Granddad?' Marcus called in *that* high-pitched voice. 'Granddad, I have a friend with me.' Mauga hesitated and looked back. 'Is it okay if I bring her in?'

'Where is she?' Suspicion was now his prominent feeling.

Marcus swung his left arm back and pointed down the short driveway to the green mini parked across the front gateway. Once again Mauga realised – and hated it – that Marcus had him snared and he couldn't get out of it. 'She's Samoan and her name's Mala and she's at varsity,' Marcus continued, strengthening the snare.

Very clever – or should he call it devious? – Mauga thought. Samoan and at university; he couldn't say no. 'Bring her in,' he called, and then

One Rule

walked back down the corridor. This was the first time he'd brought a girl to meet them.

Emelia was sitting in her chair, with the large coffee plunger and cups and mugs on a tray in front of her. 'He's got a girl with him,' he told her, and turned, and they watched Marcus and a slim dark young woman, his arm round her waist, hurrying towards them.

Emelia got up and, beaming, extended her arms towards Marcus, who was grinning widely and rushing forward. 'Good to see ya, Mama, good to see ya!' he said as he moved into her arms and they embraced.

He smelled stale, unwashed, under the strong overlay of deodorant and aftershave. 'It's been a long time, Grandson,' she whispered. 'Too long.' She meant it, and could hear the break of genuine regret in her voice.

Marcus stepped back and, clutching the girl's hand, said, 'Mama, this is Mala; everyone calls her Mal.' Dressed in tight jeans and a blue denim jacket, the girl, eyes lowered, smiling faintly, stepped forward.

'How do you do,' Emelia said.

'Glad to meet you, Mrs Mauga,' the girl greeted her. Emelia moved over and put her arms around her and kissed her on the cheek. Mala smelled heavily of cigarette smoke – and marijuana? – Emelia tried not to think of that.

'And this is Granddad,' Marcus introduced Mauga, who tried to smile as the girl moved to him and he had to kiss her on the cheek. 'Wow, Granddad, ya don't look a year over fifty!' Marcus said.

Mauga squirmed awkwardly; stopped himself from falling for Marcus's usual flattery. 'Take a seat,' he told them.

Ancestry

'What a spread, Mama, what a spread!' Marcus exclaimed, sitting beside his grandmother and pulling Mala down into the next chair.

'Thank your Granddad,' Emelia told him. 'He went and got some of your favourite things. He made the coffee and everything.'

'Thanks, Granddad,' Marcus said. 'My granddad's a great cook,' he said to Mala. 'He's the only male in our whole family who can cook.'

The only one who does, Mauga thought, as he sat down, picked up the plunger and started pouring the coffee. Certainly none of their grandchildren wanted to, despite Emelia and he trying to teach them.

'No coffee for me,' the girl said.

'Tea? We have lemon tea, green tea, Dilmah's …' he offered, noting for the first time that the girl avoided looking into his face – or anyone else's.

'Do you have some fruit juice or any cold drinks?' she asked.

'Granddad and Mama always have a fridge full of drink,' Marcus declared, but made no move to go to the fridge and get a drink for her. Emelia started to get up.

Mauga quickly went to the fridge. 'Got orange juice, blackberry juice, apple …' he offered.

'Apple juice with lots of ice,' she said.

'Thanks, Granddad!' Marcus said. 'I'll have a blackberry with lots of ice too.'

Mauga took out an ice tray and squeezed ice cubes out of it into two glasses. The clinking of the ice scraped across his teeth and he had to suppress his mounting anger with himself for allowing his mokopuna

One Rule

to treat him as their servant all these years. He put the drinks in front of them.

'Now help yourselves to the food,' Emelia said to their guests, to distract Mauga from his anger.

'Wow, papaya – that must have cost you a lot, Granddad!' Marcus took a whole half and gave the other to his girlfriend. Emelia handed them the slices of lemon, which they squeezed savagely over the papaya, and then they attacked the fruit, scooping up large hunks and thrusting them into their chomping mouths, Marcus exclaiming, 'Bloody great!'

Emelia had to turn away from watching them. Mauga's face, she observed, was a fusion of grave anger and disappointment. She poured coffee into his mug and into her cup to distract him from watching them.

As they drank their coffee and kept putting the food in front of their guests, they tried to ignore the furious, hungry, selfish manner and pace at which they were gobbling down the food. 'Always love your cooking, Granddad,' Marcus repeated between fat mouthfuls. Emelia scrutinised the girl surreptitiously, and grew more anxious when she noticed the long faint scar – knife mark? – on her right cheek, the small star tattoos on her earlobes, the amateurish 'MAL' tattooed across the back of her left hand and her refusal – or was it shyness? – to look you straight in the eye; especially that.

From the hungry way they were eating and Marcus's shabby appearance, Mauga deduced – but didn't want to believe it – they had no money and probably no jobs. And where were they living?

'Got any more bacon?' Marcus interrupted his thoughts.

Mauga glanced at Emelia. 'Sorry, there's no more,' he said, and for the first time since Marcus was born, he didn't feel guilty denying him. There, done it. 'Sorry but …'

'There're more tomatoes and toast,' Emelia interjected; she scooped the tomatoes onto his plate and pushed the rest of the toast to him.

Marcus looked disappointed but quickly hid that as he buttered two pieces of toast and put one on Mala's plate. 'May I have the last egg?' he said, reached across and, using his fork, slid that onto his plate. Mala saw the remaining fried tomatoes and onions and scooped those up.

'So, what are you doing now?' Mauga tried to sound casual about it, but was determined Marcus wasn't going to continue lying to him. There was no change in Marcus's style and pace of eating, but he caught a sharp hesitation in the girl's.

'Working on my CV, Granddad,' he replied. 'I'm applying for a Pasefika scholarship to go to AUT, where Mal is finishing her BA in management studies.' Before Mauga could react, Marcus said to Mala, 'My Granddad showed me how to write a CV years ago. He's got an MBA and accounting qualifications galore, and owned and managed an accounting firm for over forty years, eh, Granddad?' Mala smiled widely. 'Yeah, Mal, Granddad and Mama met at Auckland University and fell in love at first sight – eh, Granddad?' Marcus broke into laughter, and reminded Mauga of the way he laughed. 'Mal, did you know Mama has an MSc in biology, and was head of the research unit of one of New Zealand's biggest companies?'

'Wah, that's great, great!' Mala exclaimed, looking fully at Emelia for the first time. 'That's why I want a good varsity education,' she continued. 'Being a Samoan, I want to follow your example, Mama.'

Now it was a duet of flattery, Mauga concluded, and he had to stop himself from puffing up with it and forgetting his determination to get the truth out of his grandson. 'And what are you going to study at AUT?' he asked Marcus.

No break in Marcus's confidence. 'Business studies, like you, Granddad,' he replied. 'I wanna be an accountant and and make lotsa money.'

Emelia didn't want Mauga to continue this interrogation. In the past, it had always ended in Mauga excusing his grandson's bad behaviour and blaming himself for it. So she got up and started clearing the table, and was relieved when Mauga joined her. Their guests didn't offer to help. Mala got out a packet of cigarettes and Marcus a lighter.

'Sorry,' Emelia stopped them before Mauga did. 'Son, you know our home is smoke free.'

'Shit, I forgot,' he said. 'You and Granddad have never smoked, eh?'

'Unbelievable, incredible,' Mala sighed in supposed wonder.

A few minutes later, Mauga was washing the dishes and Emelia was drying them. Their guests came over and sat at the dining table. Emelia sensed Mauga's increasing frustration, anger. They'd raised Lagi and Errol to never sit by while their elders were doing these chores, and had tried to do the same with their mokopuna.

'Where are you living?' she asked Marcus. Again, no hesitation.

'Mala's parents have a small flat under their beautiful house in Glen Innes, and we've been living in that,' he replied. 'But it's a long way from AUT, so we've just found one on K Road, not far from it.'

He could see it coming, and was pleased it was. 'And what's the rent?' he asked, before Emelia could steer him away again. Now there was a tense, worried pause in Marcus's story. 'K Road is bloody expensive, eh?' He pursued.

'Too right, Granddad. Bloody expensive. For this one, $400 a week.'

'Must be a large apartment with all the mod cons,' he encouraged Marcus.

'Too right; it's got two large bedrooms, a kitchen and dining area, bathroom and …' Marcus itemised.

'… Laundry, a large fridge and, as you say, all the mod cons,' Mala finished for him.

'And the bond?' He pursued them. From the corners of his eyes he caught them looking at each other. 'I bet you that's expensive.' He waited.

Finally Marcus straightened and, gazing into Mauga's back while he was washing the dishes, said, 'It's very reasonable, Granddad. Bloody reasonable for the quality of it.'

'Yeah, we're getting a bargain,' Mala chorused.

Mauga finished washing the last dish, placed it in the rack for Emelia to dry, turned slowly and, leaning with his buttocks against the sink, gazed at Marcus and asked, clearly, 'Are you able to pay for it?' During the cleansing silence that occurred then, he caught Mala's knee pressing against Marcus's, urging him to answer.

One Rule

'Yeah, once I start my new job at the Warehouse and combine that income with Mal's student loan, we'll be able to afford it, Granddad.'

Mauga had to move quickly; he could sense Emelia was going to cut him off at the pass, again, and let their selfish grandson off the hook. 'In the meantime are your parents going to help you?' He refused to look away when Marcus gazed directly up into his eyes with *that* look, which he'd not been able to refuse in the past. 'Are they?' He waited; he didn't look away.

'You know what Mum's like,' Marcus whined. 'She's tight with money and expects us to pay for everything ourselves. That's why I've always come to you and Mama.'

So bloody arrogant, he thought. Did he think they were stupid and didn't know his mother had kicked him out for his lying and bludging? But before he could continue his interrogation, Emelia said, firmly, 'You're being unfair to your mother, Marcus. How much is the bond?'

'Seven hundred,' Mala intervened. 'Just seven hundred.'

'And we'll pay you back as soon as we get my first pay check and Mala's loan,' Marcus said, looking away from him. It was the first time Mauga had detected a pleading tone in Marcus's voice, and he held onto that, relished it.

'How can we trust you to pay us back when you've never done so in the past?' Mauga heard Emelia asking, and he couldn't believe she was attacking Marcus too.

'Yes, Marcus!' He reinforced her demand. For the first time Mala was gazing directly at someone, and it wasn't them but Marcus, and he discerned she was surprised, shocked and offended that Marcus's version of overgenerous, indulgent, gullible grandparents wasn't happening.

'We will, Granddad!' Marcus insisted. Mauga knew what Marcus's next tactic was going to be. 'There's no one else I can turn to, you know that.'

Mauga was deliberate. 'What about your Uncle Errol and Aunt Margaret?' He waited, knowing that after years of Marcus using his uncle and aunt, they too had told him they didn't want to ever see him again.

'You know how meanly they treat their own kids, your mokopuna, Granddad!' Marcus insisted. 'Ask Safata; they've put him in a hostel and on an allowance that he's starving trying to live on!'

'At least Safata is finishing his degree,' Emelia said.

'That's what he wants you and his parents to believe,' Marcus said with fierce relish.

What a nasty, nasty person, Mauga thought; he's even willing to rat on his cousin to try and get what he wants. 'So what's Safata doing?' he asked, enjoying Marcus's exposure of his real personality.

'Granddad, he's not going to lectures – hasn't been for months!'

'And?' Mauga encouraged him.

Emelia stopped Mauga right there: she wasn't going to see him exposing her grandson any further and then regretting it later. 'Marcus, stop right there. We're not here to talk about Safata.' Mauga turned to her to object about her rescuing their awful grandson again. 'No, Marcus. And your Granddad and I do not want to hear you lying about your own cousin.'

'But I'm not!' There was now a layer of desperation in Marcus's whole demeanour. 'Ask Mala, she knows about Safata!'

'So what about Safata?' Mauga demanded of Mala, who was clutching her hands tightly in her lap, face scrunched up as if she was foraging for courage.

Straightening her shoulders, she snapped, 'Yeah, he no longer goes to lectures and spends his time … spends his time …'

'What, doing what?' Mauga interrupted her.

'Partying and … Fuck, I've had enough of this!' She jumped to her feet, knocking back her chair. 'I don't know about you, dickhead,' she said to Marcus, 'but I'm getting out of this mean fucking middle-class bullshit!' Before Marcus could hold her back, she brushed past him and was scrambling up the corridor.

'Babe, c'mon, Babe!' Marcus called after her, and then jumped up and started after her. Stopped. 'See what you've done!' He turned on Mauga.

'What have we done?' Emelia demanded. Mauga had never seen her that enraged before. 'What?'

'Get out of our house,' Mauga said, simply, without forgiveness. Marcus looked at her, then at him. 'Go; go now.'

After they heard the front door slamming after him, they sat holding hands for a long, long time, shifting their chairs as the shade shifted according to the direction of the sun.

'You remember Bruce Stewart, who runs that marae for street kids in Wellington?' he asked. She shook her head. 'The one who got me to be the accountant for his marae?' She smiled and shook her head again. 'Your bloody memory is going just as mushy as mine,' he guffawed.

'No, mine's not mushy; it's shutting down cell by cell!'

'Anyway, the guy whose books I looked after for free as my contribution to the fantastic work he is doing with kids?'

'Oh, that *handsome* guy!'

'Yeah, *that* handsome guy, the one you used to swoon over every time we saw him.'

She started chortling. 'I could have run away with that guy, but I could never leave you.'

'Why not?'

'Cos you're handsomer, sexier, easier to con!' They whooped and laughed together for a long while. Afterwards, he went to the fridge, got a can of Heineken for himself and a bottle of Bundaberg for her, and opened them.

'Cheers, beautiful.' He raised his can and they drank together. He belched and then said, 'Anyway, Bruce and I were once discussing the rules of his marae. He told me he had only one rule: if you wanted to live on his marae you had to stop stealing. He would tell his kids, "if you want to steal, leave, go and get that out of your system and then come back. If you can't get it out of your system, don't come back."'

'And we've just done that with Marcus,' she said.

'Yes, and with our other mokopuna.'

Raising their drinks again, they clicked them together. 'Cheers, Beloved!' He saluted her.

One Rule

"Ia manuia, Handsome!' And they drank to each other, long and deep and forever. Then with beer-covered mouths they kissed passionately, embracing with their whole bodies, weaving together until they felt inseparable and aflame with desire.

'Have you taken a pill today?' she asked with urgency.

Shaking his head furiously, he whooped and said, 'But I will now!' He started hurrying toward the bathroom in their bedroom.

'By the time it works, we'll be so, so hot for each other!' she called after him.

FAMILY

Ever since his father turned eighty, Stephen has tried to visit him in the morning of the last Thursday of every month, when he has no lectures to give or meetings to attend. He parks his Soflar Hybrid in front of his father's house in O'Neill Street, a renovated villa that his father bought after his second wife, Stephen's mother, died of brain cancer and he couldn't live with her memories in their family home. As usual on his visits, Stephen inspects his father's front garden as he goes up the six front steps. Still in good order, weed-free, the flowers and shrubs recently pruned. Though he has a key to the front door and his father keeps telling him there is no need for him to knock, he never enters without knocking first. That began when, five years before, on a rainy Thursday, he'd rushed out of the rain and up the steps into the house – without knocking – and into the sitting room, where he'd found his father watching television and picking his nose. His father was *only* picking his nose – so why the shock, the guilt, the revulsion? After that he didn't want to ever accidentally intrude on his father's privacy again.

Ancestry

He knocks four times, unlocks the door and goes in and down the corridor through the scent of gardenia air-freshener. His father is the most expert cook and housekeeper Stephen has ever known, and has raised Stephen not only to be good at those tasks too, but to enjoy doing them. The house is tidy, as usual: recently vacuumed, the paintings dusted, the windows washed and everything sprayed with anti-bacterial spray and wiped clean. 'I'm here, Stephen!' his father calls from the kitchen.

Stephen is fifty-eight, yet many of his friends keep telling him his father looks more like his younger brother! While Stephen observes him making the tea at the kitchen counter, he certainly looks far, far younger than his age.

'Hi, Dad!'

He turns, long, salt and pepper hair framing his finely sculpted face, his flesh and skin without sag or ugly wrinkles and scars. 'It's a bloody hot summer, eh!' his father says, smiling that open, trusting smile that he reserves for his son. Stephen knows not to offer help when his father is making their morning tea, so he goes and sits down at the dining table. 'It's been fucking sizzling, eh?' his father repeats, carrying the tray with the teapot, milk, ginger nuts, sugar and honey, cups and saucers and teaspoons to the table. 'I keep sweating heaps. By the end of the day, I stink like hell.' He places the tray on the table and Stephen again notices his father's large, thickly fingered hands, his muscular arms and broad shoulders – not a sign of stooping. Even now, because of his father's frank language and huge frame and rugged build, people mistake him for a farmer or a builder or an ex-rugby player or, most recently, an ex-army drill sergeant. People who don't know his history would never guess he was an academic all his working life, retiring at sixty-five from his job as professor of geography at Auckland University.

'How have you been?' Stephen asks, pouring the tea.

Nodding his head, his father says, 'Good, been really good since I last saw you. Loved doing the bloody garden front and back, planted some capsicums and tomatoes. Did my weekly supermarket shopping yesterday. Fucking prices are awful. I don't know how the poor can survive this recession.' He pauses and extends the plate of biscuits to Stephen. They drink their tea in silence for a while. They've never felt awkward with each other in those silences. 'Two nights ago, I dreamt about your mother,' his father resumes. 'Would you believe it? She was bloody well stranded in the stairwell of your department, the incestuous English department.' He guffaws, and then resumes, eyes now rich with mockery. 'Why there and not in Biology, *her* department?' Stephen tries to suppress his objections to his father's disparaging remark about the English department – his father has always had a low opinion of it and, over the years, has not tolerated Stephen's attempts to change that opinion.

'You remember how your poor mother was so, so beautiful?' he is saying. Stephen nods eagerly. 'Not only was she physically beautiful, but her mind was one of the most brilliant in her field! Glorious she was until that … that cancer tumour invaded her brain, yeah, and she lost all her appetite and refused to eat and started starving to death. Over 60 percent of people who die from cancer die from malnutrition, starvation, and not from the disease.' Since Stephen's mother's death, this is the first time his father has really talked about her illness. 'And guess what? In my dream, she appeared naked in that frightening skeletal, concentration-camp shape she was in when she died – and trapped in your stairwell! What about that?' He tosses a ginger nut into his large mouth and with powerful bites loudly breaks up and crushes the biscuit, washing it down with tea.

'You don't have to talk about it,' Stephen offers, not really for his father's sake, but wanting to escape that terrible image of his mother trapped in his department's stairwell: an image that makes him feel some responsibility for her death. After all, it is his department!

'Remember how your mother became one of the leading scientists in the field of aging? How she believed that aging is a disease that can be cured like any other disease?' He pauses again; another ginger nut. 'I was passionate and devoted to my research, but compared to her, I was a fucking dabbler.' As his father details the scientific and academic career of the marvellous woman he'd loved, Stephen again recalls, with a deepening, loving sadness and admiration, the mother who'd raised him. She *was* beautiful, physically; petite, half his father's size, with unbelievable coordination. He recalls the first time he ever saw her dancing with his father: rock'n'roll at a students' function in the Student Union. The dance floor was alive with rocking student couples and his parents were the only staff among them. In their dancing, his father's massive size didn't dominate her, or make her look puny. She

Family

was the inspired, inspirational centre of their dance, the one who held it together, who guided him in their harmonious plaiting of their moves and the beat and the music and the whole charged atmosphere, until all eyes were focused on them and on her: yes, her.

'... Irony of fucking ironies,' his father is saying. 'There she was searching for cures to aging, and gets crunched by cancer of the brain, the very organ she was using to find those cures. Yes, she could have cured death –'

'But she got trapped in the stairwell of my incestuous department,' Stephen interrupts, trying to humour his father away from their huge, shared sorrow.

Laughing gruffly, awkwardly, his father says, 'Good one, Stephen, good one! Do you want to know what else was in the dream?' Reluctantly, fearfully, Stephen nods.

'Well, there she is, trapped in the stairwell, with all the spiralling stairs around her crowded with silent students, staff and you, Stephen, as a five-year-old, dressed as a girl in the sailor suit my mother wore when she was a tiny tot.' He describes the crowded stairs, the silent, motionless, black-eyed people gazing down at his wife as if they are looking into their reflections. 'Then you, Stephen, are transformed into the person you are now, and, as you bend down towards her, your right arm becomes elastic – just like Plastic Man in my boyhood comics – and *zzziiinnnggg!* it zooms down to her and you grip her thin, thin arm, gently, and, as she whimpers so helplessly, yet with gratitude, your arm de-elasticises, pulling her up into your arms.' His father stops, savouring the memory of that rescue, and then says, 'Stephen, as I witnessed that in my dream, I realised I should have loved you with the commitment and devotion she did.'

'But you did, Dad!' Stephen tries to console him. 'You do!'

'She was the bloody one who made sure you didn't go into the sciences. Did you realise that?'

'Mum loved fiction and poetry …'

'Shit, didn't she what! She read that stuff whenever she had some free time, all through our holidays here and around the world. She needed those books like they were blood transfusions …'

'And she made me love them, too …'

They talk about Stephen's mother until it is time for Stephen to go to his afternoon lectures.

'Do you need help with anything, Dad?' Stephen asks as they stroll toward the front door. 'Don't you think this house and grounds are too large now for you to cope with?'

'Do I *look* too frail and decrepit to cope?' His father laughs softly.

'Certainly not,' Stephen replies. 'You look as fit as a fucking fiddle!' Stephen imitates his father's way of speaking, and his father slaps him playfully on the shoulder.

Outside, a cloudless, dazzling sky stretches high over the city and up to the Waitakere. The air is alive with the buzzing of insects and the cries of kingfishers, blackbirds and thrushes. The muffled roar of the busy traffic on Ponsonby Road and the other main streets frames the neighbourhood.

Family

His father walks out to the car, and before Stephen gets into it, asks for the first time that day, 'How's Patricia?'

Surprised, guarded, remembering his wife, Stephen replies, 'She's fine.'

'I hope my bloody one and only grandson, the busy heart surgeon, hasn't forgotten I'm still alive.' No humour in his father's tone now.

'Sorry about that, Dad,' Stephen apologises for his son Malcolm. 'I'll talk to him.'

'Please don't.' His father's tone is now conciliatory, forgiving. 'Your mother's death really fucked him up. He was the apple of her eye. Remember how she was over the moon when he became a surgeon? They both believed they could cure death. Remember how he took leave from his job and helped me nurse her until she died? No other grandson would do that.'

On his way home, through the thickening traffic of midday, Stephen once again tries to understand why his father and his wife Patricia have never liked each other, and why, after all these years, he has been unable to change that. As always, he experiences a bitter mixture of guilt, remorse and regret.

He has just put a large dish of macaroni cheese in the oven and turned the temperature to 160 degrees when he hears Patricia unlocking the front door and entering. Her arrival home re-triggers the whole mixture of pain he'd tried coping with in the car; this time he tries not to resent her for it. Quickly he gets a bottle of red wine out of the wine cupboard above the fridge, uncorks it with a sharp pop, fills his wine glass almost to the top and stands facing the kitchen doorway. 'Where are you, Stephen?' Patricia calls.

'In the kitchen!' He stops himself from saying 'darling'. 'Right here, in the kitchen.' Right here, where I always cook our meals. Stop, stop! he cautions himself. It's unfair on her: some women, his mother for instance, don't like doing domestic chores, and they shouldn't be expected to just because they're women. 'That's fucking sexism,' he can hear his father saying.

Just as he pours a glass for Patricia, she glides into the kitchen, all five feet twelve inches of her. 'Just what I need,' she says as he hands her the wine. She pecks him on the lips and raises her glass. Her familiar scent of Poison perfume and Lux soap weaves into his nostrils. 'Kia ora!' she salutes him. He nods and they drink together. 'You wouldn't believe who came into the library today!' she exclaims, eyes wide with her secret, winding her long arm round his hips. 'Let's go into the dining room and I'll tell you.'

As soon as they settle into their chairs, she continues, 'Yeah, Stephen, one of your favourite authors, one of the ones you teach. Guess who?' He usually loves these games, initiating most of them, but he's not so keen tonight. 'Want some clues?' He nods once, and takes a large mouthful of wine. 'It's a male writer, novelist and poet, about eight years older than you.'

Trying to inject enthusiasm into his eyes and face and voice, Stephen asks, 'Is he Pākehā and, in his latest novel, writes from the viewpoint of a New Guinean woman?'

'No, not that one … whose novel, by the way, is turning into a bestseller. And no, he is not Pākehā.'

'Is it Witi Ihimaera?'

'No, not Witi, and yes, he is Polynesian.' Patricia is now almost bursting with the need to tell him. 'And he's a great performer of his own work.'

He now knows who it is, but isn't going to ruin her need to play. So he continues pretending he is trying hard to identify the author. 'Does he attack racism in his work?'

'Yes. Gets me angry every time!' she says.

He gulps down the rest of his wine, and, breathing heavily, deliberately gives the wrong answer. 'It was … it was … James George!'

Shaking her head furiously, she crunches her clenched fists against her blushing face, and cries, 'No, no, no!' She reaches forward, holds his face between her hands and presses inwards. 'And you're bullshitting me, anyway. You know who it was, eh?' He shakes his head, once, twice, trying not to laugh.

'Apirana Taylor, bullshitter!' she screeches, her fine spittle spraying his face. 'He came in to arrange a public reading. When he walked in and up to the desk, I couldn't believe it.'

He tries all through their meal of macaroni cheese – one of her favourites, especially when he makes it – mixed green salad and French bread to keep away from it, not ready to discuss it. Light-heartedly, they discuss her day at work (quite interesting cataloguing the new stock of novels), his lecture on post-colonial theory (it had gone well, but he'd felt the only Samoan student in his class didn't understand much of it), their son Malcolm and his wife Phoebe and their six-year-old granddaughter, Theresa, and the holiday they'd just enjoyed in the military-run Fiji (Bainimarama is now a dictator), and finally the movies (agreeing that they *had* to see *The Insatiable Moon*, the latest New Zealand movie and set in *their* Ponsonby).

They keep avoiding it as they clear the table. Usually she washes the dishes and he dries, but this time he says he has to ring his Head of Department, before she leaves in the morning for a conference in Canberra. 'Did you see Alistair today?' She never refers to his father as anything but Alistair or 'your father'.

Dead still, he stops three paces away from the sink and her back, which is turned to him as she washes the dishes. He can't believe it; why now, why this fucking minute when avoidance is almost complete? He's sure she can feel the heat of the fury that's surging up in him. 'He's good; looking after himself well, as always.' He listens to himself desperately suppressing his anger. He isn't going to allow her any opportunity to get at his father again – and through that, at him.

'That's wonderful, darling. So you don't have to worry about him.' She lets that slide into him slowly.

'Malcolm's been seeing him regularly as well,' he says. 'He's a very dutiful grandson.'

She knows that's not true but she's not going to say it. 'Yes, a loving *son*,' she emphasises. 'The best!'

As he hurries up the corridor to his study, the absolutely disturbing, anger-generating memories of their last argument about his father attack him again. Most unforgivable of all was her, eyes crazed with anger, shouting: 'He's a fucking narcissist, Stephen. He kept your wonderful, wonderful mother to himself and away from you and Malcolm. You fell for his whole bullshit act of being utterly devoted to her, shutting your bloody ears to the rumours – and they were true – that he was having affairs with some of his students. *With his students*. What do you think of that? And did you know, he kept telling everyone at university he was disappointed, yeah, fucking disappointed, at you being – and I quote him in that uncouth blokish language he uses – "in a fucking useless field of study, suitable only for fags and the mediocre"! How about that, Stephen?'

'Not true, not bloody true!' he'd screamed back at her.

Since his birth, Malcolm has always been his anchor, his escape from such stressful and demanding situations, and so he rings him at home and they talk about Malcolm's Fiji holiday. Malcolm's voice and manner of speaking are those of his mother, and that plus Malcolm's obvious respect and love for him soothes and dissipates his anger and frustration, finally. 'It'll be good if you can visit your grandfather soon, Malcolm.'

'I'm sorry, Dad, I've been so busy,' Malcolm apologises. 'This country is really riddled with heart disease. We eat far too much and don't exercise, so we get strangled with fat.'

'Shall we go and see him this Sunday? I'll ring your grandfather and arrange it.'

'Yeah, we can take Theresa too. He'd love that,' Malcolm says. 'The three of us guys can take Theresa to the park and have lunch there. You fix the lunch, Dad?'

Ancestry

For the first time this summer, Stephen is dressed for it, in a floppy purple t-shirt, long khaki shorts that make him feel ashamed of exposing his hairy, winter-pale legs, and thick black sandals. The Warriors cap he wears is a birthday gift from his father. Along the main walkway round the lake, he walks, self-consciously, between his father, who is holding Theresa's hand and talking animatedly with her, and Malcolm, who is dressed like Stephen and is carrying the lunch basket that Stephen has prepared. His father is wearing what, in his years of retirement, has become his outdoors 'uniform': a Warriors cap, long-sleeved blue sweatshirt (in winter he wore a thick Swanndri over that), jeans shiny with age and wear and the dark brown tramping boots his wife had bought him. Heavily influenced by her great-grandfather and his fanatical love of rugby league, Theresa is wearing a Warriors singlet, Warriors t-shirt, three-quarter trousers and Air Nikes. His size makes her look like a small doll, and draws the attention of most of the people they pass.

A strong breeze is blowing against them from the south and across the lake, bringing with it the sharp smell of wet earth and bird excrement and mud drying in the rising heat. As far back as Stephen can remember, going anywhere with his father – especially if you show you are genuinely interested in that location and ask the right questions – is like venturing out with a fabulous storehouse of knowledge and information and interpretation, the result of a lifetime of being a specialist in human geography and a ferocious, insatiable consumer of information.

Family

This is Theresa's first visit to Western Springs Park, so she is supercharged with interest in everything; the birdlife in particular. She knows the right question to ask her great-grandfather: 'What's that?'

At the start of their walk, Malcolm takes out a fat bag full of crusts and old bread. He is just about to feed the few ducks gathering round Theresa when Stephen's father stops him, saying, 'No, we'll feed them at the end.'

They stop every few paces, Stephen's father squatting down beside Theresa, naming the birds and itemising their main features. Geese, ducks, swans, teals, Australian coots, shovelers, sparrows, seagulls, mollyhawks, pigeons, mynahs, blackbirds, thrushes; he opens up the world of birds to her. Sometimes she is frightened because some of the geese and swans are larger than her and aggressive. Putting his huge arm behind her, he kneels in front of those birds, and in a gentle healing voice, his hand reaching forward and beckoning the bird to him, coaxes, 'Hey, sweetie, this is The-re-sa, and she loves you, yes, she really does.' Most of the birds edge forward, following his hand. For Stephen, it is a moving repetition of what his father had done with him and then with Malcolm years and years before.

Theresa is fascinated with the pūkeko most of all. So her great-grandfather takes her – Stephen and Macolm follow – into the cool shade of some willows right on the lake's edge, where a group of pūkeko are scratching and pecking hungrily at the grass. 'Grundad, Grundad!' Theresa repeats, pointing at the birds.

Ancestry

'Pū-ke-ko, Pū-ke-ko,' her Grundad enunciates slowly. Theresa echoes him exactly. 'Bloody wonderful!' he exclaims, ruffling her hair.

They all sit down on the long wooden bench underneath the largest willow and watch. 'They look purple but they're really iridescent, indigo blue,' Grundad tells them. The pūkeko have black wings and backs that shine with a greenish gloss, and scarlet bills and orange-red legs and feet that look far too large for them but are ideal, so Grundad explains, for their swampy and grassy environment and for swimming and running. 'They fly only short distances – when they have to. And make wonderful pets, so I've read. Now of course you can't touch them.'

Theresa jumps off the bench and now without fear walks into the group of birds. They continue foraging, without paying her attention. She squats down and reaches to touch the head of the nearest bird. As if weightless, her Grundad is immediately beside her, also reaching out to the bird. 'Here, beloved Pūkeko, beloved of our beautiful Theresa, here,' he croons. Stephen softens inside when he recognises that voice, that magic, as the one his mother used whenever she needed to calm his father. He glances at Malcolm and knows Malcolm recognises it, too.

Stephen and Malcolm dawdle behind Theresa and her Grundad, letting the sun ease in, relaxing them, massaging away that week's accumulation of job worries, concerns and stress. Most of the people they see are Indian or Chinese and other Asians, mainly in family groups. Along the lake shore and under the trees and on the wide lawns, more people are picnicking.

Family

Malcolm is nearly as tall as his grandfather but thin, gangly and bony; half his grandfather's width and build. Those who don't know him would think he is physically weak, uncoordinated and clumsy. They don't know that when he was young, he'd lived – during his holidays, spare time and extended periods when he'd 'run away' from home – with his grandparents, who were fitness and sports fanatics and had a weightlifting-fitness gym at home and who jogged every day and supported the Grey Lynne Rugby League Club. They first enrolled the five-year old Malcolm in the under-nine team and then, as he shot up in height and ability, in the heavier tougher grades. And Malcolm took to it like he and his grandmother did to anything they loved. He made the Auckland rep team when he was only nineteen and played for it for two years, until he suffered two really serious concussions – he went into tackles with ferocious, fearless commitment – and was advised by specialists (and his grandmother) to quit. He threw his passion into becoming the surgeon his grandmother wanted him to be.

'How are you and Mum?' Malcolm asks, casually, without glancing at him.

'Fine, we're fine; like every marriage, we have the usual disagreements. You know that, son,' Stephen replies, noting again that Malcolm's facial features are those of his mother.

'Still no luck in getting her and Granddad to go beyond *tolerating* each other?' Stephen knows his son can read his deepest worries because they've always been frank and open with each other, even discussing topics considered taboo between fathers and sons. 'I've tried talking to her about it; I've tried talking to Granddad about it, and,' Malcolm throws his hands up, 'no fucking luck. Phoebe and I are fed up with being at family get-togethers where everyone has to *pretend* everything is fine'

'I'm sorry, son.'

'It's not your fault.' Malcolm pauses. 'I suppose it's one of those things we have to live with for the rest of their lives, eh?'

They can see that the narrow, double-arched bridge over the last water inlet is crowded with people, Grundad towering above everyone. Stephen and Malcolm hurry towards the other two, picking their way politely through the people to hand Theresa the bag of bread crusts. The bridge is low to the dark, soupy water, and where the two arches meet at the centre of the inlet they can reach through the railing and touch the water and the milling gaggle of swans and ducks and other birds that are squabbling for the food people are tossing them.

Grundad opens the bag and tosses a few pieces to the birds, which fight for them. A laughing, dancing Theresa throws some too. Then she stops, startled, and points at the enlarging weave of eels just underneath the birds, a black-blue-flashing-white bundle of them competing for the tossed food. 'Orea, eels!' Grundad tells her. He lies almost flat on the bridge – some people have to get out of his way – and, reaching down, gently sweeps his large hand along the bellies of some of the eels. They flick away from his touch and then surge forward again for the food. Theresa squeals as the eels swirl and splash and snap at the food.

Family

Stephen looks at Malcolm. 'You remember the first time Nana brought you here?'

Malcolm nods, once.

'Do you remember what she said?'

Malcolm nods, again. 'She was never able to get away from death, from trying to save living things from death and extinction. Instead of first identifying these creatures and telling me how beautiful and alive they were, she said, "Grandson, these orea, these wonderful creatures, will be extinct in about fifty years. When they are, they will be gone forever from our planet because they exist only in our country. And why will they be extinct? Because we've reduced their habitat to this lake only, filling in their habitat with housing and roads and all the usual bullshit. And because some, some bastards fish them illegally!" Dad, back then, I could only comprehend her anger and sadness; not the information she was giving me about environmental degradation and the greed and insensitivity of humans. She told me that as the numbers of the orea decrease, their ability to increase also decreases, because the female orea spawn only once in their lifetime before they die. And it can be up to eighty years before they spawn. They're also slow-growing: one to two centimetres a year.'

'Your grandmother was right,' Stephen tries to console his son. 'Over the years since she passed away, I've noticed their numbers decreasing. Look at them now,' he points. 'They used to darken all round and under the bridge whenever we fed them; now look!'

Ancestry

Continents of clouds block out the sun and their blue-black shadows cover Stephen and his family, the whole lake and much of the park. Respite from the heat. Respite from the grim future of the orea. When Theresa finishes tossing all the bread, she and her Grundad lead Stephen and Malcolm across the rest of the bridge, and then they follow the potholed walkway round a slight bend and find a vacant picnic table under a stand of towering gum trees. It is time for lunch. For the scrumptious lunch of family favourites that Stephen has prepared with love, gratitude and hope.